THE SCOTTISH CLASSICS SERIES
NUMBER FOURTEEN

SPARTACUS

JAMES LESLIE MITCHELL
'LEWIS GRASSIC GIBBON'

THE SCOTTISH CLASSICS SERIES

1. Allan Ramsay and Robert Fergusson, *Poems*, ed. Alexander M. Kinghorn and Alexander Law.
2. John Galt, *The Member*, ed. Ian A. Gordon.
3. James Hogg, *The Brownie of Bodsbeck*, ed. Douglas S. Mack.
4. James Hogg, *Selected Stories and Sketches*, ed. Douglas S. Mack.
5. Naomi Mitchison, *Beyond This Limit: Selected Shorter Fiction*, ed. Isobel Murray.
6. John Galt, *Selected Short Stories*, ed. Ian A. Gordon.
7. John Galt, *The Last of the Lairds*, ed. Ian A. Gordon.
8. Hugh MacDiarmid, *A Drunk Man Looks At The Thistle*, ed. Kenneth Buthlay.
9. James Hogg, *The Three Perils of Man: War, Women and Witchcraft*, ed. Douglas Gifford.
10. Robin Jenkins, *Guests of War*, intr. Isobel Murray.
11. William Drummond of Hawthornden, *Poems and Prose*, ed. Robert H. MacDonald.
12. *Scott on Himself: A Selection of the Autobiographical Writings of Sir Walter Scott*, ed. David Hewitt.
13. J.M. Barrie, *Farewell Miss Julie Logan*, ed. Alistair McCleery.
14. James Leslie Mitchell, 'Lewis Grassic Gibbon', *Spartacus*, ed. Ian Campbell.

THE SCOTTISH CLASSICS SERIES

GENERAL EDITOR — DAVID S. ROBB

SPARTACUS

JAMES LESLIE MITCHELL
'LEWIS GRASSIC GIBBON'

EDITED BY
IAN CAMPBELL

SCOTTISH ACADEMIC PRESS
in conjunction with
THE ASSOCIATION FOR SCOTTISH LITERARY STUDIES
EDINBURGH
1990

Published by
Scottish Academic Press Ltd.
139 Leith Walk
Edinburgh EH6 8NS

First published 1990
ISBN 0 7073 0545 4

Introduction © Ian Campbell, 1990

Typeset by Trinity Typesetting, Edinburgh
Printed in Great Britain by
Bell and Bain Ltd., Glasgow

CONTENTS

ACKNOWLEDGMENTS

I would like to thank the following: Mrs Ray Mitchell who, while she lived, did everything to help me generously; Mrs Rhea Martin, her daughter, whose kindness to me continues; the late Helen B. Cruickshank who helped in many ways during the early years of my study of James Leslie Mitchell; the staffs of the National Library of Scotland and Edinburgh University Library; the series editors Douglas Mack and David Robb; and M. A. F. Faraday, whose help in establishing the text at an early stage was invaluable.

Ian Campbell
Edinburgh, 1989

SPARTACUS

by James Leslie Mitchell

O thou who lived for Freedom when the Night
    Had hardly yet begun; when little light
Blinded the eyes of men, and dawntime seemed
So far and faint — a foolish dream half-dreamed!
Through the blind drift of days and ways forgot
    Thy name, thy purpose: these have faded not!
From out the darkling heavens of misty Time
    Clear is thy light, and like the Ocean's chime
Thy voice. Yea, clear as when unflinchingly
    Thou ledst the hordes of helotry to die
And fell in glorious fight, nor knew the day
The creaking crosses fringed the Appian Way —

    Sport of the winds, O ashes of the Strong!
    But down the aeons roars the helots' song
    Calling to battle. Long as on the shore
The washing tides shall crumble cliff and nore
Remembered shalt thou be who dauntless gave
    Unto the world the lordship of the slave!

INTRODUCTION

The author
James Leslie Mitchell (Lewis Grassic Gibbon) was born in Auchter-less in Aberdeenshire in 1901, grew up in the Mearns he was to immortalise in *Sunset Song* (1932), then early moved to the Scottish cities for a life of largely hated journalism in Aberdeen then in Glasgow. Failure here, compounded by the Depression years, made work impossible to find and he enlisted in the armed services, working in England and in the Middle East before settling to marriage and civilian life in London, and finally in Welwyn Garden City where he enjoyed a few years of amazingly productive authorship before his sudden death through stomach trouble in February 1935. He left behind a widow and two young children; he left also a growing reputation as a major Scottish novelist whose work, crammed into these last years, was only beginning to be appreciated when death removed him from the Scottish scene. His true critical place is still being debated, though his importance is now not in question; in the 1980s he is seen as one of the major figures of the renaissance in Scottish writing of the present century.

A Scots Quair (*Sunset Song*, 1932; *Cloud Howe*, 1933; and *Grey Granite*, 1934) is his single most remembered work, now famous through repeated republication, television serialisation and teaching at school and university. *Spartacus* (1933) was to take longer to catch fire in the public imagination, and though it is repeatedly mentioned by Mitchell's critics in respectful tones it has been largely out of print since the author's death and has been overcast by Howard Fast's better-known recreation of the Spartacist slave rebellion chosen by Hollywood for the celebrated film *Spartacus*. The present publication may help to correct the picture of a 'one-book' author, for few so little fit that description as the astonishingly prolific James Leslie Mitchell. Under his Scottish pseudonym of 'Lewis Grassic Gibbon' he made *A Scots Quair* public property and established it as a Scottish classic: under his own name, which he reserved for a different kind of publication (and for the pleasure of reviewing his own work — often favourably) he published another fine book, *Spartacus*, which should in time take its place as a remarkable achievement. As Mitchell or as Gibbon, he well merits the revival of interest he is now enjoying. His science fiction (*Three Go Back, Gay Hunter*), his books of archaeological discovery and argument (*The Last of the Maya, Nine Against the Unknown, Hanno or the Future of Exploration*) and his short stories alone entitle him to serious consideration, and his other Scottish writing (*The Thirteenth Disciple, Stained Radiance*) is seriously understudied, not least since it is often all but unavailable outside a small number of specialist libraries.[1]

The 'Mitchell' books reflected a serious interest in history, social history and anthropology which predated Mitchell's army and air force years, but which was fuelled by his contact with the Mediterranean and Middle East civilisations he encountered. They reflect also a strong, politically committed intelligence, as hostile to human exploitation and cruelty as it was to the decaying capitalist civilisation of the Depression. A committed Marxist, an implacably hostile observer of the Scottish and British scene in politics and social habits, Mitchell was to find a natural attraction in the story of the Spartacist rebellion.

> When I hear or read of a dog tortured to death, very vilely and foully, of some old horse driven to a broken back down a hill with an overloaded cart of corn, of rats captured and tormented with red-hot pokers in bothies, I have a shudder of disgust. But these things do not move me too deeply, not as the fate of the old-time Cameronian prisoners over there, three miles away in Dunnottar; not as the face of that ragged tramp who went by this afternoon; not as the crucifixion of the Sparticist slaves along the Appian Way. To me it is inconceivable that sincere and honest men should go outside the range of their own species with gifts of pity and angry compassion and rage when there is horror and dread among humankind. (ScS 304).[2]

As 'blasphemer and reformer' (two terms of self-description which William Malcolm has skilfully used to analyse Mitchell's stance) he was to produce in *Spartacus* a telling indictment of men's inhumanity to those fellow-men over whom they possess total control; the dehumanising effect of such total control pulses through *Spartacus* as a constant source of authorial disgust.

'Diffusionism' in Mitchell is a clumsily-titled but not really difficult system of belief which, once grasped, is as useful for an understanding of the 'Grassic Gibbon' books (the Standing Stones in *Sunset Song,* the decadent culture of Aberdeen in *Grey Granite*) as it is to the view of Roman culture and civilisation in *Spartacus.*

To the Diffusionist historian civilisation is a slow curse which overtook an originally free and happy human race, spreading slowly from the flooded Nile valley, source of early settlements, bringing the rise of property, agriculture, militias, social systems, religious cults, slavery and the many consequences which the Diffusionist sees arising from the initial imposition of a 'civilisation' on a fundamentally free and natural human race. Civilisation was to enslave Greece, Rome and in the twentieth century the whole world.

Diffusionism, a belief passionately supported by Mitchell, sees the advances of civilisation — industrial power, machinery, efficiency, rapid transport, independence from nature in agriculture — as a hideous trade-off for the loss of original freedom, physical, societal and personal. The Churches of Christianity are seen as harbingers of guilt and hypocrisy, marriage a travesty of free sexual relations, the machinery of most parliamentary democracy a cynical device for exploiting the many by the unprincipled few. Hollywood's culture, and the grinding poverty of the Depression, seemed ample confirmation of the bankruptcy of 'civilisation' in the early 1930s and (like his contemporary Hugh MacDiarmid, with whom he produced a dazzlingly hostile *Scottish Scene* in 1934) Mitchell looked confidently to a revolution in Western society in a few years to cleanse this morass.

The past offered ample testimony to the purifying effect of revolution in a good cause. Mitchell's view of the past, as of the present, was strongly affected by a hyperactive imagination, and an uncomfortable ability to *feel* persecution and torture in a previous age. The broken leg of the horse in *Cloud Howe,* and the stinking poverty of the slums in *Grey Granite,* were real to him, the pain and the agony of the past as real as the present. The Ewan of *Grey Granite* who wanders in Paldy Slums in the summer heat may be seeing Depression Scotland in this world, but his imagination is in the dim historical past, even in the clean marble halls of Aberdeen Art Gallery.

There was a cast of Trajan, good head; Caesar — the Caesar they said wasn't Caesar. Why not a head of Spartacus? Or a plaque of the dripping line of crosses that manned the Appian Way with slaves — dripping and falling to bits through long months, they took days to die, torn by wild beasts. Or a statuary group of a Roman slave being fed to fishes, alive in a pool . . . (SQ 406-7)

If this was civilisation, plainly Mitchell wanted little to do with it. Yet his creative imagination, uncomfortably enough (for much of his work is uncomfortably full of pain and suffering), could not leave it alone. The Spartacist rebellion was plainly a subject for a historical novel he could use as a trenchant commentary on his times.[3]

Spartacus

When he began to research the background to his 1933 novel, Mitchell was in his thirties, modestly successful, rising to a small house, a small family, a small car, and easy access to the British Museum and the London world of publishers and magazines. He had come from a poor home and lived through hard times — both points which were to give pungency to his Scottish novels at a time when sugar-coated pictures of Scotland had their devotees — and he relished the opportunity to use his time to look at books, historical sources, and write the kind of book his imagination impelled him to work on.

His anger fuelled his interest. As he wrote to Helen Cruickshank in November, 1933,

I am so horrified by all our dirty little cruelties and bestialities that I would feel the lowest type of skunk if I don't shout the horror of them from the house-tops. Of course I shout too loudly. But the filthy conspiracy of silence there was in the past![4]

Art galleries of pleasingly innocuous antiquity did little to damp that anger, and the historical reading he did for *Spartacus* intensified it. A view of the past which allowed for aesthetic satisfaction in the achievements of Greece and Rome, without making room for the dripping crosses of the Appian Way, was plainly not for him. From his earliest preserved school essays, he had been fascinated by the powerful leaders of the mass movements of history, by the power of

xi

individuals, by charismatic leadership, by mesmerism; by the power of writing, too, to blur earthly definitions and to transform the commonplace to 'the wild dream of the German poet; "There is no beginning — yea, even as there is no end!"'.[5] The element of irrationality so strong in his version of the Spartacus story is perceptible in this view of history and the power of its leaders; early on described as a slave malleable in the hands of the *literatus* Kleon, Spartacus moves with maturity to a terrible power of his own beyond reason, beyond beginning and end — indeed the very last paragraph of Mitchell's story implies a circularity as the dead Spartacus and the as-yet-unborn Christ combine in the agonised Kleon's death vision.

The origin of the story came in research; from Appian, from Plutarch and from Sallust, the work of reading divided between husband and wife, bolstered by visits to the British Museum.[6]

Plutarch's *Life of Crassus* is plainly the central source[7], providing as it does the following skeleton of events and character:

— Capua's garrison is overcome.

— Clodius with 3000 troops is defeated.

— Publius Varinus enters the story: his deputy Furius is routed (with 2000 men) as is Cossinus (surprised by Spartacus) then Varinus himself.

— Spartacus seizes Furius' horse. In an interval of poorer luck Gellius falls on a slave contingent (Crixus' army in *Spartacus*) and destroys it.

— Lentulus and Gellius are then defeated by Spartacus, who sets off for the Alps, where he confronts and defeats Cassius and his 10,000 Romans.

— Crassus appointed by Senate; despatches Mummius who disobeys orders, engages with Spartacus and is routed.

— Crassus, decimating the survivors, establishes firm leadership while Spartacus heads South for Lucania and the sea; bargains with pirates but is betrayed by them.

— Spartacus camps in Rhegium; Crassus walls the slaves in with dyke and ditch; dissension in slave camp.

— Crassus begins to fear Pompey's return which would steal his thunder; meanwhile Spartacus escapes with one-third of his army through Crassus' wall. The slaves, internally riven and weakened by desertion, are beaten once and head for the mountains, then beaten again at Lucania; Spartacus is slaughtered while trying to reach and kill Crassus.

With additions and modifications from Appian and Sallust, this is to be the groundplan of Mitchell's plot for *Spartacus*. Sallust, for instance[8], gave him a keener insight into the relevance of the Spartacist rebellion to the machinations of the Roman Senate and its internal politics; the clash between Pompey and Crassus is an important off-stage element in the historical account. Appian provided a number of striking details which obviously appealed to the novelist's imagination:

— the Mount Vesuvius details
— the names of Oenomaus and Crixus
— the sacrifice of Roman prisoners in memory of Crixus
— the near-attack on Rome (not in Plutarch) inexplicably abandoned.

Appian's description of breaking out of Crassus' trap in Rhegium is full and vigorous; his description of the final battle which cost Spartacus his life so vivid that Mitchell incorporates it in direct quotation at the climax of his own battle description:

AND SPARTACUS MADE HIS WAY TOWARDS CRASSUS HIMSELF THROUGH MANY MEN, AND INFLICTING MANY WOUNDS; BUT HE DID NOT SUCCEED IN REACHING CRASSUS, THOUGH HE ENGAGED AND KILLED TWO CENTURIONS. AND AT LAST, AFTER THOSE ABOUT HIM HAD FLED, HE KEPT HIS GROUND, AND, BEING SURROUNDED BY A GREAT NUMBER, HE FOUGHT TILL HE WAS CUT DOWN.

Flexibly but skilfully, Mitchell takes what he wants from each source, altering, tailoring; Plutarch has Spartacus kill his superb white stallion for 'if they lost... he would have no need of a horse again' (S 281). The horse is there in Plutarch but not as the property of Furius. The white stallion and the superb gladiator seemed to need to be introduced earlier in the book for artistic urgency, and Mitchell simply moved them forward.

The larger context, the impact of the slave revolt of 73-71 B.C. on the volatile state of Roman politics, is very much present in the Latin sources, and very much absent in Mitchell's account. Mitchell's sympathies focus on the suffering slave, the human injustice, not on the cultured or sophisticated arguments of the Roman Senate. Not so the orthodox historians: the *Cambridge Ancient History* which was published just as he was collecting his sources saw Spartacus in quite a different light.

> Like Eunus and Salvius, Spartacus is a tragic figure, but the significance of his career is small ... the most notable legacy of the affair was its results on Pompey and Crassus.[9]

Liddell's *History of Rome* (1858), a standard source-book Mitchell can be expected to have consulted, describes Spartacus' revolt as 'a formidable outbreak that took place in the heart of Italy, and threatened for a time the very existence of the Republic',[10] yet finds room for scarcely two pages of description in a book of over 720, and much of them devoted to the wider implications Roman politics. Likewise Frank Marsh's *A History of the Roman World*, to be published in 1935, devotes one page out of almost 500 to a revolt which is not interesting so much for itself, as for its consequences.

> Rome might have breathed freely again had it not been for the fact that there were now in Italy two generals of somewhat uncertain convictions at the head of victorious armies.[11]

Examples could be multiplied of the Spartacist rebellion assuming different shape according to the viewpoint of the observer. European observers can be cited discussing the effect on the larger shape of Italian politics,[12] of the effect on the thinking of the future 'Spartakusbund' activists whose most famous representatives were Rosa Luxemburg and Karl Liebknecht.[13] As individual hero, as leader of a significant political rebellion, as potential destabiliser of Rome, and as inspiration for future class struggle, Spartacus plainly is important.

Mitchell's treatment
Clearly, Mitchell chose to write about a *rebellion*. Already we have seen his hostility towards a conspiracy which would make of history a cosy and unchallenging account of the past, and there is nothing at all about his version of the events of 73-71 B.C. which is relaxing. The inspiration of the novel is the enormous impetus given to the pent-up rebellious instincts of the slave class in Italy by the towering and charismatic leader in Spartacus the historical personality.

The plot starts with rebellion, if not with its ultimate leader; the plot has little to do with the events after Spartacus' own death, except to record in its sickening detail Rome's public revenge. The emphasis in the original historical sources is simply omitted; strict concentration on the rebellion itself is clearly the artistic intention of *Spartacus*.

The narrowness of Mitchell's treatment is extraordinary when the novel is finished and the reader reflects. By the invention and retention of the character of Kleon throughout the narrative — Kleon anticipates Spartacus and survives him, narrowly — Mitchell is released from any obligations to provide a wider contextual framework in order to make sense of the rebellion. Kleon makes sense, sense enough for his own narrow intentions and sense enough to interpret a savage, over-simplified society to the reader. The unimpassioned account of a mutilated former slave is the ideal narrative vehicle for the passionate and often repulsive material of the story. Not for Mitchell the unctuous Spartacus of Susannah Moodie, refusing to embrace his child with speeches such as this:

'Never, Elia, shall my arms embrace my child, till I am free. Thou canst pierce through the dark veil of futurity; how will the morning sun shine for Spartacus? Will it gleam upon my blackening corse, or gild my victorious arms?'

We need no prophet to tell us the outcome for Spartacus, admirable though many of the sentiments with which Susannah Moodie invests him may be. Her Spartacus is unfitted for a world where, when he enters the arena,

his eye glanced round the gay assembly, with a look fraught with contempt and hatred. 'Is it possible,' thought Spartacus, 'that man can come, with light and joyous heart, to witness the sufferings of his fellowmen?'[14]

Mitchell's hero, toughened by early hardship and unburdened by ideals plainly directed from author to audience over the character's head, accepts survival, sexual gratification, and fierce hatred and loyalty as unquestioning motives,

memories dreadful and unforgivable, memories of long treks in the slave-gangs from their native lands, memories of the

naked sale, with painted feet, from the steps of windy
ergastula, memories of cruelties cold-hearted and bloody, of
women raped or fed to fish to amuse the Masters from their
lethargy, of children sold as they came from the womb, of the
breeding-kens of the north, where the slaves were mated like
cattle, with the Masters standing by. (S 97)

Spartacus here is much closer to Ewan, whose angry rejection of art
gallery antiquity has already been referred to. Ewan's anger and
Mitchell's coalesce in Grey Granite in that art gallery visit.

Why did they never immortalize in stone a scene from the
Athenian justice-courts — a slave being ritually,
unnecessarily tortured before he could legally act as a
witness? Or a baby exposed to die in a jar — hundreds every
year in the streets of Athens, it went on all day, the little kids
wailing and crying and crying as the hot sun rose and they
scorched in the jars; and then their mouths dried up, they just
weeked and whimpered, they generally died by dark. (SQ 406)

Out of such anger, Spartacus' narrow focus of hatred and ambition
for success in the rebellion grows and achieves authenticity.

Mitchell skilfully does make some contact possible with an outside
world which is beyond this immediate artistic interest. Gershom ben
Sanballat comes in frustration to follow a leader whom ethnically he
despises, since no better may be found. Crixus and Castus plainly
follow Spartacus from a mixture of personal loyalty and sexual
attraction. Even Kleon, mutilated beyond normal passion and anger,
feels irrational loyalty beyond self-preservation to a barbarian he first
thought he could manipulate, but finally saw he must follow to the
death. Mitchell includes these outside contacts, and occasionally
replenishes them with new characters, but only very sparingly.

One really significant omission is the Romans — the Masters, as
they are universally called here. Masters they are to the slaves, and
Masters they are to the reader who never approaches them closer than
the understanding of the slave army or the superior intelligence of
Kleon. Glimpsed in the gathering dusk or in the distant dust-cloud,
occasionally eavesdropped on in council or Senate discussion, the
Romans remain in Mitchell's novel a satisfactory enigma, not under-

stood and therefore totally hated. In isolating the reader from the Roman lifestyle, which might encourage identification (and worse still, sympathy) in the modern reader, Mitchell compels sympathy with the barbarous and alien lifestyle of the slave army.

Barbarous the action certainly is. When Crassus the Lean finds his orders disobeyed, the *Cambridge Ancient History* wryly notes he found his relief in

> ... decimating an unsteady cohort — with the most beneficent results to the morale of the remainder.[15]

Mitchell's account of the episode laconically conveys not only the punishment but the complete lack of surprise or sympathy such a punishment might arouse.

> When Crassus heard this, the face of the Dives went livid with anger. He commanded that the hundred men of the velites be decimated. Then the whole army stirred at the shouted orders of the tribunes and marched north on the slave-camp. (S 209)

It was the norm of life in the army. The death of one man in ten was hardly worth commenting on, ordinary army discipline. This calculated tight-lipped description of cruelty cumulatively does much to transmit the horror Mitchell obviously felt at the circumstances surrounding the rebellion, and the society which bred it. 'Bring Cossinus' head', orders Spartacus at one point, and 'Titul the Iberian hewed it from the trunk which his club had mangled, and brought it dripping' (S 93). No comment is required for an emotion doubtless no one felt.

> The slaves implored the Gauls to free them. They were manacled one to the other, and when they were discovered with their overseer slain they would undoubtedly be crucified, as a warning to other slaves.
>
> The Gauls listened and were moved a little. But they had no time to unmanacle the gang, and the slaves of it would encumber the scouts. So they left them, hearing their cries for long as they rode round the shoulder of the hill. (S 204-5)

Laconically, Mitchell tidies up the episode a few pages later.

They passed by the field where the ten chained slaves had watched the Gauls of Titul slay the overseer. Ten shapes lay very quiet there now: already the spot was a-caw and a-crow with ravens. Gershom glanced at it indifferently. (S 212)

In catching hardened indifference to suffering, torture and death Mitchell cleverly implants in the reader's mind the ability to see the events of the novel, people and places, with the artificiality of a narrow slave perspective. Excitement is possible, no doubt, the excitement of personal loyalty to Spartacus, excitement of winning a battle over the Masters, even the thrill of seeing Rome,

> at noon, from the Campagna, from the Sabine Hills, shining below them, Mons Cispius crowned with trees and the long-roofed Doric temples, Mons Oppius shelving tenement-laden into the sunrise's place, Mons Palatinus splendid with villas, fading into a sun-haze mist where the land fell . . . Aventine lay south, and north, high-crowned, the Capitoline Hill. Rome! (S 194)

Yet the greater part of the book is calculatedly barren of excitement, barren of emotion, whether in the reactions of the mutilated Kleon, the enigmatic Spartacus, or the hardened slaves themselves.

The extent of Mitchell's calculatedly narrowed vision is seen easily enough in a comparison with Howard Fast's *Spartacus* of 1951 (source of Rank's 1959 film starring Kirk Douglas). Fast implants the story within the Roman society of the time, with flashback and forward through the experience of Crassus, Gracchus, Cicero and a young pleasure-seeking aristocratic Roman circle. Fast's narrative has its own harrowing moments, a vivid insight into the early years of the Egyptian mines in which Spartacus was lucky to survive, a dreadful description of the crucifixion scenes on the Appian Way. Perhaps Fast's most vivid achievement is to realise, in a low-key way, the full horror of *being a slave* in scenes underplayed skilfully as follows:

> The litter-bearers, weary from all the miles they had come, sweating, crouched beside their burdens and shivered in the evening coolness. Now their lean bodies were animal-like in weariness, and their muscles quivered with the pain of exhaustion, even as an animal's does. No one looked at them,

no one noticed them, no one attended them. The five men, the three women and the two children went into the house, and still the litter-bearers crouched by the litters, waiting. Now one of them, a lad of no more than twenty, began to sob, more and more uncontrollably; but the others paid no attention to him. They remained there at least twenty minutes before a slave came to them and led them off to the barracks where they would have food and shelter for the night.[16]

To describe reality with as little emotion as this is to suggest powerfully the Romans' contempt for the slaves as human beings, and their simple indifference to them. Indifference is something Mitchell and Fast both attribute to the Romans, Fast in a splendid aside attributed to Brutas waving a hand at the slave-crosses on the Appian Way,

> Did you want it to be genteel? That's their work. My manciple crucified eight hundred of them. They're not nice; they're tough and hard and murderous.[17]

Like Fast, Arthur Koestler in *The Gladiators* (1939) looks at Rome as well as at the slave camp, and produces a novel of *interplay* in a way which Mitchell simply is not interested in doing. Koestler's Rome is a city of intrigue and strife and plotting, a city where interesting and often clever Romans intrigue for mixed motives, sharing a common humanity with a casual disregard for the welfare of their fellows, slave and free. Koestler produces (in William K. Malcolm's words) a novel 'more exacting in its psychological and economic analysis of the historical situation'[18] but the epic qualities of the story are sacrificed to that complexity.

This is the key to Mitchell's success. Through savage concentration on the slave camp, with perhaps a moment's eavesdropping or one glimpse of a sunny city from a distant hillside, he suggests the world of Rome without seriously attempting to penetrate it. Mitchell's interest is in the rebellion, in the possibilities of rebellion to remedy society's injustices. He would have shared Karl Marx's admiration for Spartacus since he would have shared the grounds on which that admiration was accorded:

Spartacus is revealed as the most splendid fellow in the whole
of ancient history. Great general (no Garibaldi), noble
character, real representation of the ancient proletariat.
Pompeius, *reiner Scheisskerl*: got his undeserved fame by
snatching the credit . . .[19]

In the leader of a great rebellion, Marx finds his great historical
figure; history will work out its processes, for 'he who composes a
programme for the future is a reactionary',[20] and Spartacus comes at
the historical moment to exploit a weakness in the system. Mitchell
admired Marx and his writings, and he also possessed, closer to home,
an analysis of the world of classical antiquity which doubtless hammered home to him the importance of the right struggle at the right
historical moment.

The existence of household slaves, generally war-captives,
such as we meet in Homer, was an innocent institution which
would never have had serious results; but the new organised
slave-system which began in the seventh century [BC] was
destined to prove one of the most fatal causes of disease and
decay to the states of Greece . . .
The second half of the seventh century is marked in many
parts of Greece by struggle between the classes; and the wiser
and better of the nobles began themselves to see the necessity
of extending political privileges to their fellow-citizens.[21]

This analysis in J. B. Bury's *A History of Greece to the Death of
Alexander the Great* (1912) — a book from the Cairo Forces' library
which found its way into Mitchell's private library[22] — aptly sums up
the processes by which Roman society inherited the pent-up pressures
of the injustice of slavery. As Diffusionist, as humanitarian, as
Marxist egalitarian, as human being, Mitchell rejected the circumstances of 73 B.C. with disgust. To give concentration to his disgust,
he chose the selective treatment described here, and triumphantly
drew his readers into the mayhem with the involvement of a horrified
and unwillingly fascinated witness.

Greek and Roman societies alike provided Mitchell with an example of the kind of imposed slavery which he thought he saw in a
more abstract form in his own society in the 1930s. Slavery of the mind

is something which obviously angered him in his late teens, working in the poorer areas of Glasgow: in Scottish Scene in 1934 the anger he felt at the enslavement of a generation to poverty and despair is barely in control, giving 'Glasgow' more power than most of his polemics. For Spartacus and his band slavery has been of the body, but not of the spirit; the attack on a morally rotten Roman (or Greek) society is the coming of the historical moment where the free spirit allows the slaves to fight.

It is notable that *Spartacus* is about that moment of confrontation, the moment when a society loses control; it does not suggest a perfect or guaranteed moment of successful confrontation, the historically correct moment, for of course the rebellion — splendid in conception and gloriously described as it is by Mitchell — is a failure. The last paragraphs of the book suggest that history's moment has not come; perhaps a few generations off, a rebellion of a different kind may work. The recreation of the events of 73 B.C. is one of splendidly caught excitement and confrontation followed by an ambiguous final authorial statement (a technique Mitchell used to end *Grey Granite*). Like *Grey Granite, Spartacus* leaves the reader with unanswered questions rather than with a programme for historical or social reform; the author's deepest interest was obviously with the engagement itself, and he accepts Spartacus' defeat as historical fact. That the struggle took place, and would continue in some form, is as far as Mitchell's involvement goes. The real involvement is with the reader in the events of the moment.

Reader involvement

Two main techniques give Mitchell's account an air of the spontaneity of rebellion and revolt. One is the character of the central protagonist, war-wounded, remote, inhumanly controlled, a leader who is not understood by the followers who are prepared to go to their deaths for him. Spartacus may fascinate, but he also puzzles; by his own admission he ceases to be a statesman (S 161) in anger, he turns from Rome when he has it in his sights, he shows human feeling when it is least expected and inhuman fierceness of purpose when it is needed. Initially Kleon's puppet (or so it seems), Spartacus develops a character of his own, one which commands respect from the other figures in the story, and consistent attention from the reader. By keeping the reader at a distance from the central character, Mitchell gives the activity of the book a sense of historical unexpectedness.

The other technique is already familiar, that of the narrowing of narrative perspective. By deliberately depriving the reader of extensive areas of alternative information — Roman strategy, psychological insight into character, flashback or forward — Mitchell keeps the reader on edge for the information of the moment, which is all the reader possesses.

Both techniques serve a common end. The novel was, after all, written in haste at a period of Mitchell's life when he had limited time for research and writing, and by narrowing the canvas of his historical description he contains the necessary material and gives immediacy and focus to the progress of the rebellion. It has also been suggested that, by filtering out the normal emotions of sympathy and disgust through the hardening effect of war and repeated suffering, the novelist induces in the reader a mood in which the described emotions of the historical protagonists can be felt and understood, even if not accepted.

It is in the light of this analysis that Kleon the mutilated Greek emerges as a splendid narrative device, closer to the reader norm than many, yet decisively separated by the terrible injury which is so often mentioned by Mitchell. Even the late incident with Puculla, while serving to humanise a character too often seen as unnaturally self-contained, merely redeems rather than humanises. To some in the camp he is an object of sexual ridicule; to others such as Gershom, his harking on Plato's perfect state is mere madness. He is admired for his efficiency and his loyalty and the reader grudgingly offers identification with someone who can read and understand, within limits; while the Gauls worship the sun, 'Kleon, Gershom, and the Ionians did not worship, knowing the sun to be but a ball of fire three leagues away.' (S 34)

Kleon has specific strategies: 'Spartacus and the slaves are one . . . for the Leader is the People' (S 81) and he even wildly considers taking command should Spartacus be killed (S 172); but with maturity Spartacus distances himself from Kleon and all advisers, and finds a life and leadership all his own, increasing the admiration of a readership who can only mourn his passing.

'We come to free all slaves whatsover . . . in the new state we'll make even the Masters will not be enslaved. We march with your Lex Servorum, but we do not march with your Plato.' (S 190)

The Platonic model clearly rejected, Mitchell blends the vision of the gladiator with 'a great Cross with a figure that was crowned with thorns', and the dying Kleon 'saw that these Two were One, and the world yet theirs: and he went into unending night and left them that shining earth'. (S 287)

The reader is being urged, strongly, to accept an identification of Christ the freer of slaves with Spartacus a generation before — Spartacus killed before his time. The future is theirs; their time is not now. Again, Mitchell stops short of detailed interpretation: his intention is not to make sense of history, but rather to reflect the ambiguity of randomness of the historical process seen from Mitchell's complex viewpoint.

Style

Spartacus is told with Mitchell's characteristic verve and economy, for he was a writer who experimented through the short story to find a mature and very recognisable narrative style early in his career. There is indeed a place for good narrative style, since the novel contains very few female characters, little straightforward love interest, and a great deal of unpleasant violence. To counter the violence, to distract the reader's attention from the relatively narrow spectrum of character and incident, Mitchell fortunately has at his command a flexible and arresting prose. The basic narrative medium is well-written narrative English, the language of *Stained Radiance* and *The Thirteenth Disciple*. As everywhere in Mitchell's work, the reader is drawn without preamble into the fully-active plot.

When Kleon heard the news from Capua he rose early one morning, being a literatus and unchained, crept to the room of his Master, stabbed him in the throat, mutilated that Master's body even as his own had been mutilated: and so fled from Rome with a stained dagger in his sleeve and a copy of *The Republic* of Plato hidden in his breast. (S 15)

The style is arresting; it raises expectations; it provides essential background unobtrusively. Above all, it intimates the general scene of violence, mutilation and death we can expect from the rebellion. Two interesting points in Mitchell's narrative strategy are the references to the Masters by the slaves' name (rather than 'Roman'), setting the tone for the narrative stance throughout, and the very early setting up of a stylistic device which Mitchell exploits to excellent effect throughout. Kleon is described in the first sentence as a *literatus* without explanation: it is soon clear from context that a literatus is one who can read, but already the reader is immersed in some variety of Roman experience, the Roman term used without gloss or explanation. Latin-derived words are used exactly: 'the Way', 'casqued', 'slave-market', 'to compute' appear early in the narrative; Kleon *unwinds*, does not open a book; the perverse sexual tastes of Kleon's master are hardly explained, and certainly not illuminated by references to the tales of Baalim, Ashtaroth or Ataretos. The East is the 'Utmost Lands', the supreme deity 'Serapis'. All this functions without delay to put the reader in the position of a reader of the time.

Mitchell is doing no more here than adapting the triumphantly successful technique of his earlier success in *Sunset Song* where he had re-shaped the narrative English to the 'rhythms and cadences of Scots spoken speech' while adding a minimum number of Scots vocabulary items to produce a narrative medium which gives a warm impression of participation in a Scottish community.[23] In *Spartacus* the words and cadences are not from Scots, but from Latin, and share the same comforting feature that they operate *independently of the reader's knowledge of Latin*.

As the Scottish words in *Sunset Song* rapidly explain themselves by context, rendering glossary unnecessary[24] so the Latin (and occasionally Greek) words in *Spartacus* operate in the same way. In a description of the first century B.C. the reader can without difficulty decode references to the 'half a century of cavalry' (S 122), the sacrifices 'to the manes of dead Crixus' (S 163), to the decimation of the velites (S 209) already referred to, to Lavinia's 'himation' (S 159), to the instrument played by the 'bucinator' (S 189).

So much for vocabulary. Rhythms and cadences are also skilfully imitated from the original Latin. Occasionally Mitchell is content to intrude a single archaism:

Then said Crixus: 'We've come to the feast, but the meat is still uncooked.' Thereat he took a javelin in his hand, rode forward, stood high in his stirrups, and hurled the javelin . . . (S 97)

Sometimes the effect is denser.

The battle was to Spartacus, as once to Pyrrhus. But of the eighteen thousand Gauls and Germans a bare three thousand survived. With these fell Castus, as has been told, who loved Spartacus, and never knew him; and Gannicus, who hated the Gladiator, and was killed in his sleep. (S 261)

This is compounded of Latin translated directly into English (*the battle was to Spartacus*), commonplace tags from Latin narrative (*as has been told*), and a conscious archaism from the Bible (*and never knew him*) covering the point of Castus' homosexual attraction to Spartacus. Carefully used, the device of direct translation from Latin into English functions powerfully to give the reader a sense of involvement,

The slave horse . . . met the circling Roman cavalry, and, armed with clubs, splintered the levelled hastae and smote down the riders. In a moment the fortune of the battle changed. The Germans turned and the legionaries, caught between two enemies, struggled to reform in double lines. But this, in that marshy ground encumbered with dead, they could by no means achieve. (S 99)

This is an account which clearly draws upon an accumulated reading of Latin or Latin-inspired narrative. *Fortuna belli,* the fortune of war, is too prominently placed in the paragraph to be mistaken; even if the *hastae* or spears are not recognised, *this they could by no means achieve* is recognised for its unfamiliar syntax, even if not recognised as Latin. Retiring to a *sleeping-room* (S 112), fighting in a slave army which prepared to *receive* a Roman charge (S 150) — the effect is immersion and participation through words used in a sense slightly or completely unfamiliar.

The weakness of the style is in repetition, occasionally injudicious reliance on one effect. Kleon is too often described as cold; Gershom strokes his beard irritably far too often; the violence and the chilling lack of pity finally can overcome reader squeamishness. On balance, the style works triumphantly. Narrow, brutal, shaped by forces beyond its control, continually threatened by sudden death or agonising retribution by a ruthless army of the Masters, the slave experience which forms the totality of this narrative is caught with unpleasant but accurate focus. It was a desperate time, and Mitchell realistically recreates that desperation.

Subsequent history of *Spartacus*

Even before Mitchell's death the novel had generated interest overseas, and on 5th December 1934 Ostredni Delincke of Prague signed a contract for translation rights into Czech; one royalty payment of January 1935 (£8.16.9) suggested a prompt advance, though no further moneys reached the family. The translation *Spartakus (V Prekladu Jos. Hrusi) V Praze (Krizovatky)* appeared in Prague in 1936, 265 pages, and a copy is listed in the Library of Congress. Some tentative interest in Swedish translations, along with tentative enquiries from the BBC in 1954 and 1956, came to nothing.

The beginning of the revival of interest in Mitchell's *Spartacus* can be traced to 1959 and the film; Jarrold considered but rejected a paperback reissue. Understandably, Mrs Mitchell's feelings were regretful:

> Spartacus' reviews those I have seen have not been very exciting despite the number of stars in the film. Such a pity Leslie's 'Spartacus' failed to win the imagination of a producer.[25]

The book had been considered once, by Sir George Archibald of Pinewood Studios, but was turned down as too large and requiring too expensive a cast.[26] Thus, with the hardback out of print, the paperback 'swamped out by the Penguins' in 1937[27] and the film based on Howard Fast, Mitchell's *Spartacus* had to wait for a reprint till 1970, and for a new edition till 1989.

Now the book's stature seems beyond doubt. Spartacus has been recently described as 'Mitchell's most memorable character — and I include Chris Guthrie in this judgment,[28] and Douglas Young praised the 'simplicity and precision which convey the action and its meaning powerfully and clearly.'[29] Even with fainter praise from other critics ('too good . . . to be quite forgotten'[30]) the book has remained in the public consciousness, a 'haunting poetic idea',[31] and been warmly greeted by Francis Russell Hart as a remarkable artistic advance.[32] Now, with the Scottish fiction and the short stories firmly restored to print, and (as these words are written) a new edition of the *Quair* beginning to emerge in a series of 'Classics',[33] the time is ripe for a wider perception of James Leslie Mitchell's talents.

Egyptologist and Diffusionist, fantasist and speculator, Marxist, Anarchist, Scottish and English novelist, Grassic Gibbon and Mitchell are assured of their place. Grassic Gibbon is now a Scottish author of the first rank; James Leslie Mitchell need not stand in his shadow. *Spartacus* is evidence enough of an extraordinary talent, of a biting consciousness of features of past society and life which are easily overlooked or sentimentalised, and of a committed political awareness of injustice and brutality whose message was by no means irrelevant to the 1930s. The clear message of the closing pages of Mitchell's novel is that the butchering of the slave leader by Crassus and his men by no means marks the end of the rebellion, any more than the ghastly crucifixions on the Appian Way broke the spirit of humankind in the search for justice and freedom. *Spartacus* survives its author's untimely death as a monument to a commitment to justice and freedom, in the distant past, and in James Leslie Mitchell's own world where the fight for justice and freedom was still being fought.

NOTES

1. See Note on the Text.
2. Books are referred to according to the following code:
   Scottish Scene [with Hugh MacDiarmid] (London, 1934) ScS
   A Scots Quair (London, 1978 reprint) SQ
   Spartacus (London, 1933) S
3. The best treatment of Diffusionism will be found in Douglas Young's *Beyond the Sunset*.
4. MS Edinburgh University Library: 18 November 1933. Further details of MS locations, particularly of the partially-catalogued Mitchell holdings in Edinburgh University Library, are in the editor's *Bibliotheck* article of 1984 (see Bibliography).
5. From 'Power' reprinted in *A Scots Hairst* p. 177.
6. Mrs R. Mitchell, quoted by Malcolm in *A Blasphemer and Reformer*, p. 116.
7. *Plutarch's Lives* trans. B. Perrin (Loeb Classical Library) III (London, 1916), 335-51.
8. *Sallust* trans. J. C. Rolfe (London, 1921), pp. 65-7.
9. S. A. Cook, F. E. Adcock and M. P. Charlesworth, *Cambridge Ancient History* (Cambridge, 1932), IX, 332.
10. (London, 1855), II, p. 359.
11. Frank Marsh, *A History of the Roman World from 146 to 30 B.C.* (London, 1935), p. 145.
12. E.g. Paul Jal, *La guerre civile à Rome* (Paris, 1963), p. 20, and Robert Gunther, *Der Aufstand des Spartacus* (Köln, 1960), pp. 122-3.
13. See Malcolm p. 187.
14. Susannah Moodie, *Spartacus: A Roman Story* (London, 1822), pp. 7, 27.
15. *Cambridge Ancient History* IX, 331.
16. H. Fast, *Spartacus* (New York, 1951), p. 51; (London, 1952), p. 38.
17. Fast p. 23; (London, 1952), p. 31.
18. Malcolm pp. 116-7.
19. K. Marx and F. Engels, *Correspondence 1846-95* ed. D. Torr (New York, 1934), p. 126.
20. R. Humphrey, *Georges Sorel, Prophet without Honor* (Cambridge, Mass., 1951), p. 192.

21. Bury, p. 118. Mitchell's copy bears the stamp of Central Education School, Zeitoun, Cairo no. 49.
22. Now in the editor's possession.
23. From 'Literary Lights', ScS, 205.
24. *Studies in Scottish Fiction: 20th Century*, Vol 1., ed. Horst W. Drescher and Joachim W Schwend, Scottish Studies no 9, Frankfurt, Bern and New York, 1990, pp 271-287.
25. MS Edinburgh University Library. To Helen B. Cruickshank, 13 December 1960.
26. ibid.
27. MS Edinburgh University Library. To C.M. Grieve, 23 February 1937.
28. Malcolm p. 120.
29. Young p. 73.
30. M. Lindsay, *History of Scottish Literature* (London, 1977), p. 415.
31. D. Gifford, *Neil M. Gunn and Lewis Grassic Gibbon* (Edinburgh, 1983), p. 49.
32. F.R. Hart, *The Scottish Novel, A Critical Survey* (London, 1978), p. 231.
33. *Sunset Song*, ed. T. Crawford, appeared in the Canongate *Scottish Classics* in Spring 1988.

NOTE ON THE TEXT

The novel was typeset once for the Jarrold edition of 1933 (in the author's lifetime), and a second time for the Jarrold Jackdaw paperback reprint of 1937 — without the author's supervision of course. In 1970 Hutchinson published a reprint, the text photographed from 1933. The textual history of the novel is thus, on the face of it, uncomplicated.

After Mitchell's death, however, Mrs Mitchell came across a complete typescript of *Spartacus* 'which Leslie [Mitchell] had typed here in Welwyn Garden City'[1] — an interesting ambiguity which (as will shortly be seen) could be important. Presumably this is the typescript which survives among the Mitchell papers now in the custody of the National Library of Scotland. Mitchell was a quick, tidy and thoroughly businesslike worker, and the survival of a complete typescript is significant.

The Jackdaw came out by 17th February 1937[2] and did achieve some success — the editor's copy is of the 42nd thousand. Likewise the 1970 reprint achieved some success, but by April 1978 Mrs Mitchell was sadly reporting to C. M. Grieve that poor sales meant that this edition, too, was shortly to be allowed to go out of print.

Why then should a complete typescript of the novel survive among the author's papers? We know that Mitchell typed his own work, despite the astonishingly cheap rates he could find for occasional professional retyping[3] but this is a *fair copy retyping* bearing none of the marks of the heat of first composition, but frequent changes of mind both in ink (in his hand) and in overtyping on the same machine. The ribbon was changed during the job, and there are instructions typed in to compositors which would have disappeared had the typescript been copy-edited in a publisher's hands.

Perhaps most interestingly of all, Mitchell typed a page of prefatory matter listing other works as follows:
Books by J. LESLIE MITCHELL published in America
Hanno — E P Dutton
Cairo Dawns
Three Go Back — Bobbs-Merrill
The Lost Trumpet
and under the nom-de-plume of Lewis Grassic Gibbon
Sunset Song — Century Co.

The clear implication is that Mitchell had typed up and kept a copy for the US market, should success in Britain warrant his trying-out the book on US publishers. This would be consistent with his wide experience of US publishers, and his keen commercial sense.

The fact that the typescript remained in Mrs Mitchell's hands at his death suggests that the typescript (which appears to bear no marks of editing by any other hand) never left his desk. It does complicate the otherwise simple textual picture of *Spartacus* in ways which can be briefly described.

The published version (1933) includes some changes made by Mitchell on this new typescript (TS). TS p. 49 as an afterthought makes the phrase 'Hating all Greeks' start a new paragraph, accepted by 1933. TS p. 69 superimposes the phrase 'Now, he shouted aloud' on a much more complicated original version, and 1933 accepts this change.

This strongly suggests that the typescript was made before 1933 was published, and that the carbon was the basis for the typesetting at Jarrold's. The top copy was thoughtfully retained for future submission to US publishers. Even apparent errors in the typescript appear in 1933 uncorrected.

However, the 1933 text has also had corrections made independent of the typescript. Mitchell typed 'assailling' on TS p. 285, and the printer has corrected this (p. 240 of 1933) to 'assailing'; and minor changes are made — 'pectorale' on p. 58 of TS becoming 'breastplate' on p. 55 of the published text, and the tribune who is 'killed' on TS p. 65 is 'down' on p. 61 of the final text.

The typescript is thus probably Mitchell's top copy of the final version the carbon of which went to Jarrold's to be set in type, where it was edited and corrected. Had Mitchell lived, he would probably have marked those corrections on to the typescript and sent it on its way to the US for publication.

A comparison of this unique copy with the published 1933 text suggests few changes, though interesting ones. In the absence of proofs of 1933 (which do not seem to have survived) the text of this reprint is the 1933 version, as being overseen by the author — and without proofs we cannot tell which divergencies from the typescripts are Mitchell's, and which the publishers' own suggestions. The 1937 version, while catching some errors, offers no significant improvements, and the 1970 version repeats the text of 1933 by photographic reprinting. In the present edition, obvious misprints have been silently corrected.

NOTES

1. MS Edinburgh University Library: To C. M. Grieve, 28th November 1960.
2. MS Edinburgh University Library: To C. M. Grieve, 17th February 1937.
3. See Ian Campbell, 'Gibbon and MacDiarmid at Play: The Evolution of *Scottish Scene*', *The Bibliotheck* 13 (2), 1986, 44-52.

AN INTRODUCTORY BIBLIOGRAPHY TO J. L. MITCHELL

For lives of Grassic Gibbon see I. S. Munro, *Leslie Mitchell: Lewis Grassic Gibbon* (Edinburgh and London, 1966); Munro also edited *A Scots Hairst* (London, 1967) with reprints of biographical and autobiographical material from *Scottish Scene* (1934). Further important biographical and critical material is found in Douglas F. Young, *Beyond the Sunset* (Aberdeen, 1973) and W. K. Malcolm, *A Blasphemer and Reformer* (Aberdeen, 1984). There is a trenchant chapter in Douglas Gifford, *Neil M. Gunn and Lewis Grassic Gibbon* (Edinburgh, 1983). Substantial sections appear in Alan Bold, *Modern Scottish Literature* (London, 1983), F. R. Hart, *The Scottish Novel: A Critical Survey* (London, 1977), I. Murray and Bob Tait, *Ten Modern Scottish Novels* (Aberdeen, 1984) and R. Watson, *The Literature of Scotland* (London, 1984). Full bibliographies have appeared in a series of articles in *The Bibliotheck*, themselves listed and complemented in Ian Campbell, 'Lewis Grassic Gibbon Correspondence: A Background and Checklist', *The Bibliotheck* 12, 1 (1984), 46-57. An authoritative overall guide is W. R. Aitken, *Scottish Literature in English and Scots,* vol. 37 of *American Literature, English Literature and World Literatures in English* (Detroit, 1982). Malcolm's 1984 bibliography is up-to-date and lists most fully the Grassic Gibbon and Mitchell publications. D. M. Budge has a good paperback anthology of short stories and essays in *Smeddum: Stories and Essays* (London, 1980). Mitchell died with his papers in some disarray, and the article on his correspondence cited above gives some introduction to that subject: a further treatment is in 'A Tribute that never was: the Plan for a Lewis Grassic Gibbon *Festschrift*', *Studies in Scottish Literature* XX (1985), 219-30. Also among the papers was the novella which has appeared as *The Speak of the Mearns* (Edinburgh, 1982). Patricia J. Wilson has an excellent article on 'Freedom and God: Some implications of the Key Speech in *A Scots Quair*', *Scottish Literary Journal* 7, 2 (December, 1980), 71. The most recent, and very valuable discussion of Mitchell appears in 'Novelists of the Renaissance' by Isobel Murray, a chapter of vol. 4 of *The History of Scottish Literature* ed. Cairns Craig (Aberdeen, 1987, 103-17). For further discussion by the present author see 'Chris Caledonia, the Search for an Identity', *Scottish Literary Journal* I, 2 (December, 1974), 45-57; 'James Leslie Mitchell's

Spartacus: a Novel of Rebellion', *Scottish Literary Journal* 5, 1 (May, 1978), 53-60; *Kailyard: A New Assessment* (Edinburgh, 1981) and *Lewis Grassic Gibbon* (Scottish Writers Series, 6, (Edinburgh, 1985)).

I. INSURRECTION

The Gathering of the Slaves

It was Springtime in Italy, a hundred years before
the crucifixion of Christ

(i)

WHEN Kleon heard the news from Capua he rose early one morning, being a literatus and unchained, crept to the room of his Master, stabbed him in the throat, mutilated that Master's body even as his own had been mutilated: and so fled from Rome with a stained dagger in his sleeve and a copy of *The Republic* of Plato hidden in his breast.

He took the southwards track, not the Way, but the via terrena, hiding by day and walking swiftly by night. His face was pallid, his eyes green and weary. He had no faith in the Gods and could know no pleasure in women. Under his chin was tattooed in blue the casqued head of Athena, for he was of Athenian descent, though sold by his father in the slave-market of Corinth in time of famine.

Purchased thence, he had been for twelve years the lover of a rich merchant in Alexandria. The merchant was brown and stout and paunched, holding faith in forgotten Canaanite Gods, for he had been born in Tyre. Kleon he had taught to read and write, to compute, to play upon the lyre and to dance in obscene measures with the women of the household. Frequently, under the surveillance of the merchant, he was stripped naked and beaten with a fine wire whip, till the white flesh of his young body quivered under a thin criss-cross of fine blue weals. Watching, the merchant would quiver ecstatically in harmony, and then order the boy to be bathed and scented and fairly clad. Then, at nightfall, under the golden haze of the Alexandrine stars, he would come to Kleon.

And Kleon forgot the starings of childish wonder, and his mother's face, in tears, and the ways of little beasts and birds on the blue hills of Corinth.

In the afternoons, in the courtyard of the merchant's house, Kleon would sit at the feet of his Master and read aloud to him, unwinding and rewinding the scrolls in the manner he had been taught. He read in Greek, in Latin, and in Syriac; and for his Master's delectation he sought assiduously in the bookshops for those tales that

3

the merchant loved: Tales of the Baalim, of Ashtaroth and the obscene fecundities of the Mother Gods; the *Nine Rapings* of the Greek Ataretos; nameless works by nameless men, translations and retranslations of all the dark and secret and ecstatic imaginings of men who pondered on women. Arab and Indian tales he read, though their origins were long lost, tales from the Utmost Lands, from China and beyond. The merchant would nod and groan in pleasure, and drink from a bowl a mixture of honey and water, flavoured with aniseed, for he was an abstemious man.

And Kleon had forgotten love, but he had not forgotten hate. Yet that in time went by as well, even while he knelt and the wire-whip sang. For he read other books than the women-tales and saw that hatred was foolish. Great men had enquired in the meaning of Life, the nature of Fate and the loves of the Gods, the why of pain and terror and death, men slaves to lust and men slaves to men. And these things they had discovered were part of a divine plan.

For a while thereafter, conceiving Serapis, the Supreme Deity, to be insane, Kleon believed in him.

But at the age of twenty-one he and a Negro named Okkulos, too old to give pleasure to the merchant, were sold to a circus-trainer from Rome. In the course of the voyage Okkulos succeeded in breaking his manacles and freeing Kleon. Together they strangled the captain of the ship and threw overboard the circus-trainer from Rome. They were joined in revolt by the crew, and sailed to the White Islands, joining the pirate fleet of an Iberian named Thoritos, a tall man lacking a hand. He was said to worship in a cave a pointed stone fallen from heaven, and had gained great treasure in the Social Wars.

Thoritos had many wives, captured in his raids. Two of these, of whom he was weary, he presented to Kleon, for he grew to love the wit and learning of the Greek. And Kleon looked on the women and shook, and the pirates shouted with laughter. And Kleon took the women to his bed, in hate and a white, cold lust: and they kissed him, apt in love, to tears, and the wall of ice broke round his heart.

Now ten years passed on the great White Islands and the secret sailings from their windy coasts. Thoritos levied tribute across many routes, and his riches grew, and Kleon became his first captain. Yet he had no love of ships, though the sea he loved, sight and sound and smell of it in the long, amethystine noons, when his bed was set on a

4

westward terrace and the world of the Islands grew still. Crouched at his feet one of Thoritos' women would sing and brush the flies from his face, and bring him cool wine to drink when he woke from his daytime dreams. And Kleon would drink and doze again, though he slept but little, lying still instead, companioned with thought. And the women would hear him groan as he lay, and think that a God was with him in dreams.

But he thought instead, till his thoughts were as knives: Why did men live and endure it all? For to-morrow came up with the self-same sun, the night went down with the self-same stars, there were neither Gods nor beginnings nor ends, plan in the blood and pain of birth, plan in the blood and pain of death, only an oft-told tale that went on and knew neither reason nor rhythm nor right, men as beasts that the herdsman goads, the Herdsman himself but a slavering lout. And he thought of his captured stores of books, and the dream the great Athenian dreamt, of Herdsmen wise in the perfect state; and he knew it only an idle dream, yet he loved it and turned to it for ease; or woke and pulled the woman in his bed and buried his face in the peace of her breasts.

And the years went by like a fading breath, till he woke one dawn and found himself, in company with a score of others, redeemed the cross because of their strength, standing with white-painted feet in the ergastulum of the Roman slave-market. They had been captured by a disguised galley in an attempted raid on the Alexandrian wheat-route.

The overseer of Lucius Julius Pacianus bought him and three others and took them to the villa on the Palatine. Pacianus himself came out to inspect them. He had dull eyes and a grave mien and believed that he should have been made a consul. Standing in the sunlight, his green tunic edged with silver, his beard combed and oiled, he pointed first at Kleon and then at another.

'That one and that. They will be safer so.'

Not until two grinning Libyans approached, and seized him and threw him on his back, did Kleon understand. Then he saw that they had brought an iron bowl where water steamed, and with it two small knives.

And suddenly, vividly, with an intensity that wrung his heart, he remembered the smell of the sea, and the smell of women, and

5

never again so remembered them.

(ii)

Three mornings after setting out on the road to Capua he awoke on the edge of the dark and found two men bending over him. One held a pliant cord in his hands, and stooped with drooling lips. The young sunlight dappled Kleon's face and he smelt the dew-wet vines. He laughed and stretched himself and bared his throat.

'I am ready,' he said.

They drew back, startled, threatening. Thereon Kleon suddenly leapt to his feet and struck at the nearest with his dagger. The man swore and jumped aside. Kleon laughed again. The roll of *The Republic* fell from his breast.

'Slit throats are to the swift, you swine.'

Then he stood and considered them. They were shepherds, clad in grey felt tunics, with bare feet and legs and conical hats. One was tall, red-haired, an obvious Gaul, with sleepy eyes and curling lips. The other was of lesser stature and different breed, and he it was held the rope. His forehead and chin sloped steeply away from the line of his straight, keen nose. And, looking in his eyes, Kleon was aware that they were the eyes of one aberrant to the point of madness.

'Why the stranglers' rope?' the literatus asked.

'Why not?' said the sleepy-eyed shepherd, looking at his companion. The short man bared his teeth.

'It's fit end for a Roman slave.'

'Aren't you also slaves?'

'We were — yesterday.'

'Then you've heard of Capua?'

At that the eyes of the sleepy Gaul lit up. 'We are making Capua,' he said; and added, with simplicity. 'So we were to strangle you, to prove ourselves freemen and worthy to kill.'

Kleon picked up his copy of *The Republic*. 'I also was a slave. I am going to Capua. Come with me. We'll be crucified near one another.'

They scowled at him and stood fast. The short man's lips parted again, shewing decayed teeth.

'You're mad, a fool, or an ill augur. Pity you woke so soon. I was

6

to open your chest and offer your heart to Kokolkh — though Brennus, being but a Gaul, was against that.'

'A sacrifice?' Kleon was coldly amused. 'I hadn't heard of your God. Tell me of him as we go. This is a poor place to hide, and we must make the hills.' He added, as an afterthought, coldly, 'I carry a charm that twists in agony the entrails of any who seek my life.'

High up on a hill-ridge they found a grassy dip and squatted there throughout the hours of the day. Below them the country lay blue in the Spring-time warmth. To the north a ribbon of river glinted. Once a kid strayed near them and the short man leapt out upon it, strangled it with his hands, and brought it back to their hiding-place. They drank its blood, but their throats were too parched to swallow the raw flesh. The short man speared the kid's heart on a flake of stone and held it towards the sun, ceremonially. Brennus grinned. Kleon squatted cross-wise and regarded the proceeding with passionless gaze.

'Who is Kokolkh?' he asked.

'I come from the northern seacoast of Iberia,' the short man said, 'but I am no Iberian. My name is Titul and my people are the last of a race that lived on the world's edge, far in the Western Sea. This people was a great people: but they neglected to sacrifice to the God Kokolkh. So he whelmed their country in mud and sand; and the seas rose against it and devoured it.' He paused ceremonially, being mad, and chanting an oft-told tale. 'But my fathers fled in boats and them Kokolkh allowed to escape. They saw him, the God visible, in the lightning fires that smote the islands. He was bearded with serpents and on his head were the feather-plumes of the sun.'

Kleon nodded, as the slurred chant ended. 'It was the island of Atlantis, for so Plato tells. Of him you've never heard. And why worship this ill God?'

'He is Pain and Life,' said Titul, and ate the heart ceremonially, watched by Brennus the agnostic and Kleon the atheist. The sun wheeled westward. Brennus clasped his hands round his knees, and sang a song in the broken Latin of the vulgares slaves:

'These are the things I desire:
The city of stakes
And the darkened rooms

7

Of my home,
And the curling smoke,
And the moon;
Wild cattle low in the woods:
Shall I not return?'

'He's a poet,' said Titul; and fell to his drone. 'Mighty were the poets of old in the vanished Western Isle.'

Brennus yawned. 'They were fools. For they were drowned. Let's sleep.' He yawned again, and shaded his eyes and looked south. 'There's a big farm across that stream.'

Kleon nodded. 'We'll try to get near at dusk, and free the slaves. If we form a large enough company, we can march openly to join the Games men.'

Titul licked his thick lips and also peered through the haze. 'There may be women there — women of the Masters.'

Stretched full-length on the sun-warmed grass, Brennus purred drowsily. 'No women are like the Gaul women. Oh, Gods, Gods, none at all! And I haven't had one since they brought me south, four years ago this Spring. Deep-breasted and with wide full hips; and we used to raid them. Gods! for a strong, warm woman to weep under your hands!'

'In the Western Isle,' said Titul, 'there were mighty women.'

(iii)

A day later Kleon halted his band by a river ford. With him were forty men and three women. More than half of the men were Gauls, tall, thin, and black-burned by the sun. Shepherds, they were matted still with the filth of their night-time kennels where every sunset they were led and chained when the horns of the horreum sounded. They had ceased to weep and sing and stare, and challenge one another to racings and wrestlings. Now, wearied, Brennus elected their leader, they lay down at halts and cast lots for the use of the three women captives.

Since daybreak they had marched through a country deserted. Like droppings of blood long shed, the grapes hung heavy in abandoned vineyards. Flocks strayed without shepherds and the horrea were found fast-locked and barred. These buildings the Gauls fired and looted, gathering bundles of grass and piling them under the wooden eaves. In stone-built houses which would not burn they defiled the atria with excrement, and smeared it upon the faces of the statues in the peristyles. Far across the countryside as the day waned other fires broke forth at intervals.

The Gauls had been shepherds and labourers, but the others vulgares of the household, ostiarii, pistores, coqui, bed-chamber slaves and slaves of the bath. Nine of these were Greeks, slaves from slave mothers, pale men with black hair and keen eyes and a high, shrill laughter: as though they knew this freedom a dream that would not endure, and shivered in the winds of the open lands. Their backs were scored with cicatrices, for their mistress had been Petronia, wife of C. Gaius Petronius, strong in belief that a well-flogged slave was a willing slave. Now, clad in a single linen shift, dust-covered, blinded, she was dragged forward by the hair grasped in the hand of a giant Gaul. He had cut a switch from a thorn-brake and at intervals raised the shift and smote the woman with the full strength of his arm. Her two daughters, with faces engrimed and staring eyes, ran by the side of their mother. Them the Gaul did not beat, for he desired them.

Five of the men were Negroes, cooks and men of the bedchamber, who slobbered a strange, half-intelligible Latin and stared appalled on the spaces of a countryside they had seen but seldom in their days of toil. One had been the household executioner. In the sleeves of his girt-up robe he carried two swords, and marched and smiled with a vacant intensity.

But the women slaves of the household had been left behind, at the order of the literatus Kleon. For they would delay the march. They had wept and followed the company many miles, some carrying children, some loot from the rooms of Petronius. Then they were lost behind in a stretch of marshland.

Now it drew towards nightfall again, and at the halt by the ford Kleon gestured Brennus and Titul to his side. Since they freed the slaves of Petronius, these slaves had elected them leaders without demur, and Ionians Kleon and the Negroes Titul. Some already had heard of the Gladiators' revolt, others believed it only a tale, and the cross the end of the day's revolt. These it was who wrecked their fury on the countryside and the body of their stumbling mistress.

Brennus came sleepy-eyed from the midst of his Gauls. He wore the sandals of Petronia, strained and split on his shambling feet, and about him had girt the green robe she once wore, for he had been the first to reach her room. In his belt he carried a dagger, a sling, and over his shoulder a pouch of clay pellets.

'Look there,' said Kleon.

They shaded their eyes with their hands and looked into the sunset quietude of Italy. Against it was a glitter of metal. A band of soldiers was riding towards the ford.

'The Masters,' said Brennus, his hands trembling. Kleon looked at him with a cold contempt, unstirred by either fear or hope, and Brennus caught that look, and ceased to tremble. 'Well, here's an end to women and freedom.'

'We'll cut the throats of the women,' said Titul, licking his lips. 'But first we'll fight.'

At the order of the three leaders the company climbed a knoll that overlooked the ford. Upon its summit were great stones, ruins of a temple builded by ancient men. With these stones the slaves set to building a wall. Flinging back the long hair from their faces, the sun-blackened Gauls lost their fear, and toiled with obscene jests and panting breath. Then they unwound their shepherds' slings, and laid in each leathern thong a round clay pellet, such as were used against flock-raiding wolves. The Negro executioner drew out his swords and laughed with a vacant fury towards the ford. But the Ionians were silent, toiling to erect the stone wall. Then one, the youngest, said to the others:

'I'd thought to see the ships in Delos harbour of which our mothers told.' And he smiled upon them a strange, frightened smile. And the older men muttered and turned away their faces, to hide the ready Greek tears.

The three women crouched in the hollow on the summit of the knoll. Petronia knelt and stared with half blind eyes. A Negro flung filth in her face and promised her jackals instead of men to share her bed by the morrow. Kleon smiled coldly and looked down on the ford.

Now the horsemen rode near. They numbered half a century, and were heavy cavalry, armed and armoured in the new fashion borrowed from the Greeks, with iron leggings and breastplates and crested helmets. Two officers rode at the head of the company, men of

10

high rank, middle-aged and grave. The sunset was in Kleon's eyes, but his company and the hasty defences were plain to the eyes of the soldiers. A shout arose.

'Slaves!'

With this came a roar of laughter. The horsemen splashed through the ford. Then, at a word, they wheeled and halted below the knoll. One of the officers held up his hand, stilling his soldiers, and addressing Kleon.

'Excrement: a hundred lashes and the mines for those of your following who surrender. For such of the others as escape our swords — the cross. Choose. Quickly.'

Behind Kleon the giant Gaul who had beaten Petronia throughout the march laid aside his switch and wrenched a great stone from the ground. Before the officer had ceased to speak the Gaul swung the stone twice and thrice till he reeled in the momentum. Then he hurled it from him. It soared through the air, struck a soldier from his horse, and broke the back of the animal, which neighed a shrill scream. Wild laughter broke from the slaves. All seized stones and hurled them upon the horsemen, Kleon alone standing inactive, watching the horsemen scatter. As they did so, slaves and soldiers alike were startled by a woman's scream.

'Father! Petronius! My father!'

One of the daughters of Petronia attempted to climb the wall at the summit of the knoll. Titul seized her hair and held her. Weeping, she knelt and flung out her arms. Titul licked his thick lips.

'It's Petronius himself.' He laughed, and snatched one of the swords from the Negro executioner. Then, twisting the girl to silence, he rent her robe from her shoulders and bent her back over his knee. In the half-dusk her body shone white, and the sword, a moment ceremonially poised in the sun's last rays, descended to sever her breasts. But Kleon leant forward and held Titul's arm.

Then he called to Petronius: 'We hold your wife and daughters. Come nearer and we'll cut their throats.'

Petronius, the officer who had threatened them with the mines or the cross, gave a cry and fell forward in his saddle. Two soldiers went to assist him. He was an old man, in the Social War notorious for his cruelties. From the knoll Kleon watched him recover and again sit erect in his stirrups. His face was now indistinct, as were the faces of all the soldiers, but his voice carried clearly uphill in the evening quiet:

'If you'll surrender the women you can go.'

A howl of laughter rose from the slaves. Titul, with mad, drowsing eyes, again swung up the sword. But again Kleon the literatus held him.

'And what's our surety that you won't follow?'

The soldiers debated. 'The surety that a body of slaves, too strong for us to assail, is camped three miles beyond the ford.'

Kleon looked into the darkness where the sunset had been. The Romans spoke the truth, for he saw the glint of watchfires. He decided quickly, with a cold amusement that he ordered the Masters.

'Withdraw your soldiers, Petronius, and we'll send down your daughters. Beyond the ford only we'll release Petronia.'

The body of horsemen manoeuvred dimly. A segment of it trotted away, with rhythmic hoof-beats, into the darkness. Kleon freed the girl from Titul's clutch. Half-swooning, she staggered down the hill. Then the eunuch literatus became aware that the Gauls, laughing, had surrounded Brennus and the other girl. In a sudden, sick distaste he thrust through the group. At the girl he did not look.

'Run!'

She sped down the hill towards the ten horsemen who still waited. Singing and laughing, the slaves descended the hill in her rear and splashed through the ford. Petronia, fast-gripped by the giant Gaul, was dragged in their midst. They had gained the further side when a rhythmic beating of hooves again arose to their ears. Then, out of the darkness on either side, burst the horsemen who had ridden away. At the same time Petronius and his ten charged through the ford.

Too late Kleon realized his own simplicity. He screamed:

'Scatter! Westward is the slave camp.'

Then the horsemen were on them. With shrill screams the Negroes fled, all except the executioner, who swung his swords and disembowelled a horse. A moment later, clawing at a pilum buried in his stomach, he fell into the water and was carried away. Maddened, the sun-blackened Gauls stood fast and fought, or, running to a little distance, swung their slings and poured a volley of clay pellets into the mellay. Each pellet was of the hardness of stone and fashioned to

12

ensure straight flight. Several horsemen fell from the saddles, and an Iberian and a Greek, struck by these projectiles of their fellow-slaves, were killed instantly. Then the horsemen wheeled and charged again, and the Gauls, drawing their short knives, attempted to hamstring the horses. A sickening smell arose from the slicing of warm flesh. Then complete darkness descended.

(iv)

In the darkness a half-mile beyond the ford Kleon stumbled upon the Ionians. One of them limped and another was attempting to staunch the flow of blood from his neck. Him Kleon bandaged with strips torn from his tunic. Then they listened, but now the night was void of sound.

Yet presently there neared the noise of a galloping horse.

'The Masters!'

Kleon listened, panting, having fought at the ford, not only run from it. 'There is only one. I'll stab the beast in the belly.'

With his short dagger in his hand, he crouched by the side of the track. The horse shied in alarm from his leaping figure. Then Kleon saw it was no Master, but Titul. The Iberian grinned with gleaming teeth.

'I dragged down a soldier and dashed out his brains with a stone,' he said. 'His helmet cracked like a shell. Then I stole his horse.'

'Brennus?'

'Brennus is dead,' said Titul. 'For I saw him killed. As for the other Gauls, they're also dead and doubtlessly in hell, being men without GODS.'

'They were heroes,' said one of the Ionians, a clerk, a thin man who had run with rapidity. 'Such men they bred once in Greece.'

'Mighty in valour were those of the vanished Western Isle,' said Titul, being mad.

Kleon clung to the horse's mane. The Ionians trotted behind. The darkness began to clear and soften till, brilliant and white, the stars came out. Up the hill-side a wolf howled long and piercingly.

'The wolves are late about,' said Titul, 'for the flocks are unguarded.'

Again the long howl, wild and cold and cruel, arose. It was a

13

lone wolf. None of its kind answered it.

'It may be the Wolf of the Masters herself,' said Kleon, 'come down from Rome to bay.'

The Greeks shivered, believing it a werewolf. Remote in the distance, they heard a last howl, then the beast left them.

Suddenly one of the Greeks, a young man, stumbled and fell. Titul halted his horse and Kleon went back and bent over the man.

'What ails you?' he asked.

Then he saw it was the young man who on the hill-top had spoken of Delos harbour. Now between his lips his breath blew out in a bloody spume. The eunuch squatted beside him and wiped his mouth.

'I'm wounded in the breast. But I said nothing. Lest you leave me behind to die. Alone. In the dark. Like a slave.'

He coughed and murmured. Broken Greek came to his lips, though he had never seen Greece. The spume grew to a warm stream. Suddenly he gripped Kleon's arm.

'Oh, the sea!'

Then Kleon knew that he was dead, and a sad and terrible anger stirred in his frozen heart. But there were no tears in the body that had lost its manhood.

(v)

It was near to dawn and the morning cold with a drizzling rain before Kleon, Titul, and the four Ionians came to the slave camp. They had twice lost their way, wandering up stark ravines or into cane-brakes. By accident they stumbled upon the camp, nor did they know it the camp at first, for the fires were long dead, no sentries placed, no trench had been dug or stake-fence erected. The slaves were men from the Eastern world, and they slept under dripping sycamore trees, shivering, numbed in their dreams. But one was awake and he challenged them on the verge of the camp, in a whining, sibilant Latin.

'We're slaves,' said Kleon, peering at him in the dawn-gloom, 'seeking freedom and empty bellies, not to mention a band of Gladiators.'

The man held an axe in his hand. Now he came from under the dripping fronds and looked at Kleon with a frowning face. The Greek saw before him one stout and black-haired, with a curling beard and

14

a curling nose, bright, scowling eyes as black as his hair. He was clad in an ill-fitting toga, edged with a senator's fringe.

'If you seek empty bellies you've been misdirected, for these hogs are filled with the wine we looted. As for the Gladiators of Capua, they've surrendered at last, or so it's said, betrayed by a Thracian who led them.'

The eunuch shrugged. 'Then we don't seek the Gladiators. Couldn't the fools find a leader other than a Thracian savage? And who is your leader here?'

The bearded man scowled upon the morning. 'I am the leader — may Jehovah give me wit. Half of these' — he waved an arm at the dim groups huddled under the trees — 'are Bithynians, newly-come from Brindisium and speaking no Latin. I and twenty household slaves of Crassus the Lean freed them, for we surprised their guards on the marsh and strangled them.'

'That was well. I am Kleon of Corinth, a Greek.'

'That's ill, for I've no love of Greeks. I am Gershom of Kadesh, a Pharisee and a Jew.'

In revolt against Jannaeus and his Hellenistic priests, Gershom ben Sanballat had twice raised the standards of the Hasidim, and twice had been defeated. But so dourly had he held his own in the mountains around Kadesh, that the King had been forced to grant him a pardon, and thereafter left him in peace. Gershom had retired to cultivating his farms and engrossing himself in the Ochian mysteries of the synagogue. These practices lost him his following. In two years' time Jannaeus died and his widow Salome Alexandra reigned in Jerusalem. Among the first to fall was Gershom, secretly seized and sold into slavery in Syria, from there re-sold to Rome, from there re-sold to the household of Marcus Licinius Crassus. For less than a year a slave, his iron spirit was but faintly bent when he heard the news of the Gladiators' revolt, and stirred his fellows to emulation. Now he fronted Kleon, unclean, a Greek, the old, strong Gentile hate in his face, that hate forgotten while he was a slave, stirring now to a flame from old embers.

But also, the Greek had a strange attraction. The flame died down. Scowling, Gershom raised a hand to head and heart. Kleon responded, and they then touched hands, watched by Titul and the Ionians. But Gershom secretly cleansed his palm against his tunic,

15

remembering that the touch of a Gentile was defilement.

'This is an Iberian,' said Kleon, pointing to his company, 'and these are Ionians.'

'There's Greek wine under these cloths,' said the Jew. 'And unclean meat. Eat, if you're hungry.'

Titul and the Ionians squatted on the ground, and drank, and were warmed with the strong Greek wine, choking and gulping on the mouthfuls at first, being slaves unaccustomed to wine. Famished, they tore with their fingers at the roasted meat, Kleon eating but sparingly, hungered though he was. For even hunger in his mutilated body was only a faint ghost of the lusts he had known. Slave or free, that would alter never, and a moment that thought came twisting his mouth. Then he filled a silver cup with wine and went to Gershom, who had drawn away.

'This is a fine cup of good workmanship,' he said.

'I stole it from the pantry of Crassus the Lean,' said Gershom, moodily. 'He will crucify his overseer because of its loss: unless the man has fled. Which is unlikely: for he was a fool.'

'Why is he named the Lean?'

'His soul is lean,' said Gershom. 'May it howl for ever in the wastes of Sheol. Which is hell.'

A taciturn and calculating man, the attraction of the Greek was growing upon him. Looking at Kleon, he combed his curled beard with long, brown fingers, and sighed, remembering Kadesh, though memory and heart and soul alike were encased in an armour of iron. Kleon drank the wine in a cold amusement, and answered with sardonic politeness.

'I hadn't heard of your hell. Also, but a little while back you spoke of an unknown God. Who is he?'

'Jehovah, the One God. Your Greek and Roman Gods are but idols of demons. No idols are reared to the One True God — unless by Salome's Hellene rats.'

'There are no Gods,' said Kleon, 'but Time and Fate. I worship neither, which doubtlessly vexes them. This Iberian also has a new God — with a name like a cough and a serpent's head and its home, I gather, the sea.'

'Doubtlessly it is Behemoth, the Beast of the Waters,' said Gershom, looking at Titul contemptuously. 'For he is a Gentile.'

'He is also mad,' said the eunuch, indifferently, and looked about him. 'Your Bithynians are awakening.'

The rain and the morning gloom had passed away. Above the ridged Italian hills uprose the sun, trailing a translucent veil that shivered and faded like a bubble-wall. In the air was the smell of green life rain-drenched. From under the trees the slaves thronged forth to stand by Gershom and peer into the East. As the sun rose full and rested upon the brow of the hill, round, splendid and scintillant as a new gold coin, the shivering Bithynians droned an Ormuzdic hymn, their arms upraised in adoration, their mouths engaged in singing and yawning. Titul, the Iberian, prostrated himself, howling at the sun like a dog. But Kleon, Gershom, and the Ionians did not worship, knowing the sun to be but a ball of fire three leagues away.

One slave still lay asleep under a sycamore. Yet presently he awoke and looked at the worshippers, companioned by those who did not worship. One of these attracted his attention. He crawled to his feet and came softly behind Titul.

'As big a fool as ever, Iberian. Your God's a slave like yourself, and cannot keep his bed.'

His sleepy bass laugh boomed out, disturbing the hymn. Then he turned his face towards Kleon the eunuch, who saw that it was Brennus.

His tale was short:

'At the ford I broke the knees of a horse. Horse and rider fell on me. I took the man by the throat and lay with him under the horse, strangling him. I held his throat till he ceased to move and his skin grew cold in my hands. Then the Masters came slicing their swords in the dead and cutting the throats of the wounded. So I feigned death, but looked out a little, the shine of the moon was on us by then. Petronius and his wife stood by the ford and near them stood two others. Petronia wept like a bleating sheep, and knelt, and wrung her hands. The two other Masters cried out at Petronius, and pleaded with him, but he grunted and spat. Then he put his arm round Petronia and drove his dagger in her heart. I hid behind the dead horse and saw no more. She was strong in love, as I found that night I took her in bed. But a bitch.'

He ruminated a little, vexed with some memory. 'I didn't mean to hurt her then — overmuch. Pity that that fool should kill a good

17

bedmate. He'll not spare the daughter either, if she tells — Gods, she was ripe and fair!'

'Fair from the womb were the children of women in the vanished Western Isle,' said Titul, being mad.

(vi)

At noon Gershom ben Sanballat marshalled his Bithynians. One man who was quarrelsome he slew with his own hands. Then he marched southwards, resolved to seek some stronghold, and from there escape to the sea.

With him went Kleon and Titul and Brennus. They marched until sunset, and then, hard by a marsh, came on the rout of a battle. Horses, riderless and ridden, streamed north in drumming flight. Already wolves howled on the verge of the dark. Seeing the fugitives soldiers of the Masters, the Jew flung his company upon them, slaying many and possessing themselves of armour and swords.

Only then they learnt that this rout from the Battle of the Lake had been wrought by the Gladiators, still undefeated. Their leader had fallen on Clodius the praetor, taking him unawares and scattering the half-legion he had brought from Rome.

Gershom halted his company and waited till dawn. But from east and west and south, all that night, the slaves gathered by rumour and an insane hope, marched into the camp of the Gladiators.

The Gladiators

(i)

A YEAR before the Battle of the Lake there had arrived in the ludus of Batiates at Capua a Threce called Spartacus, condemned to death ad ludam as a bandit. One side of his head was split with a great sword-wound, and he sat long hours on the benches, saying nothing, staring at the clang and wheel of the training Games-men. He was young and bearded, heavy-chinned, with a brow that rose straightly to thick-curled hair. The thick-lipped mouth was set evenly, his eyes were clear and grey. Batiates stared at him move and saw the hunter's stride. No story came with the slave from the barbarous land where he had been a bandit. Then presently, in the idle gossip of the ludus, the story spread that the bandit himself remembered nothing, the sword-wound had destroyed his memory.

Presently the wound healed. He was quick and strong, his grey eyes cool and patient, his hands learned readily the grip of the gladius, the shameful, curved sword of the Games-men. Batiates matched him with mirmillones, then with a retiarius, both times in test. But a madness came on the Threce, caught in the retiarius' net. He dropped his wooden sword and caught his opponent and strangled him to death ere the lanistae could save him. Panting, he flung the body on the ground while all the school gaped and Batiates smiled. With a thorough training this slave would earn a good price for the Circus at Rome.

It was a time of hardship and heavy taxes. Batiates cut down the supply of meat to the men in the ludus. Accustomed to flesh, not corn, the Gladiators grumbled and dozed in the sun, unheeding the shouts of the lanistae. Batiates had these armed with great wire whips, and the Gladiators driven again to their exercises. Watching them, Batiates would calculate on each the profit, and retire at night, satisfied, to the arms of Elpinice.

She was sixteen years of age, a Greek slave, and four years the mistress of Batiates. She was Athenian born, the slave-master had affirmed, as she stood naked, with white-painted feet on the platform of the ergastulum. Batiates, in need of a mistress, had kindled, grunting, but demanded if she were yet a virgin. Reassured, he had

19

bought her and taken her to his bed. His slaves heard that night sounds that rang through the ludus. But by morning she had learned the place of a bed-slave. In the months that followed she was quiet and demure, with ivory skin and deep red hair, and dark brows meeting intently, Greekwise, across her nose. Hated by the rest of the slaves, she kept Batiates' bed and his favour. Wakeful in the middle of a night, she would hear the drone from the sheds of the Gladiators, and a God of horror havoc in her heart as she looked on the sleeping Batiates.

Winter went by. The food grew worse. Now, roused, the Gladiators were like half-tamed beasts snarling at the sight of Batiates. But he kept them patiently, awaiting the sales of Spring. Elpinice fed the Gladiators with scraps from the kitchen; and stumbling through the sheds in the dark found herself by the chained Thracian.

He spoke to her in halting Latin. 'What is your name?'

'Elpinice. And yours is Spartacus.'

She put a hand on his head. He put up a chained hand on her arm. She shivered in his sudden, wild grip.

Lovers, she found in his bed delight, not agony. He found with her something that cleansed the dark gloom from his eyes. Lying together, they planned the revolt, with the restive mutter of the Gladiators around them.

Elpinice brought the keys in the dead of one night, and unlocked the chains. Shouting, the Gladiators poured into the kitchens and fed their starving stomachs with meat and filled their hands with spits for weapons. Roused, Batiates called out the lanistae, and a desperate fight broke out in the half-dawn, the Thracian leading the Gladiators, Elpinice crouching in the sheds and watching. Presently the lanistae broke and fled and the Gladiators threw aside the spits and armed themselves with the abandoned weapons. Gannicus, a German retiarius with palms sent down to the ludus for re-training, would have made himself leader, but the Gladiators shouted for the Threce Spartacus, and placed themselves under his command.

Ere Batiates could rouse Capua, the Gladiators marched from the city in a compact body, armed with the weapons of the lanistae, led by the Thracian bandit, the woman Elpinice in their midst.

Waking the morning after the Battle of the Lake, she crouched by Spartacus and remembered these things. They seemed part of a far tale now. Between them and now lay the first wild days in the crater of Vesuvius, unsheltered, when a troop of velites was sent against them, and routed, and five centuries of legionaries routed as well: between them and now lay the days of starvation when Spartacus had fought, possessed by a God or a demon, to keep his fellows from surrender: between them and now lay the perilous descent of the lava crags, at night, by ropes, to a sleeping countryside and food for the seizing: between them and now lay the days when the slaves round Capua revolted and joined them, and decimated the half-legion that Clodius had led.

The camp was silent in the hush of the dawn. Elpinice knelt and stared at the face of the Gladiator, he had turned uneasily in the night, throwing the cloths from his face. Now the great wound was no more than a faint, dark limning on the dark-bronzed skin, on head and chin and breast the hair curled blue-black and metallic, the face had a terrifying simplicity in sleep, so that Elpinice remembered the great stone faces she had seen in her childhood in Athens. She shivered and drew the cloths about her, and watched through the tent-opening the coming of the dawn.

It had been Clodius' tent, captured with much other gear in the Battle of the Lake. All night it had sheltered a Threce Gladiator and an Attic slave-woman, the leaders of the servile host. For the rest, the slaves had flung up shelters of earth and grass, and slept in these, or rolled themselves in the garments stripped from the Roman dead, and lain in the lee of the waving clumps of rushes. But Gannicus, the German retiarius with palms, elected strategos under Spartacus, had erected a skin tent in imitation of the Thracian. The third strategos, Castus the Gaul, had patrolled the camp.

Hating the Roman titles and ranks, the Gladiators had named their leaders strategoi, as in the armies of Greece, and elected each from day to day. The girl, looking into the morning and the future, saw trouble awaiting that order of things: till the Masters marched down their legions and crowned the revolt with the cross.

For that was the certain end. No armies yet had withstood the

21

legions, despite the chance defeat of Clodius. He or another would return, and unless the servile host dispersed, seeking the mountains or the sea —

Elpinice turned. Suddenly, through the stir of the slave-camp outside, a bucina roared. Then the pad of hurrying feet came near.

'Strategos!'

(iii)

Spartacus, buckling on his Threce armour, gained the middle of the camp within a minute of the bucina sounding. Running to him came Castus and Gannicus. The German grinned like a wolf.

'Nearly two thousand of them, so a shepherd says. There — you can see the gleam of the standards. The ravine still hides the main body.'

The Thracian bandit looked and saw the morning dazzle on weapons. It was an ill place to be taken in battle, with the marsh behind them. Then he smiled. There would be no battle. He turned his dark, staring eyes on Gannicus.

'We'll not fight.'

The retiarius, a Teutone, with grey eyes and red hair, heavy of jaw and bearded again since his escape from Batiates, swore, the blood running red across his forehead.

'By the fat-bellied Gods of the Baltic, are you afraid? You'll surrender?'

'Not even by those Gods. Look, it's a party of slaves, with stolen armour.'

All looked again. So it was. The party marched undisciplined, shield-flourishing. The red did not recede from the brow of the Teutone. But Castus laughed.

'We still dream we're in the arena. All but the Strategos.'

Gannicus' temper went again. ' "The Strategos?" Aren't we also strategoi?'

Castus was cool. 'We are. Also, we're fools. Had you or I acted as Strategos, Gannicus, we'd by this time have fallen on those two thousand slaves — who seem to number about three hundred.'

'More Eastern rats,' growled Gannicus, standing arms akimbo

and surveying them contemptuously. For he had little faith in Eastern men.

The company of Gershom ben Sanballat entered the camp and looked around. For a little there was silence, the Gladiators and their allies leaning on their weapons, the Bithynians doubtful, half eager, half hesitant. One man of the company rode on horseback. It was Titul, the Iberian. He pointed towards the three strategoi.

'The middle man with the gladius. He is the Captain. Mighty—'

"Were the Captains of hosts in the vanished Western Isle",' said Kleon, hastily. 'Even so. But they neglected to sacrifice to Jehovah. Or was it Kokolkh?' To Gershom: 'I think these Gladiators are more likely to welcome us as slaves than as allies.'

Grinning, the Gladiators and those who had recruited their revolt before the Battle of the Lake, surrounded the Bithynians. Said one, a Gaul, 'These are small men, but valorous. This one was a cook. He'll slay the Masters and pot them.' A Thracian, with the hair on his chest matted in filth, glared and spat, for he had been a retiarius in the arena, and had conquered many with this glare. 'Monkeys from the Circus. Hell! Are the apes also in revolt?'

A grinning Gaul wandered round the band, surveying it jeeringly. But suddenly he cried out in Gaulish, forgetting his Latin, and seized on one of the strangers, a tall man with large feet and a flaming head of hair, clad in a stained woman's robe. At this onslaught on Brennus Titul snarled and leapt from his horse with drawn knife. Then he stood aside, and a mutter of astonishment rose.

For Brennus and the Gaul were embracing, breast to breast, and weeping and laughing. Brothers and twins, they had slept in the same stockade of northern Gaul, had been captured and enslaved in the same raid, had together heard the aurochsen low that last time they were marched south on the road to Rome.

At sight of the brothers' meeting, the enmity of the Gladiators vanished. With laughter and horseplay, they embraced the Bithynians, rolling them on the ground, or weeping large, mock tears of rejoicing. The Bithynians grinned and submitted, chattering unintelligibly. Titul replaced his knife. Gershom ben Sanballat, tugging at his beard, pushed his way through the tumult, and stood at the foot of the central mound and looked up in the faces of the three Gentile strategoi.

23

He looked on the face of Castus, the Gaul, an ordinarius of the arena, the reputed lover of Spartacus — a young face, uncruel and uncertain. And the Jew thought, 'No leader.' Then he looked at Gannicus: 'A bull, and brave as one. Pity he isn't in Jerusalem. Salome dotes on bulls.' And he scowled, for he did not share the doting.

The two strategoi of the Gladiators returned his gaze watchfully, as men prepared for treachery. Only the third stared over his head, with dark, blank eyes — dreaming, drunk, or was the slave mad? A queer conviction came on the Jew guerilla that he had seen that face before, and with the conviction a faint hope kindled as well. Disregarding the other two, he saluted the Strategos in the middle.

'I am Gershom ben Sanballat, a Jew. I was a slave of Crassus the Lean. I've brought these slaves to join you, if you'll have them.' He scowled irritably. 'Which Jehovah knows will be a favour, for without you the first band of horse will cut us to pieces.'

'You are welcome, Gershom. I'm Spartacus, a bandit. These are Generals of the Gladiators, Castus and Gannicus.'

Gershom combed his curled beard with thin brown fingers. 'They may be Generals of the army of hell, if it please them. I surrender my leadership of these Bithynians to you, not to those: who are doubtlessly very worthy men.'

Anger flamed afresh across the face of Gannicus. But Castus laughed. 'Thereby you show your sense. We two mistook your band for the soldiers of the Masters, and would have fallen on it, but that Spartacus held us back. You already owe him your life, Bithynian.'

'I am no Bithynian,' said Gershom ben Sanballat, 'but a Jew.'

Castus was indifferent. 'A Greek folk?'

The face of the Jew aristocrat flushed with the old Hasidim rage. 'My fathers were worshipping the One True God ere the Greeks came wallowing from the slime of their origin.'

The giant Thracian stared the simplicity of a half-awakened child, Castus shrugged, Gannicus sneered clumsily. 'I've heard of your folk in Rome. They worship trade and usury, and an ass's head for a God.'

The Thracian began to speak:

'We have little food, and by this marsh we're likely to be trapped. Elpinice thinks that another praetor may be marching against us. Camp your Bithynians, Gershom, but be ready to move.'

24

'First I'll deal with this Gentile swine ——'

Spartacus stared at him with blank, dark eyes. 'Camp your Bithynians.'

For a moment the Jew returned that gaze. Then he saluted again, and turned to obey.

(iv)

Gannicus, the Strategos for the day, set sentries on the neighbouring hills. Then the bucina blew again, summoning the slaves to a council. Meantime they had eaten, and new bands of slaves, herdsmen and hunters, had entered the camp. The most of them were Germans or Gauls, and drifted into the sub-camps of Castus and Gannicus. Looking on this gathering the eunuch Kleon spoke to Gershom.

'Most of these are northern barbarians, with little desire to return to their own lands. They'll mingle ill with your Bithynians.'

'Or with your Greeks,' said the Pharisee Jew. 'But that's a small matter. This army is a gathering of fools, as I'll say aloud in this council. Now the Masters have twice suffered defeat they'll move more slowly. In that space this army should split into fragments, and each band escape to the sea. There's no hope else.'

Kleon smiled coldly, indifferently. 'There's little hope even so. To kill as many of the Masters as we may, and ourselves in the end be killed. . . . What of the leaders of the Gladiators?'

'Two are wise fools: and the third — I don't know.'

'That third — the dark barbarian? Who is he?'

'Spartacus, a Thracian.'

Kleon, being Greek, looked contemptuously on Thracians. 'They are savages, eating horses and worshipping their dead.'

'They may eat their dead and worship horses, if it please them,' said Gershom. 'If this leader Spartacus will show good sense in his leading. I: I am for the sea.'

'And I: I am for nothing.'

In great circles, squatting on the grass, the slaves gathered to listen. Some gaped astonishment at the number of their fellows; some sat and rubbed at their eyes and broke into strange peals of laughter; some sat scowling, gripping their weapons, with twitching faces and

25

eyes on the hills; some lolled half asleep in the sunlight, their scarred limbs showing through the rags of their clothing, resting and resting in blessed ease from toil and the whine of the lash. Half at least were slaves born in slavery, men of the fields and plantations and households, with uncertain Gods and rules and beliefs, fear for an urge by day, exhaustion their urge by night, uncertain their fathers, but glimpsing their mothers, mating a matter of stealth and chance unless they came from the great stud-farms, where children were bred with the care of cattle and sheep. Yet even so, alien to their own lost lands, they remembered dimly their rules and creeds, in which women were lesser beings than men, without reason, and voiceless in public places. So now they stared their astonishment at the centre of the circles where, on a pile of Roman loot, the Strategos Spartacus sat.

For a woman, a girl in a Gladiator's tunic, had come threading the lines of squatting slaves, and now sat by the side of Spartacus. A murmur arose from the Gauls and the Eastern men, and all, save the Gladiators, looked on her in surprise and anger, or greedily and with desire.

The woman paid them no heed. She sat in the sunlight, by the side of the Thracian, her small face cool and composed under the dark line of brows. Presently the slaves saw a Gaul rise up. It was Brennus.

'A woman for the brothel or a woman for the hut — yes. But a woman sitting in a council of war — no.'

With this, winking his sleepy eyes, he sat down. Growls of approval arose from the shepherds, mingled with the thin, tenor laughter of the Bithynians. Then a Gladiator spoke:

'I'm of the men who came from Capua,' he said. 'We defeated two armies and camped by a marsh. And in the aftermath certain herds of asses wandered into our camp, braying "We have come with our valorous aid. But of this one and that of your band we do not approve." Now of asses I know little, except that their smell is bad. But of Elpinice I and the other Gladiators know much.' He looked towards the motionless figure by the side of the Thracian. 'Who unlocked our chains in the ludus of Batiates? Who twisted the vine-ropes for our descent of the crater? I do not mind it was this Gaul. No doubt he was overbusied in hut or brothel.'

At this the jeers and bull-laughter of the Gladiators broke out, and the others were silent. Still neither the Thracian nor the woman

26

spoke, though Gannicus laughed aloud and looked on Elpinice sneeringly. Castus the Gaul, who cared nothing for women, sat with his arm flung round the shoulders of Spartacus and his head bared in the sunlight. For a little, in the silence that was on the slave gathering, they could hear across the marsh the bleating of strayed and untended herds. Then Gershom ben Sanballat stood up, irritably tugging at his beard. For a moment his anger was quelled in scorn, looking at the slack slave mouths and leering eyes. What could these scum ever achieve? Then his anger was finding his lips.

'By my God, are we here to quarrel over women and asses? There are too many of both in the world. Strategos' — he addressed the Thracian Gladiator directly. 'What is your plan? Where will you lead us?'

Elpinice bent towards Spartacus and whispered. He nodded. 'That is for this gathering to decide,' he answered the Jew in that remote, brooding voice that came so strangely from the lips of the bloody leader who had held the passes of Vesuvius single-handed while his followers retreated, who had commanded the Gladiators with courage and skill at the Battle of the Lake. Gannicus spoke next.

'The Masters won't leave us unmolested long. Let's march to the nearest town and take it by stealth or assault. There are women and plunder in plenty in this land you've helped to till.'

Murmurs of approbation rose from the squatting, scratching, ill-weaponed slaves. For all desired women and plunder, save the eunuch Kleon, who had use for neither, and the Gaul Castus, who loved Spartacus, and Gershom ben Sanballat, who loathed the thought of a Gentile woman as he loathed the thought of a Gentile Master. Then Titul spoke.

'We'll keep the women, but the men we can sacrifice to our Gods, and so ensure victory in the future. Gladdened is the heart of Kokolkh by a sacrifice of blood.'

And to many who listened this seemed a good plan, remembering dimly their ancient Gods and the cold still faces in the peristyles of the enemy Gods that the Masters followed. Now out of nights and days made free of toil, strange, lost Gods arose to memory again, giving new fears to the dark of the slave shelters, new fierceness with the mutter of half-remembered chants. Then they turned their eyes as the Jew rose again, and a murmur of his name spread round the

27

circles, the Eastern slaves had heard of the Jews with a name through Asia for pride and ferocity, cunning and greed.

'Let us split into many small bands and escape to the sea. There we may seize ships and so escape Italy.'

But at this the Gauls and Germans cried that they were being deserted, and broke into an angry clamour which Gannicus made no attempt to still. The Gladiator who had spoken in defence of Elpinice pulled at the Gladiator's tunic she wore.

'Shall we Games-men quieten these shearers of sheep?'

Spartacus was standing up. Silence fell at his first word, for most had already seen him and all knew of him.

'I remember hunting wolves,' he put up his hand to his head, 'long ago. When the packs were about us in the winter-time I and the others kept in a band and reached home in safety. We neither stayed among the wolves nor scattered and ran ——'

He stopped, staring, a troubling, tremendous figure to the eyes of the slaves; and then sat down. Elpinice stood up, her woman's voice strange and mild in the bass rumblings of the ragged horde.

'The Wolf is Rome. Spartacus will lead us from Italy, but only as a united army. Let us march and meet the next army of the praetor's.'

'What will that help?' asked Gershom ben Sanballat, and he voiced the slave-army.

'If we defeat the Masters we can arm ourselves and be strong enough to fight a way through Italy.'

Hearing this, the slaves were again divided, some favouring the boldness of the woman, others crying that she was mad. In the warmth of the increasing day, a dull stench arose from the squatting circles. Hunger came on the slaves and certain of them drew away, lighting cooking-fires. The hum of argument rose and fell, with occasional wild bursts of laughter from a group of demented slaves who had escaped the mines. The literatus Kleon had stood on the verge of the gathering, listening in a cold amusement. Now he made his way through the circles to the side of Gershom the Jew.

Hating all Greeks and loathing eunuchs, the haughty Pharisee shivered with a secret repulsion whenever Kleon approached. Yet also, himself dazed in the discovery, he would look on the Greek with an angry, wondering compassion doubtlessly planted in his brain by some wandering Italian devil. Kleon looked in the Jew's heart, cold

28

and amused, passionless but for the ice of his hate to the Masters, yet sometimes teasing the haughty solemnity of the slave-aristocrat as a wasp a tail-switching leopard. He did so now.

'I thought you found this Spartacus a possible leader? He's no more than a savage, uxorious at that.'

The hill-leopard struck back. 'The last at least is denied you, Greek.'

Kleon's pale face barely twitched. Gershom's swarthy face flushed. He spoke again, angrily at unease, as the other said nothing.

'I have spoken with these Gladiators. This woman is favoured by a God, some devil of these heathen lands. In my country she would be stoned till her shameful body was hidden from the sight of men.'

'A meek and gentle people, your countrymen,' agreed Kleon. 'How came the woman to join the revolt?'

'Of that there's that tale and this, each of these Gladiators being a bigger liar than his neighbour. Some say she was a concubine of that Batiates whom they've escaped; others that Spartacus was her lover for years, and they bandited together in Thrace. While this new-come scum maunder as slaves will, being fools.'

'You yourself are a slave, Jew.'

'I am a noble of the Maccabees.'

'Who sold you from Bithynia to the Roman slave-market!'

'Some day I'll redress that, with a forest of spears against the Bitch in Jerusalem.'

Kleon squatted on the ground and drew forth the roll of *The Republic*. 'Then you're in need of advice on how to model the perfect state. I'll read to you now from Plato the divine.'

'No, no.' The wasp had stung again. 'He was doubtlessly a very worthy Greek, but I've no taste for his counsel. Some other time, when we are out of Italy. Here comes a sentry with two more recruits. Gauls both, by their look. Which is no great accession.'

For Gershom ben Sanballat had little faith in Northern men.

(v)

A German posted on the outlying hills by Gannicus, the sentry came striding through the squatting slaves. With him came two men, small men and dark in the Celtic way, clad in short linen tunics. They

29

were clad in the armour of mirmillones, with images of fish on their iron helmets, and decorated leg-sheaths shielding their knees. Those of the slave-host who had escaped the school of Batiates stared at the newcomers and their shameful armour. For since the rout of Clodius all the Gladiators had flung away their arena weapons and re-armed themselves as legionaries.

Spartacus sat staring blindly, intently south, seeing nothing of the approach of the sentry. A German and a mines-slave, the latter halted in front of the seated Strategoi and addressed only Gannicus.

'These Gauls say they've come from Capua and that they have been Gladiators.' He sneered. 'Myself, I believe they've been bed-men.'

Gannicus laughed, surveying the small men without pleasure, for his humour was evil. 'Where did you steal the arena gear?' he asked, jeeringly.

The younger of the two Celts, slight and dark and mild of face, had long lashes drooping like a woman's over mild eyes. He looked through those lashes at Gannicus and stroked his chin.

'Where Gannicus won his palms — when his adversary stumbled. In the arena. I've watched you there at Rome with net and trident, and wished for you as opponent. For I'm a timid man who desires to live long.'

'You Gaulish swine ——'

The little Gladiator held up a mocking hand. 'Now you're angry. Yet this sentry tells me you're a strategos, a word for a captain, I believe. An ill choice, for I see you're a man of little wisdom.' His eyes strayed to the silent Spartacus. He suddenly saluted. 'Thracian, we heard of you and came to join you.' The banter came into his voice again. 'And for reward we seem like to be killed and, for all I know, roasted and eaten by a red-headed Teutone.'

A smile came seldom enough on the thick lips of Spartacus. It came now. Crixus watched it come, and relaxed that watchful tension his banter had barely concealed.

'We were mirmillones, Crixus and Oenomaus.'

'You are welcome. I was a Threce, Spartacus.'

'Now I know we are really free, Oenomaus. All the way in the ditches and thickets that line the road from Capua I've sworn it a dream; once I frightened a flock of goats half-way over Campania when I pricked myself with my gladius in order that I might wake.' He explained to the blank stare of Spartacus. 'We were at Rome and heard nothing till we were brought back to Capua and the school of Batiates. There they told us the news and how it was now impossible to escape, such precautions were taken. So Oenomaus and I, one misty morning, gained by stealth the rooms of Batiates himself, and forced him at the dagger-point to lead us out by a private gate. Or at least Oenomaus forced him, for I hung back, fearing strong men with beards. Then we hid in a wine-cart that was making out from Capua, and so escaped the city. For the rest, we've wandered and hid and fared ill till this morning when we came on three scouts of Furius, the legate of Varinus. Two of those scouts we slew by stealth; the third we put to the question. From him we heard of Clodius' rout, and that Publius Varinus, the new praetor, has been sent south by the Senate, with a legion and a half, to eat up and excrete all the rebel slaves in Italy. So we tied this third scout to a tree and came away. Then we fell in with this German and prevailed on him not to eat us, though as yet we're untried men and he a veteran.'

But Castus was on his feet. 'Masters? How far away is this legion and a half?'

'Four leagues, I'd say, or less.'

(vi)

The clamour of the roused camp around them, Elpinice sat in the tent with the head of the giant Thracian in her arms. He had ceased to groan and claw at his head in that madness that had come in him as he stumbled into the tent from the sunlight. But now a torrent of broken Latin poured from his lips.

'But I can't understand! Who am I? I can't remember! Darkness ... and the forests, and waking. Night killing of men. Why should I kill them? I want only to hunt, to swim in the rivers, and lie in the hunt. I cannot kill them. Why should I kill?'

She had heard this raving before, though never in such frantic tones; she had soothed him from it before, the strange alien barbarian who, with his sword broken, had broken men with his bared hands and torn at their throats with his teeth; and who, outside the blindness of fighting, shuddered from the thought of killing like the frightened girl she herself had long ceased to be. Who was he, what origins had been

31

his in that wild Thrace where he was captured?

And sometimes a terror would come on her, bright and dreadful, yet with joy in it also, as the great, glazed eyes turned to her for help, and the great hands held her, in appeal, in the lazy play of a drowsing beast that sheathed its claws and played in the sun, in the urgent hot hours of desire when she quivered alive as never before in the hands that had held her throughout four years. Dim and remote her own beginnings, she yet remembered again and again those faces in stone in the Violet City, and would sometimes shudder and stare at the Thracian. What God had stolen his reason and set there the strength of a lion when roused at last, the cunning and speed of a striking serpent — these, companioned with the dread of a child?

So she soothed him now, as before, and he sighed, holding the hands that held him. Then he raised his head and smiled, suddenly, as on Crixus.

'Better now. Elpinice, there are forests where I'll take you and we'll go alone, only the bears and the deer are there; and caves; and the moon coming at night.' His face crinkled in sudden anger. 'After. There are the Masters who would stop us.'

She helped him with his armour, and armed herself; and as always, he plotted a plan in his mind, and traced it aloud, a hunter's plan, one who had hunted and waylaid beasts. She whispered beside him, agreeing, amending; till a bucina captured from the Roman rout roared outside the rallying signal of the horde.

And Elpinice, once mistress of the lanista Batiates, raised up her small head, her young eyes old. And she knew that bucina ended a phase: the revolt was over, it was WAR that began.

The War Begins

(i)

THE Senate had despatched Publius Varinus, with nine thousand men, to retrieve the shameful defeat of the Battle of the Lake and free the land from the threat of another servile war. Varinus, a tall, melancholy man weighted down with debts and the caprices of a young and unvirtuous wife, went forth slowly and reluctantly, and took the southwards road.

Presently he was in a land that another army seemed to have devastated. Houses stood looted and roofless, with the smoke still curling from the charred beams and starving dogs snuffling amid the ruins; farms were deserted, the storehouses sacked, gates open and herds straying untended. For the slaves, deserting to join the Gladiator revolt, had maimed or mutilated that which they could not carry away. Cattle, slashed and hamstrung, lowed amidst the hills; milldams had been raised and vineyards flooded; the statues of the Gods overturned or defaced with filth. And, seeing these things, the heart of Varinus kindled to a slow anger, and he forgot his debts and the lovers of his wife.

With him, as his legate, rode Furius, a young man who had lately served in Iberia with Pompeius, and before that had wandered many years in Greek lands, and more eastwards still, through Asia to the Persian kingdom. His slim figure was enclosed in a breastplate of silver, sewn on a leather coat. Ocrea of the same metal were bound on his legs. He wore a Greek helmet with a horsehair crest, and rode carelessly a great stallion from Cisalpine Gaul, white, with a bristling mane and red-rimmed eyes and over-ready hooves, as the legionaries knew.

Beside him, dropping vindictively, rode Varinus, unadorned and in plain armour. Behind, rank on rank, marched the legionaries, short brown men bearing the Samnite shield and the Spanish sword, adopted by the Republic after Cannae's rout. On each legionary's back five stakes were strapped to erect on the palisades of the nightly camps.

It was bright weather. The great southwards track that left the Appian Way grew thick in dust, so that Furius, cursing, maintained

33

he would rather march with a company of scavengers. He had little respect for Varinus, who was no soldier.

'Scavengers we are,' said Varinus, looking at him sourly, 'and on no holiday jaunt. If you cared so much for soldiering you'd have done better to stay in Iberia.'

But Furius yawned. 'The Gods — the dear, old smutty Gods! — forbid. I'm no more a goat than a scavenger. Clambering Iberian mountains in pursuit of the unscrubbed savage wearies me. Given flat country, the chasing of runaway slaves should yield twice the sport.'

'It was the slaves who did the chasing at the Battle of the Lake.'

'So Clodius said. For a fat man, how he must have run! He was puffing even when he arrived in Rome, thirty pace miles from the battlefield. If it *can* be called a field. They say he is still hiding in the baths, afraid to return to his wife, though freely forgiven by the Senate. The man is no more than a slave himself.'

But Varinus answered nothing, himself knowing the affliction of a lawless wife. Furius glanced at him contemptuously and then rode on singing, for his was a gay heart. On the road they came on a party of women slaves deserted in the flight of their menfolk to join the Gladiators. One of these women Furius singled out and ordered to be carried along for himself. The rest, with a great roar of laughter, were caught and distributed among the marching troops. Varinus rode frowning.

So in this way they marched south for the space of three days. On the morning of the third they were stayed by the velites falling back. Light-armed Iberians, these soldiers had been scouting in advance. Several had pushed forward many leagues and now brought the news that the Gladiators, reinforced by many slaves from the farms, were still encamped near the Lake where Clodius was routed. Learning of the nature of the ground, Varinus made his plan, and Furius agreed to it, contemptuously and indifferently.

Taking the half-legion the legate would make a detour and come up behind the slave horde. Yet he was not to attack immediately: rather, rigorously to avoid an open engagement. Meanwhile, the praetor would delay for a day and then advance with his legion and offer battle. The legate's half-legion could then cut off the fleeing slaves at the hither side of the marsh.

So they agreed, and Furius rode off gaily at the head of his three

34

thousand, the while Varinus encamped for that night, for now he believed he held the Gladiators in a cleft stick. With Furius went the female slave, a Gaul, whom he had allotted to himself. He carried her across his saddle and sang for her Eastern songs. Small and lithe, she lay rigid and listened, being afraid. But when the legate kissed her, she returned his kisses.

Seeing these things, the tribune and centurions, grey, scarred men, shook their heads. Things were differently managed in the great campaigns: the women captives, when they'd given their pleasure, had their throats cut or were sold as slaves. For Furius to carry a woman on his saddle shocked and angered the half-legion.

So Furius guessed, and cared nothing. For he came of a great family and the Senate was friendly to him. Moreover, he believed that he himself could defeat the Gladiators and their allies, and so win credit from Varinus.

With this thought, he marched throughout the night, spite the grumbling of the heavy-laden legionaries. Once or twice in the night-march he meditated ridding himself of the girl, then relented, for she was desirable. At dawn he halted under the spurs of a mountain, and three of his scouts fell back to report: The Gladiators still held their camp, they were less than a league away.

Three of the scouts had not returned: but Furius was carelessly unanxious. Summoning his officers, he told them to halt the legionaries and feed them. In an hour they would march on the Gladiators' camp.

One centurion, a young, coarse-featured Lucanian, protested against the short time of halt. But as he spoke a curious thing happened. His eyes and mouth opened very widely, as though stricken with a wild surprise. Then he swayed and gurgled blood while the others stared. There was an arrow in his throat.

The bucinae blew. Furius looked about him, coolly. Nothing. No one. The mountain reared in wild crags above them, deserted, sun-glimmering. Cattle lowed. A lark was singing high in the white heat. The bowman was nowhere to be seen.

Then, from a distant ledge, the legate saw an unhelmeted head cautiously projected. At the same moment a shower of arrows whistled down on the half-legion. Some stuck quivering in the ground; some rang on iron helmets like hail; each pierced through the eye by chance

35

missiles, the screams of two legionaries came to Furius. But the majority of the legionaries, accustomed to barbarian warfare, unslung the great Samnite shields and held them ready for another volley, and jested on the death-screams of their fellows.

Furius called up from the rear two centuries of Iberians. It was his intention to set them storming the mountain spurs and so drive out the archers. But before this could be executed, there came from round the mountain base the noise of a thunderous trampling; it grew to a rhythmic beat that shook the earth. Then a herd of maddened cattle, propelled with shouts and spear-thrusts, and leaping from ledge to ledge of the mountain-base, poured like an avalanche on the halted legion.

The legionaries stared and howled and beat their shields; too late: in an instant, with curses and laughter, they broke and scattered before the lowing, maddened charge. Like rushing water either side of a rock the herd split before the neighing stallion of Furius, which wheeled and lashed at the beasts with iron hooves. Quieting his mount, the legate suddenly grew tense and shouted unheeded orders.

For, low-bent, half-concealed in the dust, in and out among the leaping beasts raced companies of half-naked slaves. Howling like wolves they raced, and in a moment, wielding clubs and axes, fell on the legionaries. Two of them sprang on the legate, one a great Thracian, one a starved Bithynian.

It was too late for Furius to draw his sword: he thrust his dagger into the Thracian and the man rolled under the stallion's feet which pranced him to a bloody pulp. But the Bithynian, foot on stirrup, clung to the legate's left side and struck at him again and again with a sliver of sharpened stone. Each blow dented the legate's armour, and, try how he would, he could not come at the man because of the burden of the Gaulish girl. Then one of the centurions, leaping amidst the cattle, came to the rescue and slew the Bithynian with a blow that tore open the thin brown throat, and drenched the girl in blood.

Then Furius looked about him.

The herd had passed in dust and noise, though here and there a hamstrung beast strove to rise from the ground. The legionaries, scattered and taken by surprise, were falling back before the desperate attack of the slaves. Loud above the din rose the wailing 'Hui! Hui!' of the Thracians. Then the tribune caused a bucina to blow, and the

36

soldiers, cursing and fighting, fell into rank.

Furius spurred the white stallion back, broke bloodily through the onset of the slaves, and in a moment was again at the head of his men. He tossed the girl to the ground, drew his sword, and slung his shield on his left arm. In front of him a man, drawing back, whirled a great sling in his arm. Something sang through the air and Furius reeled as the stone glanced from his silver helmet. But behind him an Iberian, bending his bow, pierced the slinger through the throat.

Over a hundred of the Romans were down. The slave attack seemed to falter a moment, and then was pressed with redoubled fury. Half-armed men flung themselves on to the Roman swords. Transfixed, a slave would seize his assailant by the throat and seek to strangle him. Others charged yelling, and then, at the final moment, hurled themselves to the ground and grasped the feet of the soldiers. By this means many legionaries were dragged down and despatched by the blows of knives driven through their armour.

Cursing, Furius thrust and thrust, but contemptuously, for the slave-reek offended him. Half clad, half armed, it was evident that the slaves could not long keep the field. Jesting, the legionaries smote and smote with pilum and sword till their assailants reeled back in the beginning of rout.

Abruptly, from the mountains a horn blew wildly. At that sound panic seemed to fall on the slaves. With yells they turned and fled, and after them, Furius on his stallion in the van of the pursuit, swept the legionaries. The stream of flight swung round the mountain-base a full hundred yards; and then, for the second time, the horn blew. Furius found the tribune clinging to his stirrup.

'Back, back, Legate! Look to your right!'

Looked Furius, and strove to rein in the stallion; looked the other Romans, and strove to wheel to the right in ranks. But it was too late, and the order too scattered in the pursuit. The body of three hundred Gladiators, fully armoured, and armed with the long Etruscan hastae, smote through the disordered Roman line like the blow of a gigantic fist, then turned and smote again. At that even the veterans among the legionaries knew themselves lost, and, smiting their way out of the press of battle, fled northwards.

Furius was hurled from his stallion and killed by a giant Gladiator wielding an axe: he grasped the stallion by the nostrils and

37

clove down Furius in one blow; the Gladiators roared at the sight. The
tribune was down, and within five minutes rout as complete as that
which had overtaken Clodius at the Battle of the Lake fell on the half-
legion of Furius. The aquila of the three thousand was captured and
torn from its pole and smashed in the mud. Then the din and the dust
died off as the sun stood at noon.

(ii)

Gershom ben Sanballat had charged in the shelter of the cattle
with his Bithynians, and was the first of the slave commanders to beat
his men away from plunder and the killing of the wounded to make
account of their losses. Wielding a great whip, as long before in the
guerilla wars of the Hasidim, the Jew commander marshalled his
panting, ragged horde into straggling lines. There he found that over
a hundred of the company he had led from the north were dead; over
a score had wounds of such nature that recovery was impossible.
Himself half-naked, bleeding from a wound in his shoulder, his curled
beard torn and dusty, the Jew walked up and down the ranks and
tugged at his beard with an irritable hand. Then he gave an order, and
turned the cold back of a Pharisee on the ranks while it was executed;
for this order was against the Law, and a Gentile abomination.

The Bithynians surrounded their wounded comrades, chattering, weeping, and kissed them, and made pretence to serve them. But
the wounded had heard the order, and panting, bared their throats to
the knives. So they were slain that the slaves might march unencum-
bered.

On that sight Kleon of Corinth came to look with cold, amused
eyes. The Jew turned and saw him and scowled, for the Greek had
neither armour nor sword, and still carried no more than his knife. He
bore as little sign of battle as that morning he had entered the camp
of the Bithynians.

'I see you sacrifice to Jehovah, Jew — or is it to Kokolkh?'

But Gershom did not look towards his company. 'Sacrifice? I am
no baal-worshipper. What could I do? These men were unfit to march.
Would you leave them for Varinus to be tender with?'

'Oh, it's a good killing. All killings are in this country. I think the
God of its land drinks blood. A bloody people and bloody Gods. But

38

what do you think they've profited, those slaves you liberated five days ago?'

The Jew forgot his anger in weariness. Suddenly, in the blood and din of a thousand little fights, he saw, hopeless, the road to Kadesh. 'What profit is there under the sun? wrote a King of ours. What truth is there in a Greek?' His heavy lips curled. 'Or valour?'

The eunuch's cold look of amusement did not change. 'With his manhood, no doubt. I'm classed with the women, Jew. What would one of the Mutilated do in a battle?'

Gershom ben Sanballat flushed with rage. 'Now, by God, did those Gladiators refuse you a sword? I'll teach the slaves courtesy with the edge of mine.'

Kleon's laughter was the shrill, high laughter of the Mutilated ere he bit it to silence on his lips. 'Keep your sword for the throats of your wounded, Jew. I need neither your help nor your pity.'

He turned away with twitching face, and Gershom stared after him angrily — angrily at the pity that twisted his own heart. Were he himself so defiled would he keep a quiet temper? And he shuddered at that thought, and passionately, a moment blinded his eyes in prayer that whatever end awaited him in this revolt, the cross, the stake, or the mines, it might not be that mutilation which would cut him from the kingdom of the Elohim, alone and lost and defiled in this heathen land.

And it was then that he swore to himself that wherever a Jew slavewoman should join them, he would take that woman to his bed, be she Samaritan or Sadducee, that the seed of his loins might not be lost and the eyes of a son remember him.

(iii)

In an orgy of hate, the slaves flung themselves on the legionaries, captured and wounded. A Roman, a centurion, who resisted was surrounded and torn piecemeal by a pack of Germans, with a wrenching of tearing flesh and a crackle of breaking bones. Coveting a helmet, Brennus the Gaul seized a prisoner and drew him aside, and attempted to rive the stout leathern bands from under the captive's chin. They were clumsy to move and he drew his knife, sawing at them. The legionary screamed and writhed. The Gaul held with a

39

vacant grin, still sawing with his knife while the screams went on. Then the other slaves saw that the Gaul was hacking off the captive's head with his helmet, and screams of laughter arose. Pallid and filthy, denied the sun, denied the remembrance of wine or warmth, the slaves of the mines went mad in a lust of revenge, delighting in torments, bathing their arms to the shoulders in blood, tearing the entrails from still-living bodies. A pandemonium of howlings arose afresh from the battlefield a moment quieted. Then a murmur spread and Spartacus appeared.

He it was who had led the Gladiator charge and smitten Furius from the saddle. Now, he shouted aloud. The slaves stared their incomprehension and then, as he sprang among them, desisted from their torment of the legionaries, seeing that a God of madness had seized the Strategos. For all had sought or taken vengeance, and the strange Thracian Gladiator looked round about him at circlings of faces still fired in the heat of cruelty, saw Crixus himself unbend from thrusting a dagger in the heart of a legionary, saw Gannicus strapping bloodstained ocrea to his legs, saw Elpinice, who had charged with the Gladiators, cleaning her knife in the sand. She had cut the throat of the wounded tribune.

It was as though a dark cloud fell over the sun of their victory. All stared, Spartacus now silent, with strange, glazed look and heaving breast. Then they turned their gaze to the giant stallion which stood shivering beside him. Its nostrils were still in the grasp of his great fingers, and as the general of the slave-host groaned, his knuckles whitened and the stallion groaned beside him. And, because of that terrifying sound and sight, the slaves drew away from their prey, staring at man and stallion. Slowly his grasp relaxed and the Gladiator looked up in the eyes of the great beast he had held. Those near at hand cried out to Spartacus to beware, but he did not move, staring at the stallion. It heaved its head and snorted, and snorted with quivering nostrils between its knees till its white knees were spattered with a bloody foam. Then it raised its head and slowly, hesitatingly, made a step towards the Gladiator.

The leader of the slave-horde had found a mount.

40

By mid-afternoon the slaves had marched away, all marching in ordered companies in imitation of the iron-clad Gladiators. Laden with weapons and armour, they marched with great carrion-birds already a cloud overhead. The Roman dead were left unburied, the Roman wounded that survived unharmed. But the dead of the slaves Spartacus buried in a great mound; thereon was heaped a pile of stones and at the foot the fragments of the broken aquila strewn for a memory. Into far years that cairn survived, long after the name.of the battle was lost, and all that they did and suffered there.

At nightfall Varinus' legion came up and heard the news from such of the wounded as still lived. Thereat Varinus cursed coldly his dead legate, Furius, with regret that he had not lived to meet torment in the hands of the Gladiators or the mines-slaves. Then he desecrated the mound of the slaves, left his wounded to care for themselves, and pressed on all that evening in pursuit of Spartacus.

But he was too late to come up with the horde that had routed Furius. By the falling of dusk, in sight of the marsh, he was aware of lines of entrenchments and the burning of watch fires. The slave-leader had left behind him the Gauls to entrench the camp while he fell on Furius.

Cursing, Varinus gave orders to camp for the night. The legion-aries dug hasty earthworks against a surprise attack, then lay down and slept in weariness under the deepening frosts of Spring.

And at length it drew near to dawn.

(v)

A figure muffled in a grey abolla came hastening through the dimness, passed a watch-fire and stood by the side of Kleon. The eunuch leaned on his pilum and looked towards the Roman camp. As the muffled figure approached he turned round indifferently.

'Time?'

'The horses are waiting. Come.'

They passed through the camp together, skirted the edge of the marsh, crossed the last line of entrenchments, and came to a thicket. Here three great horses were tethered, Roman horses from the rout of Furius' half-legion. They stood with bent heads in the darkness. Kleon

41

groped to an unaccustomed saddle. The muffled figure, hand on the saddle of another horse, made a gesture.

'Not yet. He's waiting the light.'

The eunuch looked up at the sky. His head ached under the weight of his helmet and the effect of the stifling marsh air. But now, faint, a ghostly whisper, he was aware of a little wind that arose. The reeds sighed underbreath, moved by the God, and the thicket shook beside the horses. In the east a dull pallor overmantled the sky.

The night was lightening; and with a feebler glare burned the fires. Kleon and the other looked back on the slave encampment.

It was completely deserted.

Yet not quite. As they looked they could hear the ringing tread of one who wore greaves and carried armour. Then, against the Roman camp and the reflection of the dawn on the dark western horizon, across the deserted lines of the slave-horde, they saw a great figure pass and vanish into shadows. Kleon shivered, for the cold bit into his bones. Why ever had he volunteered this wearying watch?

Then he felt against his breast the crinkle of the roll of *The Republic*, and smiled with a chill amusement for his plan.

Beyond the thicket rose a sleepy cheeping of birds.

The footsteps of the giant figure drew near. Now he himself was at hand and the horses pricked startled heads. Kleon soothed them and was aware of a giant pair of hands reaching for a bridle.

'Don't mount yet. Walk the horses softly.'

Hand beside the moist mouth of his beast, Kleon led the way. Each crunched twig underhoof seemed to him thunder-loud. The dead reeds swished as they passed. Far off in the east a wolf howled.

They held along the south border of the marsh, till the darkened water lay entirely between them and the Roman camp. Then the giant spoke:

'It will soon be light. Ride.'

Now the eastern sky was stippled in crimson. Mounting, the three looked back. The watch-fires of the slave-camp had died to a smouldering glow where all night the three had paced to give the illusion of an army still camped there.

Kleon yawned.

'Vale, Varinus!'

Then the three of them rode south.

South to Lucania

(i)

ALL that morning they rode, while the light paled and grew and was touched with gold; and the sun, unseen, crept up behind the bastion of the eastern mountains. They passed down wild and deserted valleys, skirted long necks of swamp, rode soft with muffled bridles by villages and great farms. Ever the sky brightened and presently the sun was on them, and the white hoar under-hoof began to thaw. A thin mist rolled over the Campanian land. The eunuch hung wearied in his saddle, but the other two pressed on untiring.

Still holding south, they held by the banks of a river for many pace miles, on a ragged via terrena fringed with rushes. Once or twice they sighted boats: once, in a forest clearing a gang of slaves at work. Still they rode undetected.

Sleep came and went before the eyes of Kleon. Now and again he would jerk to a vague wakefulness: once dreamt himself again at sea with the pirate ships of Thoritos. In a clear moment he spoke to the others.

'We've surely missed the track. They cannot have passed this way.'

The giant eased the pace of his horse, a great white stallion. He turned his face. It was the Gladiator Spartacus.

'They passed this way.' He rode for a little looking at the track they followed. 'See.'

Kleon for a moment saw something in the path ere his horse was beyond it. Then weariness fogged his eyes, sick of the jest and the plan he had planned.

'What was it?'

The third rider, still muffled in abolla, answered him:

'A slinger's pellet.'

The speaker pushed back the hood of the abolla then, for the day promised heat. It showed the young-old face of Elpinice, weariness-pinched, her gaze on the riding Gladiator.

The three rode south.

The slave-horde had passed that way. But at legionary's pace they must have passed, for there was no sign of them. They had set out

43

silently as soon as night fell, under the leadership of Castus and Gannicus and Crixus, with the little company of Eastern men commanded by the Jew ben Sanballat. The three had remained behind to patrol the watch-fires and deceive the watching Romans.

Few of the slaves, stealing away in the darkness in long files, realized that they left the Strategos himself behind. Several of the leaders even did not know. Some said two Italian shepherds, men well acquainted with the country, remained. But Elpinice was the second, and Kleon, moved by the plan of his humour, the third. Riding now, he cursed that impulse. Would they never halt?

Yet this at last they did, at an open and deserted horreum, away from the river track and with the Lucanian mountains looming in view. Beyond the horreum itself, through a fence of osiers, the steadings of a farm loomed. Though no smoke arose and it also seemed deserted, they did not approach. Instead, Spartacus hobbled the horses in the shelter of the overhanging eaves of the building; Elpinice disappeared. Kleon staggered inside.

The floor was thick with the chaff-winnowings of many a harvest. In one corner mouldered a heap of straw. To the Greek eunuch it seemed he would never reach that straw. Lying on it, it seemed he had slept but a moment when a hand shook him.

'Time to ride south again.'

(ii)

He rose and followed the Gladiator out of doors. The sun was again low in the sky. The great white stallion stood tail-switching, snuffling at the necks of the other horses. Elpinice squatted near. In front of her was a heap of olives and a goatmilk cheese, at which she hacked with the dagger that had cut the tribune's throat. She pushed a handful of olives towards the eunuch.

'Where did you get the food?' he asked.

'At the farm while you slept. It is deserted, so I stole the cheese and olives.'

Kleon looked at her in cold puzzlement. 'Didn't you also sleep?'

'Like the dead — after Spartacus awoke.'

The Gladiator stood unhelmeted by the open door, staring into the sunset peace with his dark, blank eyes. The wind moved the strands of his great beard. The stallion ceased to snuffle at the necks of the other horses and thrust its muzzle into the hand of its new master. Spartacus did not move. And to the woman who looked at him there came back again a memory of those faces in stone on the terraces of the Violet City. She ceased to eat, sitting still and clasping her knees.

The eunuch glanced from one to the other — the slave bed-woman of a lanista and the taciturn Thracian savage. And for a moment a cold wonder held him. How had these two come to free and lead the Gladiators, to gather about them the beginnings of the slave-revolt? How came this savage to show the generalship he had done in two battles? And he remembered the saying of the Jew ben Sanballat that the ordering of these battles was the ordering of a hunter planning a battle, their success the success of surprise against known tactics in marshalling a battle. How long would these successes continue with the half-armed rout that already called itself Legio Libera — the Free Legion?

And he knew it likely that another month would see that legion dispersed or enslaved afresh. The Republic as yet had hardly moved. Now, with the rout of Furius, the Wolf would howl her packs to the hunt and the slaying. But ere they gathered. . . .

That would be a good play to play. And the Greek eunuch thought with a twisted mouth how the divine Plato would have stared in amaze had he heard it proposed that a Thracian savage, a slave eunuch and a courtesan hardly more than a girl should set to organizing the Republic which he had planned! Yet, ere the Romans gathered and ended the revolt for ever, the Gods might laugh at that jest — if he could prevail on the Thracian to play it.

'Strategos.'

Spartacus turned round slowly, the stallion still nuzzling his hand. For a moment Kleon felt a strange pity for this black-staring barbarian with whose heart and head he planned to play. Then he saw, as Elpinice herself had seen, that the Thracian was altering. He had altered in the space of a day, it seemed, the blankness was fading from the deep, dark eyes, there was a wakening purpose there, a fresh set to the giant head, the bearded mouth grown stern. Elpinice gave a cry, staring. Her child-savage possessed by a nameless God: he was changing and transmuting before her eyes.

45

Kleon said: 'When we reach Lucania — what then?'

'We'll march to the sea and seize a town. Then we'll seize ships, and each return to his own country.'

Elpinice recognized phrases of her own, whispered in the kennels of Batiates. But now they were said with a purpose and deliberation that made them Spartacus's own. Kleon laughed his shrill, high laugh, squatting and eating the olives.

'Each his own country! And aren't the Masters waiting in each country? The Wolf has conquered the world. There's a Roman Army in Thrace, I've heard. What better will you be?'

The girl's young-old eyes turned on him under her straight line of brows. 'At least we'll be out of Italy.'

'And still: What better will you be? Listen to me, Strategos. I'm a eunuch and no-man, from whom men and Gods turn their faces. But I'm a literatus as well — one who has read and pondered the thoughts and plans of many men. Slaves have risen before against the Masters, in Italy and in Greece. For a little while they've held their own, but never for longer than a little while. They've wasted the early days of revolt either in looting and rape or in seeking escape to that land that lies neither in Thrace nor under the Nile Cataracts: but elsewhere.'

'Where?' Elpinice asked, for the Gladiator stared in silence.

Kleon pointed west, where the sun already rested on the hills.

'The dead go there, they used to tell. Beyond drowned Atlantis, the Islands of the Blest. Nowhere, in fact.'

Then the girl with old eyes, the slave bedwoman of a Gladiator-farmer, said a thing as unexpected by the Greek as a blasphemy on the lips of a woman.

'I think it's neither in Thrace nor your Islands, this land you mock. It lives in our dreams and our hopes, and maybe we'll never attain it. But — we broke out of Batiates' ludus to *try*.'

'Then let us try here — in Italy. Given a leader strong and skilful, given men who will follow him without question — the land we dream is Italy, *we* its Masters, not its slaves.'

Still Spartacus said nothing. Kleon stirred a little, even he uneasy under that uncanny stare of a wakening child or a wakening beast. Again it was Elpinice who spoke.

'And this leader and his men?'

Kleon had finished his olives. He wiped his fingers on his thighs, and rose up slowly, his twisted smile on the Gladiator with the giant stallion behind him.

'There is your leader. He might change the order in Italy as no man before, casting down the Masters and raising the slaves, for the Republic is weak and its armies scattered, he could seize and hold all Southern Italy, and carve it out the state that Plato dreamt.'

Elpinice would have spoken again, but Spartacus motioned her to silence, his eyes on Kleon.

'Of this matter we'll speak while we ride. Now we'll ride.'

Elpinice looked at him wide-eyed. And it seemed to her in that moment, being wearied, that the God, nameless, terrible, endearing, had left him at last and for ever. In his place rose sure and sane and strong — alien and strange, the King of the Slaves.

(iii)

A mist and a light, warm rain came down with that sunset. In a little at a trot, the three slaves had left the horreum behind, and went south with the shadows in pursuit till those shadows overtook and devoured them. And presently Elpinice, riding behind, heard the high shrill voice of the eunuch raised eagerly in explanation.

All that night he talked, as they still rode south, into the mountains of Lucania. Then, in the morning, they learned from a shepherd that they had missed the track of the army, for the slave-horde had swung east. So eastwards turned the three, and Elpinice, in weariness, heard still the shrill of Kleon's voice, and unceasing throughout the hour, the Thracian question him.

So, in a night and a day, he crossed a great measure of country.

And at last, late in the afternoon, they rode into the camp that Crixus had entrenched under the spurs of Mount Papa.

(iv)

The slave-army had marched from Campania without a casualty; but the most of the slaves were in rags, their feet torn and bloody from the wear of the rough tracks crossed, their throats and voices choked with dust. Even the Gladiators grumbled, and unending in the baking heat of the march the dreamings went on in each man's head;

47

dreamings in German heads of the sound of the Rhine and its steel-blue splash, the easeful scrunch of pine cones and mists that hid off the sun; dreamings in the heads of Eastern slaves of the yielding sands and a bright, white glare; black men's dreamings of blue-shadowed forests and the rich mould lands that slope by Nile. Only the Gauls and Thracians and Iberians were unvexed by the mountains, and hailed them with cries, some thinking them the veritable mountains of home.

In their three days' march into Lucania the country had cleared before them as dust clears before a broom. Twice they had come on deserted villages, tenantless and foodless, waterless even, the wells filled up to hinder the slaves. One of these villages the Gladiators fired, hearing that it belonged to Licinius Crassus. Gershom ben Sanballat had looked on, keeping his Bithynians under sharp surveillance, his black beard curling in haughty contempt for this childish display of servile spite.

Though meat was plentiful enough, for they drove a great herd in the van of their march, the slaves grumbled continuously for lack of clothes, for tents such as strategoi and Gladiators used, for the comforts that most of them had known but seldom in all the years of their slavery. They had tasted freedom and raved to devour it, starved men set down at a giant dish. Rumours and scandal spread through the host. Were they being led into Lucania to perish? Why had they not scoured the land in their march, for clothes and gear and the Masters' women? Where was the Strategos Spartacus?

And concerning him tales grew and grew, some saying he had returned to the Masters, others that the Gauls had killed him — the Germans — the Iberians — the Thracians, each and all blamed by return of rote by the others whom scandal accused of the crime. The Germans under Gannicus clamoured to be led north again.

Castus rode brooding and absorbed, with his Gauls. Crixus made friendly overtures to him, but met with little response to these — instead, a stare of suspicion and dislike. Where was Spartacus? Was not Crixus the last to see him?

Crixus had shrugged and gone off with a smile. Yet, the evening of their halt under Papa's spurs, when Gannicus secretly approached him with a project, Crixus refused to listen.

'Wait for Spartacus,' he advised. 'Deserting him, we're lost.'

Gannicus, bulky, Roman-armoured, a splendid figure, sneered, and played with his tribune's gladius.

'He's well enough, the Thracian, but that he's mad and a woman's man. How do we know he'll ever reach us here? We've left no easy track. I think he may have been slain by Varinus, him and the woman and the Greek.'

For it was now known that Kleon and Elpinice had stayed to patrol the camp with Spartacus. Crixus's jesting face grew rigid.

'Gannicus, if that's as you dream, I'll gather what men I can myself and hunt down Varinus like a dog a deer.'

'You'll not gather the Germans for the hunt,' said Gannicus, and turned away.

So, on the afternoon when Spartacus and his two companions rode into camp, they saw a diminished force; and were greeted with the news that on the previous afternoon the Germans and Thracians were found to have deserted the camp. But news of them was not uncertain. They had marched south with intent to fall upon Metapontum, taking it by surprise. Gannicus led them; and with him, strangely enough, had gone Oenomaus.

'Of this intent I knew nothing,' said Crixus to the Strategos, 'else I'd have strangled Gannicus with his own beard.'

'For a little man,' growled the Jew ben Sanballat, standing by, 'your heart is high.'

'My father was a butcher,' said Crixus, modestly, 'and I am accustomed to killing cattle.'

Beside Spartacus was the pale-faced eunuch Greek. 'If this Teutone fool takes Metapontum we can expect no Italiot allies!'

'Italiot allies?' said Crixus. 'Who seeks them?' and he looked at the giant Gladiator. Spartacus smiled his dark smile.

'We seek them, the Legio Libera. Varinus is following us without any doubt, and if we destroy Metapontum we'll be in a land of enemies. Gannicus has done ill.'

'Shall I follow him and cut his throat?' asked Brennus the Gaul, who stood near.

The Gladiator looked at him with undreaming eyes. 'You'll slay when I bid you slay, Gaul.' Then he turned away to his tent. All stared. Some strange thing had come on the Strategos.

Irritable, Gershom ben Sanballat stared after him. What had wrought this change in the Gentile barbarian? He accosted Kleon with the question, and met the usual cold, twisted smile.

'Not *what*, but *who*. I.'

'You?'

The eunuch nodded. 'This barbarian Spartacus is more than a mere brute beast of the ludus, or a lion that plans a killing. So I'm teaching him and finding him apt. It was just such material that Plato looked for to build up the New Republic.'

'I remember now that I've heard of him,' the Pharisee mused. 'He believed in enslaving all men. Slavery's well for the rabble: *I* am a noble of Judaea.'

'You're an escaped Roman slave, one of the rabble yourself. And unless it ceases to be a rabble—'

The Jew laughed, angrily. 'Are these the words you spoke in the camp by the Lake?'

'I'd not thought of amusing myself with this little game then. What does it matter one way or the other, when all we do or dream are but blowings of dust?'

The guerilla leader of the Hasidim knew otherwise. 'There's the Law — of which you know nothing, being a Gentile. We nobles of Judaea worship no planless God, but one terrible in Will, with the Jews his people.'

Kleon smiled politely. 'A peculiar God.'

(v)

In his tent Spartacus ate and drank, Elpinice serving him. Then he sat for a while with his head in his hands, deep in thought; and looked up at her with that sharpened gaze of the last two days. Far leagues from the gaze of the giant child who had held her in love in the sheds of Batiates.

Yet she regretted nothing, loving him still, perhaps now with a deeper passion that he stirred and moved from her side, he whom she had comforted, herself uncomprehending, from his horror of blood and war. And, whatever this wakening had brought to him, he desired her still, and hungered for her breast and body, if no longer her hands in pity. But a strange thing she noted even while he held her in passion, a changed passion and possession that minded her with a stab of hate of nights in the hands of Batiates. It was the lust of a man who sought

50

lust for a food, not the dream passion of the slave God-possessed.

'Send for Crixus the Gaul,' he said.

So Elpinice sent that message, and Crixus came, and saluted the Strategos, cheerful and fat and short of build, with a heart in which sat, so alien to the land and time, a humour simple and kindly. Spartacus looked up at him.

'I intend to make you tribune of the Free Legion, if you'll take my commands as its strategos. We cannot longer remain a rabble, leaderless and planless, or with leaders rising in a night and marching off half the slave-host in an hour. I in future command without question. Will you be my tribune?'

The little Gaul pulled at his lip with a troubled finger. 'I'm no general. But I'll be your tribune — if it's in your power to make me so.'

'I have the power.'

Thereat Crixus swore to take his commands as strategos of the Legio Libera, swearing mistily by the names of two Gods, one of Gaul and one of whom he had heard in the sheds of the Roman arena. Then Castus was brought and swore the same obedience, a fellow-tribune to Crixus. Kleon the eunuch stood in the background, listening and watching with a cool amusement this play of slaves who played to be Masters. Yet — they might succeed. And the game had its humour.

'It would be as well to swear also Gershom the Jew,' he said, 'who was a noble in his own country, and a commander of barbaric armies.'

So Gershom was brought from outside the camp, where, under the frown of the Papa spurs, he had set to training his Bithynian company. They were armed now with long hastae, round shields and short breastplates, and the one-time leader of the Hasidim planned to use them as the Greeks their peltasts — scouts or legionaries, as the need arose. Chattering and docile, the Bithynians obeyed his commands, wheeling and charging in running columns, forming and kneeling in solid ranks to meet the charge of imaginary horse, breaking and flying in feigned retreat. Cursing the laggard and urging the eager, Gershom pulled irritably at his curled beard when the message from the Strategos interrupted his training. Nevertheless, he went with the messenger, through the lounging lines of the other slaves, who attempted no training but slept in the sun.

The Pharisee listened with a haughty scowl as the Thracian spoke, and looked round the tent at the listening Gauls, the Greek, and the woman.

'To make of the slaves an army at all is foolishness, as I've always said. And I've no great wish to tribune the fools. Even so, who are you to swear by, Gladiator? If I swear by Spartacus do I swear by the slaves?'

'You swear by the best of them, at the least,' said Crixus. 'Swear by Spartacus.'

'Spartacus and the slaves are one,' said Kleon. 'For the Leader is the People.'

Then Elpinice spoke, strangely, as once before in Kleon's presence.

'Yet I think a time will come when men will swear by the people alone.'

Gershom ben Sanballat looked at her, with veiled eyes, for she was a woman. 'That is your counsel, then? I should swear by the slaves, as their tribune, and not by your lover, as their Strategos?'

'That's for you to decide. Yet in your case I'd not swear myself the Strategos's man.'

The Jew shrugged. 'This may be good sense or a lovers' quarrel. I have nothing to do with the squabbles of the bed. But I take the sense of it, agreeing with mine. This is where I stand, Spartacus: A section of the slaves has made me their leader: all the slaves have made you their strategos. Good. So long as you remain that strategos, I'll take your orders, whatever the grace. But I'll lend no aid to setting up this Gentile kingship of slaves.'

Gershom laughed, his eyes on the Thracian. Kleon's lip curled. Castus, hand on his dagger, half rose.

'I think, Bithynian, you're tired of the sun.'

The Jew laughed contemptuously. 'I am tired of many things, Castus. Most I am wearied of fools.' With a sudden motion he held the arm of Castus and those watching saw the veins stand black on his forehead. 'Do you think I've marched from Campania in order to die with the dagger of a savage in my throat? If you're the type of Companion our new Alexander swears to his side, it'll be long before the Republic trembles.'

With that he flung Castus aside and left the tent. Crixus' eyes followed him admiringly.

'There goes a true man, Spartacus, and one that'll stand by you when I and this Greek run as fast as deer. You did ill to threaten him, Castus.'

'Do you lead here, or does the Strategos?' The blood of anger, unusual enough, mantled the face of Castus. Then Elpinice spoke.

'Neither, it seems. There's fear and hate and suspicion to lead, since we swear by leaders and not by a plan. I didn't climb the ledges of Vesuvius for this. Who did?' She looked at Kleon and he saw the eyes of the woman who had cut the tribune's throat. 'It was a pity they didn't put a knife in your neck when you came to our camp by the Lake that day.'

Spartacus, not looking, put a hand on her shoulder. He had heard the debate with a shining calm that reminded Kleon of a waiting snake. Now the snake had moved. Elpinice shivered.

'*I* am the Leader. Kleon, watch Gershom. If his words mean deeds, kill him at once.' He looked at Elpinice with bright snake's eyes, and she saw the horror of the threat that was there, no hate or anger, but a bright, cold purpose. A mist of sweat came out on her forehead. Spartacus dropped his hand from her shoulder.

'Sound the bucinae. We march after Gannicus.'

(vi)

Spartacus marched on Metapontum, intent on seizing it before Gannicus and the slow-moving Germans should make their surprise.

But swiftly though the Strategos marched his Gauls and Eastern men the retiarius Gannicus at length had moved. In the early hours of a misty dawn he fell upon Metapontum. It was feebly garrisoned and unsuspecting, for, though the news of the slave exodus from Campania into Lucania had spread over the countryside, the Gladiators were believed to be encamped near Papa. The citadel was stormed and fired; then the Germans turned their weapons on the town. By full day Metapontum was blazing murkily, and Gannicus, his army laden with spoil and women-captives, withdrew again to the hills.

Leaving the smoking wilderness of Metapontum on the horizon, the Thracian marched rapidly after the German retreat. Late in the afternoon the entrenched camp of Gannicus was sighted, and the German, awed by the superior numbers of the slaves who followed Spart-

53

acus, came out and greeted him. The Gauls clamoured for their share of the women.

What passed in the tent of the leaders none knew, but Gannicus marched back his host to Mount Papa under the leadership of the Thracian. Spartacus had suppressed the first revolt, and not for the space of a score of battles while Italy reeled under their marching feet, was any to dispute his leadership.

Kleon had a metal-smith beat out insignia for the slave army, standards to be raised against the Wolf and the Eagle of the Republic.

And the sign of the slaves was a Snake.

II. LEGIO LIBERA

War in the Mountains

(i)

HOT-FOOT on the track of Varinus, Cossinus was sent up from Rome with a further half-legion to reinforce the praetor. The latter he found encamped over against the mountain-range which hid the dark countryside dominated by the slaves. From out that tract amidst the mountains came rumours and refugees without end.

Both bore tales of horror. In their camp the Gladiators had elected as their leader a savage Thracian, who tortured his captives and had virgins brought to his tent in order that he might violate them publicly. Also, he ate horses. Metapontum had been looted and fired at his orders; and he designed to increase the slave-hord until he might make his way to the coast, seize on a fleet of ships, and so cross into Greece and conquer it.

Woven of such fabric grew the legend of Spartacus. Up and down the lands of the great Republic of the Masters the tale of the rebellion rode the winds. And to some it was a tale of horror and to some a tale of hope. From towns and farms, mines and plantations the slaves slipped away by twos and threes and made their way southwards to join the host of the horse-eating Thracian whose standards bore the insignia of a Snake.

Burning homesteads and looted orchards marked the passage of such bands. Even the companies of brigands who preyed on the roads and had done so from time immemorial abandoned their routes and marched to join the slaves with the hope of greater plunder. Meantime the light troops of Varinus, scouting beyond the mountains, brought back strange and contradictory reports. One day it appeared that the camp under Mount Papa had grown into a great town, strongly entrenched and provisioned, where the slaves and their savage leader designed to await attack. Another, and it was certain that the entire slave army had marched away, to the east, designing to cross the great Way and lay waste the lands of Calabria.

Soured, irritated, but determined, Varinus organized his forces. Meantime, he succeeded in intercepting and capturing stray bands of the slave reinforcements which straggled towards the camp of the Gladiators. He spared none. For this the Senate reprimanded him,

57

pointing out that the supply of slaves was small and that the lash or torture, not death, was sufficient to break their spirit. Finally, because of the clamour of the town-dwelling property-owners, the full cost of a thousand vulgares was charged against his private estate.

Hearing this, Varinus, with thought of his wife's extravagances which had already impoverished him, cursed the Senate and crucified outside his tent a dozen of new-come captives. Then he took the legions under his personal command and marched into the mountains of Lucania, determined to come to battle with the Gladiators.

Cossinus he left behind, to the satisfaction of both Cossinus and his troops. Their orders were to forestall any retreat of the slaves northwards into Campania again. Encamped at Salenae, with the sea-water near at hand, the men of Cossinus doffed their armour and swam, or lay on the sands and made obscene jests on the ventures of his wife while Varinus slave-hunted. Cossinus himself had a great pavilion erected, and sent for his bath-attendants at Rome. Then he prepared to rest and recuperate, thus combining his usual autumnal health treatment with the rigours of war.

A man learned in the Greek tongue, he treated his slaves and soldiers with great kindness. His friend, Kharmides, was a freedman, and this friend he brought to Salenae. Together, sitting in the pavilion, they read Aeschylus and laughed over the freakish ancient world portrayed by Aristophanes; they read and debated in Hesiod and Ovid the Golden Age of Justice and Kindness that had once existed, a well-known fact, ere Jupiter in Egypt rose against the good King Saturn. Kharmides had recently met in Rome the Greek noble Hiketas, renowned alike for his wanderings in distant lands, his blasphemies against the Gods, and the fact that he lived in incest with his sister. This Hiketas was newly returned from a long year's voyaging up a great river from the Euxine. Beyond the land of the Scythians, in a land of eternal forests, the Greek noble told that the Golden Age still reigned: he himself had lived with a forest people who knew nothing of war or government, cities or arms, masters or slaves. Many in Rome believed this tale a lie, and Cossinus himself was doubtful.

'Even were it true it is a tale of barbaric folk, living far from the lands of the Republic. How can it help or hinder us in Rome?'

Kharmides agreed that it helped nothing; then told (the jest of the Roman baths) the further tale that Hiketas had spread: that the Thracian savage who led the slaves was himself no Thracian, but a tribesman of remoter people, strayed southwards and captured from the Golden Age. This accounted for his strange conduct in the ludus of Batiates and the fashion in which he had spared the Roman wounded at the Battle of the Mountain.

Cossinus laughed: 'Then the Iron Age has engulfed him rapidly.' And thought. 'As in Hesiod it tells that that Age did to our own ancestors long ago, letting loose on the world a cruelty and rapine unknown to the Simple Men. If Hiketas tells true this Spartacus is all men in one, with the Golden Age lost.'

Meantime his soldiers, grown lax, slept on their rounds at night and the winter drew on. Kharmides was sent back to Rome to bring warm robes and skins from the villa on the Palatine; also, Cossinus gave orders that if the roads were not impassable his mistress, Lavinia, should join him.

The autumn seemed to pass reluctantly. Days of warm weather intervened and in these Cossinus, a strong swimmer, would hold far out into the bay and then return to lie on the sands and think of his mistress. And thinking of her, his desire would mount, bitter and sweet, and his hands grow unsteady. She had been his mistress a bare three months, having abandoned Fulvius when that merchant was broken by the failure of his wheat-ships to escape the galleys of Thoritos.

'I shall send him a talent for that service,' Cossinus thought. 'Even though it seems my Lavinia brings death wherever she bides, like Helen of old. But that was no fault of hers — Fulvius and his gushing veins. Soon Kharmides will bring her, this slave-hunt end, and I'll buy the Thracian Spartacus, make him my body-slave and debate the life of the Golden Age while he rubs me in my bath. And I'll take him and Lavinia to Sicily, and leave Rome for ever and forget it. I'm weary of the false faces that sneer at one in the Forum, the base faces of the plebs, the thin-faced slaves, the cruel dull faces of my kin who rule. Out on them all! I'll till the olives of Sicily and watch my slaves at the wine-press and swim in the blue Sicilian seas. And all will be well with me at last.'

And he closed his eyes, dreaming of Lavinia. From that dream he awoke to the roar of the bucina, and his tribune, a veteran from

Syria, shouting in his ears.

'Cossinus! The camp is attacked!'

(ii)

But it was already too late. In the evening haze, over the palisades stormed the attacking bands of slaves, men miners or shepherds or porters a month before, now ragged, well fed, and a storming fury. The sunlight was ruddy upon them, and Cossinus, no man of action, stood staring aghast a long moment.

Again the bucina roared under the standard and the soldiers, snatching armour and swords, ran for the palisades. Reformed within the palisades they had crossed, the slaves greeted the legionaries with a shower of javelins and stones: then charged. They were bands of Gauls, armed with great swords forged in the wilds of Lucania. Swinging these with both hands, their charge was irresistible.

In their van raced a giant, dark-faced, dark-haired, swinging a giant axe, clad in the armour of a Roman tribune. He clove down the centurion who guarded the standard, hewed down the standard pole with one sweep, then smote in through the hesitant Roman ranks. Cossinus heard armour crackle under that axe: a slave-titan, that, and a general to boot.

And, being a valorous man, for all that he knew nothing of war or leadership, he took his sword and helmet from the pavilion and ran swiftly towards the battle. But by then it was no battle. Here and there, in groups, the legionaries still fought, but already the slaves swarmed over the camp, killing stragglers and the wounded. Beside Cossinus ran a centurion: towards them leapt two of the attackers. One of them was a tall man, with large feet and hands and braided red hair. A Gaul, he swung the sword of his tribes. The centurion thrust at him, missed, and rolled headless from the stroke of the sword. The other was a lesser man, and as he came at him Cossinus noted the peaked, chinless face and the stare of demoniac eyes. Twice Cossinus thrust at the man, and twice the man leapt back with reddened tunic.

He was armed with great wooden club, set with gleaming blades of flint. Snarling, he halted and swung this club till the glassy blades shimmered and it gathered momentum. Then he hurled it at the Roman general. Right athwart the body of Cossinus it came: stagger-

60

ing in amaze, he looked down at the entrails spurting from his own body. Then a light flashed and flashed and he thought, 'Sicily,' and fell and was trampled as the last of the scattered fighting ebbed and rolled down to the beach.

So died Cossinus at Salenae. Spartacus, bloody to the elbows, unwounded, unwearied, though his axe was twisted upon its haft, had his horn-bearer sound. Slowly the Gauls, burdened with spoil, collected from the four corners of the camp. So rapid had been the attack that few of the slaves had died at the palisades — even within their casualties had been few enough. Since morning they had lain hidden, at the orders of the Strategos, in the brush that overlooked the Roman camp, waiting for the Roman hour of siesta and slackening. Few had slept in that waiting time, excepting the Strategos himself, watched over by Castus. Now Castus, also unwounded but with a broken shield and reddened hands, came panting to Spartacus.

'Shall we burn the camp?'

The Thracian shook his head. 'That would warn the scouts of Varinus, unless he still follows Crixus and our main army. Are there any prisoners?'

There were three. They were brought in front of Spartacus. One was a centurion, the others Balearic legionaries. The centurion faced him fearlessly, for he was a Roman: but the legionaries stared at him with the fear of death and torture in their eyes.

'Bring Cossinus' head,' said the Strategos.

Titul the Iberian hewed it from the trunk which his club had mangled, and brought it dripping. Carrying it, he sang the sacrificial song to Kokolkh, being mad. Spartacus looked at it, the dropping eyelids and the bloody grin; and suddenly shivered and a moment hid his face in his hands. Then he remembered the words of Kleon and the taste of power already strong in his mouth.

'The legionaries will carry this to Rome, a gift to the Senate from the Legio Libera.'

The centurion and the two Balearic legionaries took the northwards road. In a package they carried the head of Cossinus. The raiding slaves vanished into the mountains, leaving Salenae despoiled.

61

Unaware of the end of Cossinus, the praetor Varinus marched ever deeper into the wilds of Lucania. For three weeks he wandered there, and, despite his velites, found himself unable to come up with the Gladiators and their allies, or force them to battle. Under the brow of Mount Papa he found their camp deserted. Marching northwards again, in the trail of the elusive slave-bands, he forded the river at Paestum only in time to see the leaping flames from the houses. Pushing on quickly, he overtook at dusk a considerable body of men, and these turned to give him battle, holding his legion in a cleft of the hills till darkness fell. Then they melted away with singing and mocking laughter.

Only then did he learn that Paestum had been occupied, looted, and fired by a small body of Eastern slaves, numbering less than three hundred: and that they had deliberately led him on for two long days, the while the main body of the insurgents still eluded him.

He camped a night in Paestum, and from Lucerius Piso, an aged patrician almost blind — as he had been for many years — from a loathsome disease, he learned of the advent of the Eastern slaves. They had captured Paestum without a blow being struck. Their leader had been a tall, black-bearded slave, evidently of different race from his followers. These he had held well in hand, only one of the inhabitants of the town being killed: and he because he threatened the slaves from afar. Thereat the black-bearded slave leader had snatched a bow from his back with incredible swiftness, and, bending it, pierced the breast of the mocker with an iron arrow.

Then, summoning the chief men, of whom Piso was one, he had demanded a small store of corn, all the money and jewels in Paestum, and the liberation of the slaves.

All his demands except the liberation of the slaves had been agreed to when the troops of Varinus were seen approaching. Thereat the black-bearded slave had marched his company away, he himself riding in the rear. An arrow fired after him, though striking between his shoulders, had fallen blunted to the ground. He was evidently protected by some alien God.

'Or by armour beneath his tunic,' said Varinus, sourly. 'Couldn't you have closed the gates and held three hundred men?'

Piso blinked with lashless eyelids. 'No, for few of the plebs have arms.'

'You are fools,' said Varinus.

'So the bearded slave said,' remarked Piso reminiscently. 'He was a short-tempered man, like yourself, Varinus, and swore by a God called Iavē.' He chuckled. 'I'd no mind to risk a slit throat for the sake of the Senate or a few slaves. How fares your wife, Varinus?'

But the praetor had turned on his heel and left him. Next morning, dour and unshaken, he turned southwards again. As he marched news was brought to him by a Gaul, a slave who had deserted the insurrection, that the Thracian Gladiator, whose name was Spartacus, had detached a party from the main slave horde and was marching swiftly towards the sea in order to engage Cossinus. Hearing this news Varinus altered his line of march, left the Gaul hanging crucified on a nearby tree, and pressed westwards towards the coast.

But at midday, in a marshy plain amidst low foothills, he found a considerable body of men waiting to give him battle. For the first time in a month his face lighted up. He saw that the campaign would end here, now that the rebels had come into the open.

His cavalry, a small body of four hundred horse, the Roman commander divided and placed on either wing of his main battle. They were heavily armed and armoured and well mounted. In the centre he marshalled the Tenth Legion, with gladii, breastplates, and bearing the short pilum: these men were the stay of the Republic, short in stature, brown-skinned, disciplined as no other troops in the lands that fringed the Middle Sea. They halted motionless, in taciturn silence, in contrast to the light-armed troops from Cisalpine Gaul, who clamoured with the usual din of velites. Beside these Gallic troops Varinus placed a body of slingers on the flanks. Then he took heed of the ordering of the slave-army that opposed him.

A small man, evidently a Gaul, and mounted on a small and shaggy horse, marshalled the slaves. It was Crixus, helmeted and in Roman armour. In the centre, opposing the Tenth Legion, and grouped around the Snake standard of the slaves, he set the Gauls and Germans, the first under Oenomaus, the second under the scowling half-mutiny of Gannicus. For the German, believing that the command should have been deputed to himself by Spartacus, had marched

63

sulkily since sunrise. His Germans also considered that their leader had been slighted and so drew away from the Gauls.

Seeing that his centre was likely to split even before it was attacked, Crixus sent a Thracian, Ialo, to watch by the German leader, and, at the first sight of treachery or cowardice, to drive a knife in his throat. Suspecting the intent of Ialo, Gannicus, albeit still sulkily, held the Teutones in check. Further, he hated the Masters more than he hated either Crixus or Spartacus, and the blood of his unquestioned bravery began to beat across his forehead.

In their ranks the marshalled slaves fidgeted, with twitching faces. For it was the first time, unshielded by ruse or hill or lake, they had faced that dread of the Middle Seas, the legionaries of the Masters. At first there was almost panic in the ranks, as those men from the vineyards and mines and warehouses gaped open-mouthed at the enemy they fronted, and remembered the sting of the lash on their backs, and the averted head of a slave in the presence of a Master. And then, in a kind of glad despair, they realized they must stand and fight, there was no escape.

With that realization there came on the slaves hate with re-membrance — hate built on memories dreadful and unforgivable, memories of long treks in the slave-gangs from their native lands, memories of the naked sale, with painted feet, from the steps of windy ergastula, memories of cruelties cold-hearted and bloody, of women raped or fed to fish to amuse the Masters from their lethargy, of children sold as they came from the womb, of the breeding-kens of the north, where the slaves were mated like cattle, with the Masters standing by. And a low, fierce growl of hate rippled up from the marshalled slaves, the hiss and rattle of the Snake that faced the Wolf.

For a little, out of sling and arrow-shot, the two armies halted motionless. Then said Crixus: 'We've come to the feast, but the meat is still uncooked.' Thereat he took a javelin in his hand, rode forward, stood high in his stirrups, and hurled the javelin whistling through the air. It buried itself in the breast of a front-rank legionary and slew him instantly. On an eminence to the rear of the Roman force, Varinus saw this play and smiled with a sour contempt. He had already gauged the quality of the slave leadership, and ordered his horse to feign a frontal attack.

Out from either flank they swept and poured across the dusty

64

turf upon the slave front. The sods dashed high from the racing hooves, and the soldiers rode with levelled hastae, low-bent in their saddles, silent. They brushed through a curtain of arrows, scraped the Gaulish front, and fell on the men of Gannicus. With a roar the Germans leapt forward to meet them.

Crixus rode like the wind till he stood beside the standards of Gannicus. 'Keep fast in your ranks, retiarius. It is only a ruse.'

Circling like swallows, the horsemen drew off, leaving here and there a hamstrung horse or a slain rider. But Gannicus's ranks were broken, and, looking up at the words of Crixus, the German slaves beheld an unexpected sight.

Shielded under the cavalry ruse, Varinus had set the legion in motion. Rank on rank, steadily, Samnite shields poised to guard the right breast, and elbows crooked behind pila for the thrust, they advanced at a pace that grew ever swifter. Swallows skimmed the near-by hills, there was a drowsy hum of bees in a tree, a slave coughed and coughed, with dust in his throat. The Germans gazed appalled.

In a moment the crash of the Roman attack echoed up through the valley like the noise of a comber on a shaking rock. Now the inferiority of the newly forged long swords of the slaves became plain. Hacking and hewing, the slaves fell back before the deadly inthrust of the pilum. Cleft through the breast in the moment of swing or recovery, they fell like butchered cattle. Round on the left wing of the slaves rode the Roman cavalry again, and the defeat turned to rout. Screaming, the Germans fled from the terror of the Masters' attack.

Crixus sat his horse behind his Gauls and ate pensively at a handful of plums he had stolen from an orchard.

'Were Kleon the Greek here he would tell me that the battle is lost. But I am no General. Therefore I think it is won.'

Too late Varinus perceived the same. Like an avalanche the Gauls, wheeling at the roar of their horns, fell on the flank of the pursuing Romans, for Crixus, seeing the lie of the land, had placed them a little in advance of the Germans, though this fact was inapparent from the Roman stance. The slave horse, negligible in number, but composed of great-limbed Thracians, miners and lumbermen, met the circling Roman cavalry, and, armed with clubs, splintered the levelled hastae and smote down the riders. In a moment the fortune of the battle changed. The Germans turned and the legionaries, caught between two enemies, struggled to reform in double lines. But this, in that marshy ground encumbered with dead, they could by no means achieve.

Varinus rode from the field with a hundred horses and took the northward road. Ten stadia away he halted and at nightfall the survivors of his force began to straggle back. A legionary of no rank, a Gaul, saved almost a third of the infantry, fought a way out of the slave-press, and escaped to Varinus in the dusk.

Overbusied in looting the dead and killing the wounded, the slaves did not pursue. Further, Crixus, having obeyed his orders to hold Varinus, made no attempt to pursue him. Instead, he encamped on the battlefield, sending messengers to Kleon in the Papa camp, and to Spartacus, hurrying from the slaying of Cossinus.

Varinus and his rout laboured half the night at the erection of a trench and stockade. Hourly they expected the slaves to attack, but the night about them remained void and voiceless. Waiting, Varinus sat down to his tablets and penned to the Senate the news that the band of escaped slaves had grown to an army, strong, ferocious, and well led. He made no mention of his defeat, but only that he had drawn back and awaited reinforcements. These he urged should be sent at once.

Next morning his scouts reported that the slave army had vanished again into the Lucanian hills.

The Pits of Death

(i)

TWO men, helmetless, but with long swords girded to their shoulders, lay in a cane-brake near the camp of Varinus. All day they had lain there, and all the previous night, suffering the dews and the mists of morning with a hardy indifference, for they were slaves and Gauls. One, red-haired, large of feet and hands, had snored so stertorously in the hours of the night that his companion, wakeful, had frequently kicked him also awake. Lest the Romans hear.

This companion was a smaller man whose left cheek had been branded with a slave iron, and so twisted his face in a humourless smile. He ate olives endlessly and threw the seeds at the birds which hopped and chirped near the brake with bright, curious eyes. Already the earth was thick with stained leaves and the browns of autumn were on all the land.

Through the shielding walls of the cane-brake came the sounds of Varinus' encampment, and sight of a high stockade over-topped by the eagle signum.

Brennus yawned. 'Gods, but I'm wearied. When next we come to a farm, I'll drink hot milk from a horn and share the bed of a woman. If there are any women left.' He yawned again. 'I'd give my life to lie with a girl in a withy stockade and hear an aurochs low.'

His brother, grimy with leaves-stain, frowned grotesquely. 'I'm not minded to die till I've cut more Roman throats.'

'They should be cut in the interest of peaceable men sleeping,' said Brennus, listening with closed eyes to the mechanical shoutings of the centurions from Varinus's drill-ground. 'Is this Master never to move after the Free Legion?'

'He'll move when the new men come from Rome. Till then we stay here, as Crixus bade us.'

'Gods, don't I know it? Wake me if they ever come, or if another wearied man strolls out to rest near our shelter.' He looked back at a dark, shapeless heap behind him, already smothered in drifting leaves. 'You had all the sport last time.'

When next he awoke it was with the urgent hand of his brother upon his arm. Noon had passed. From Varinus's camp came the same ceaseless hum except that it seemed to have increased in volume.

'The legionaries have come from Rome. The Seventeenth Legion, I think. Sh!'

Suddenly the brother slid from his crouching position and lay flat. Brennus followed his example, and then peered through the interstices of the cane-brake.

Two men, both carrying swords, but without armour or helmets, walked side by side. They were deep in converse, and Brennus, recognizing the nearer man, strained his ears. It was the commander of the Romans, Varinus.

Closer they came, then passed. Then wheeled and passed again. Brennus's hand stole to the hilt of the long sword that rested across his shoulder. At the movement his brother gripped him again.

'O son of foolishness and a forest bitch, is this the time to play with a sword? Didn't you hear?'

'I heard, O brother of the son of a forest bitch. Now I'd end their planning and make south to Crixus.'

'And won't the legions remain and new leaders be found? Any fool may lead an army. Now of *these* leaders we know the plans. Of the plans of their successors you'd know nothing, being by then poison in the stomach of some Lucanian wolf.'

Brennus growled, but withdrew his hand from his sword. They watched the slow stride of Varinus and his companion back to camp. Then Brennus glanced at his brother.

The latter nodded and rose cautiously to his feet. He spoke one word.

'South.'

Brothers, and rivals since infancy in the games of chidhood and barbaric youth, they made south, each at his uttermost speed, running shoulder to shoulder, in the huntsman's long lope. Finding that their new swords encumbered them, they threw them away, retaining only their knives. Hours passed, but they did not ease their pace, encouraging each other with taunts and jests. With the fall of darkness they were many miles south of Varinus's encampment, and came to a deserted village in the hills.

There they found a stray goat, milked it, drank its milk, slew it, broiled and ate its flesh: then lay down to sleep. At moonrise the indefatigable brother roused Brennus, and they sat out again.

68

They slept once more, in a sheltered ravine, just as the dawn tipped the eastward mountains. Awaking, Brennus pointed to a far summit that rose like a copper dagger against the blue bowl of the dawn.

'Papa.'

(ii)

Crixus had entrenched the camp of the Free Legion in Gaulish fashion, dyking it with sloping sides and setting thorns in place of a stockade. So strong was it now that many of the slaves believed it would repel even the attack of a legion. Within its bounds all the warring and raiding parties had reassembled in the last few days, Crixus from his defeat of the Masters in the Battle of the Gauls, Gershom ben Sanballat from his sytematic raiding and looting in the foothills, Oenomaus from a sudden descent on Thurii. Amazed, the slaves awoke to the sudden plenty in their camp, food, weapons and clothes, and stared at these things, stuttering, and turning shamed, hesitant faces from unaccustomed garments and unaccustomed comforts. Then they would remember the Battle of the Gauls, where they had faced a legion in the open and defeated it: and in all the slave horde a strange new spirit stirred, with no longer the bravery of desperation, but instead a pride and a wild hope.

Walking the bounds of the camp that morning, Crixus the Gaul hailed Gershom ben Sanballat, the commander of the Bithynians, who was stalking past him in silence, his fierce eyes fixed on the ground.

'You are early abroad, Bithynian.'

'As you are, German.'

Crixus laughed. 'German? I am a Gaul.'

'And I am no Bithynian. I am a Jew.'

Crixus nodded. 'I'd forgotten. A very worthy people, though they eat horses. Or am I thinking of the Thracians?'

'My people were eating of the bread of God when yours were starving in their northern stenches.'

'A very desirable and praiseworthy God,' said Crixus, politely. He cared nothing for Gods. 'Could you not make him a sacrifice and bring him over the seas to help us now?'

Gershom ben Sanballat looked at the heathen with the old Pharisee arrogance.

'He is the God of Israel alone.'

Crixus signed. 'That's a pity, since He specializes in bread. He might have helped in the feeding of this gaping camp. The country is as bare as a desert for a score of pace miles around.'

Gershom nodded: 'Then let us move.'

'Where?'

'To the sea and disperse.'

The Gaul shook his head. 'That we can't do, unless Spartacus orders it. We've sworn to abide by the orders of the Strategos alone.'

'*I* have sworn no such oath.' The Jew combed his black, curled beard with irritable fingers. 'This Thracian is our leader for as long as we please, not a King whom we cannot depose.'

'Yet I heard of a tribune of the Free Legion who beat one of his men — a Bithynian, I think — who had spread the rumour that Spartacus intended betraying the slaves to the Republic.'

Gershom shrugged impatiently, but made no answer, tall, black-haired, black-bearded, incongruous in his Roman armour and silvered Greek helmet. Crixus looked westward and spoke almost to himself.

'Yet we can't stay here long, as Spartacus knows. He must return within a few days, he and the Greek.'

Gershom was blunt. 'What is this Greek eunuch to the Strategos? His lover?'

Crixus laughed again. 'Many men love Spartacus. Even you, I think, Jew.'

'Many men love a maid: but she beds with but one. This Kleon is with the Strategos night and day. He came back from the killing of Cossinus and I saw the Greek meet him. They talked together, then summoned you to their tent. Then I heard the sound of a company leaving, and saw the Strategos and the woman Elpinice, together with the Greek and a score of Thracians, setting out southwards. How do we know they haven't fled to the sea?'

'Spartacus or Elpinice desert us? Ask the Gladiators who were with them in Vesuvius. You know little of either, Jew.'

'I know little, else I'd be neither a fool nor a slave — nor a so-called tribune in an Unfree Legion commanded by a barbarian who withdraws from the camp when he chooses, and where.'

'He has not withdrawn far. Listen: but don't spread the news about. They have crossed the hills to the great Stone Way to lie in wait for a tribute-train coming from the East through Brindisium. The Greek learned of this train's arrival, and laid the plan for its capture. With its treasure Spartacus is to buy the help of the Italiot cities and make payment to each slave as a Free Legion soldier.'

Then the Jew saw clearly. 'So will it cease to be the Free Legion. We'll wander this land, fighting small battles and storming small towns, seeking alliances that never mature, seeking never to escape from Italy. Till the Republic awakes and crushes us as a man walking through grass crushes an adder.'

Crixus cared nothing for the morrow. 'So be it. Any death is a good one if it isn't the Cross. And I'd rather any day go into the dark with a gladius in my ribs than escape to Gaul and grow old, and die of old age and hunger in some forsaken hut. Especially if the dark, ill Gods of whom they speak lie waiting one at the thither side.'

He fell silent a moment, straining his ears, listening; then looked at Gershom with bright, mocking eyes. 'But Spartacus and the Greek have other plans. They talk of upbuilding another Republic in opposition to that at Rome — a Republic here in south Italy to which the Italiots will cleave.'

'A Republic in the skies,' said Gershom. 'Are these fellow slaves of ours allies that the Italiot cities will welcome? Especially after Metapontum — not to mention Paestum. Were I a free man I'd rather seek allegiance with a herd of swine.'

For even yet there were moments when the sight and smell of a fellow-slave disgusted the one-time aristocrat of Kadesh — disgusted him both as ruler and Pharisee, he who had twice defeated the Hellenizing Jannaeus, and then turned and ground under-heel the revolting serfs of Kadesh. He was amongst them, but not of them, himself seeking only escape, return to Judaea and a secret passing to his mountain folk, there to raise again the standard of the Hasidim against the unclean Salome. Marching his Bithynians through Lucanian towns, he had freed the slaves, as his own men clamoured, but coldly, contemptuous of those he freed. Half at least that he freed had been slaves from birth; slavery he thought their apportioned lot.

Yet also (and this startled his haughty heart when he thought

71

of it), there were long stretches of days and hours, when he sank himself in the mood of the slaves, moved with their anger against the Masters, with their compassion for the fellow-enslaved. Gannicus the Teutone had now a fine tent, and two Roman captives who served him at meat: for that he was hated throughout the camp, perversely, the slave-horde pitying the Romans. Gershom joined in the hate like a slave; looking now towards the quarters of the German slaves a thought, unbidden, came sharp on his lips.

'If the Strategos were wise he'd have his German tribune impaled on a stake ere he started the campaign.'

Crixus laughed. 'What, in the Free Legion? Gannicus had done better to die as a slave.'

'He has the heart of a slave. As have too many of the Legion. See to it, Gaul: no man may ever be a slave but he bears the stigma until he is dead. And that stigma is on his soul. We are no free men. We are rebel slaves.'

For a moment it seemed to Crixus that he was aware of a bitter truth. Then the sharpness of it faded from his mind. He laughed again.

'I am no slave: I have no slave-stigma on my soul. I hate the Romans as I hate an enemy, not as a slave his Master.'

'Then you are a fool,' said Gershom, and turned away. Then halted. 'Here come your two spies.'

'Brennus and his brother? Where?'

Gershom pointed across the entrenchments to two far figures that neared the camp with speed. The Gaul nodded.

'You have keen eyes, Jew.'

'Though a dull heart, Gaul. Heed to me, Crixus. If you and I led this Free Legion, were there in it no Gannicus, no dreaming Spartacus or Kleon, we might save it yet.'

Crixus shook his head. 'I've sworn an oath to the Strategos; which is nothing. But I love Spartacus; which is much.'

Then he went forward to meet his panting spies.

(iii)

Early that same morning a band of twenty, on horseback, forded a river and rode north-westwards into Lucania. They drove a long train of laden ponies. All of the band was mounted, mostly on small

72

horses, long-maned and long-tailed, Calabrian bred and hardy. Each rider carried a shield and javelins. Some were in armour, some not. Some rode half naked, their garments torn. Some had their bodies bound with bloody cloths. One rolled in his saddle, held there by a fellow-rider. It was the slave-band of Thracians, returning from its raid on the great Stone Way.

At the head rode their solitary scout, a small man with retreating chin and forehead. It was Titul, the Iberian. In the rear rode three who every now and again looked over their shoulders at the plains retreating and fading in the haze of the brightening sun. The tallest rode in the middle, a giant, mounted on a giant stallion, unwounded, unwearied, his great body cased in gilded armour. A magnificent figure, the Strategos Spartacus, commander of the Free Legion, once a slave in the ludus of Batiates.

So Kleon thought, riding on the Thracian's right side. But more than merely magnificent, the Thracian. In the space of three months he had changed from a wild, brooding slave who sought no better future than freedom in Thracian forest to a General, a statesman, archon with strategos, to the seeming, inward and outward, of that Prince whom Plato the divine had sought in sun-washed Syracuse. A feat for a eunuch to perform, this, while the Seeker slept with the shades!

Elpinice rode on the Gladiator's left. Since dawn she had ridden in agony, cloths wound tightly round her body, her armour long since thrown away. With lips compressed, she had felt the pain surge over her and set her teeth, and said nothing. For they could not stop in the plains, and she knew that the pains were but early ones, and her body would tell her in a keener agony when her ultimate hour had come.

At the first, in the marching and riding from Papa, when that knowledge had come on her in a night that she bore in her womb the seed of Spartacus, fear and anger had come with the knowledge. By means that were known to many women, in Rome and Capua and the white-walled houses that rose in all the cities of men that girded the Middle Sea, she had taken heed in her nights of old that she should give no children to Batiates. Then in her madness for the Thracian Gladiator, in the wild rides and hidings that followed Capua, when the world gaped to engulf their revolt, there had seemed no purpose to guard herself afresh. The days and the nights of the Thracian's love

73

would endure but a shining space ere the dark came down.

But the dark had not come. In Lucania the Masters still failed to subdue the slave-horde. It waxed daily in size and strength. And with it waxed the fruit of that first strange night when the Gladiator took her in the kennels of Batiates.

So she had sought to kill the thing, riding as a centurion in the company of Castus, engaging in the sprawling guerilla warfare that Spartacus and Kleon waged on the Masters the while they tried to rouse the Italiot cities against the Republic. But it would not die, though she slept unshielded at night, though she lay in the ice-cold water of pools, though twice, dismounting, she had fought in the slave-ranks. Then a calmness had come on her, albeit fear also; and with widened eyes she watched her body change and grow strange. In the dark of the night, by the side of Spartacus, sometimes a wild, dark anger held her, breaking the calmness; sometimes, strangely, tearing her heart, a nameless thing that might once have been pity.

Pity for herself, for the giant head of the Gladiator, fast and secure in sleep, for all sleeping horde about the tents, for all life sleeping and waiting the day. In those dark, lost hours she groped back again through the curtains of years to the tears and touch of a woman half remembered, long before, in Athens: through the curtaining times that had set in her eyes, frozen, the stalactites of hate; that had put in her heart that cold delight that had urged her to cutting the tribune's throat, that had urged her in company of other slaves to nameless tortures on captured Romans, till the blood and the sweat stood out as a rain on their skins, tormented, and they groaned and died. And beyond those curtains she seemed to find, white-faced, a self that wept and, weeping, brought down its hands from a hidden face and laughed with the joy of careless child.

And with that lost self to companion her, she had ceased her ridings from Papa camp, abiding there while the Gladiator rode, hither and there, on missions and raids with the eunuch Kleon his companion-literatus. And the eyes that looked on Elpinice when the Thracian returned from those journeyings she saw awakened to a lover's eyes, not with the lust of the mad, strange child: he would lie and speak, with his head in her lap, of the world of the cities that awaited their coming, of the State that he and the slaves were to build; and she saw in him Power, like a quiescent Snake, and wondered over him while he slept; while the Masters armed and prepared in the north; while his seed would stir and turn in her womb.

He went unaware of her unborn child, as the slave-host did, with no eyes to see, death and the chances of War in their eyes; except for the eunuch Kleon, she thought, reading in the cold, amused eyes of the Greek a hint of the knowledge he shared with her. Yet even when they mooted the plan to raid the great Stone Way for the treasure-loads, and she had said she would ride on the raid, Kleon had said nothing, his eyes had not changed. She had thought it likely she rode her last raid: she had not known that her time was so nigh.

So Elpinice had crossed the mountains, into the green Calabrian land, hiding by daytime as did the others, marching and riding swiftly at night, going without food and long without drink, lying a fugitive in the rains. Behind: the slave-host was perhaps dispersed, perhaps they alone survived the revolt. But Spartacus and Kleon had taken the chance, knowing that Crixus was cautious and skilful, and Varinus still unreinforced. So they kept by the Way and fell on the train, taking it after a scattered fight. Now for two days they had been making their way back to the slave-camp under Mount Papa.

In the afternoon they were forced to turn north to avoid a band of Roman velites whom Titul had spied ere they spied him. Till sunset they made a wide detour, and were presently riding through the mountain-country grown familiar enough to the slaves since the Spring-time exodus from Campania. Here they descried a runner approaching, a solitary figure in a short grey tunic and carrying only a knife in his belt. It was a Gaul and he brought to the Strategos a message from Crixus under Mount Papa.

'Haste and return. Varinus has been reinforced at last, and we have news of his secret plan.'

But Kleon pointed to Elpinice.

'The woman can go no further.'

She was reeling with weakness. But she read in the cold Greek's eyes his plan. It was to have Spartacus abandon her.

Spartacus seemed to awaken, looking at Elpinice in frowning wonder, his ears still filled with Crixus' message. Then he and all who had ridden with her became aware of the thing of a sudden. They had ridden with her unnoticing for days, thinking of her as Elpinice, a Gladiator almost, no woman at all. Now they stared open-mouthed at a woman pregnant, and near to her time of travail at that. Around stood the halted pack-train. The sun was low, in the air a chill. The horses stood drooping-headed. Somewhere at hand a waterfall splashed ceaselessly over hidden rocks. Through a mist of pain Elpinice heard the Gaul messenger speaking.

'There is a house back there in the hills.'

She became aware of the horses in motion, of an arm thrown about her, iron and sure. Winding down through a pit in the hills, they came to the deserted villa. It had been the country-house of some rich Lucanian of Thurii or Metapontum, now fled the slave-occupation. The door of the fauces hung ajar and from the kitchen on the right arose no smoke or the sound of slaves at their toil. The Gladiator kicked wide the doors and went in, carrying the bed-woman of Batiates. For a moment he stood in the gloom of the atrium, looking round him in wonder, for he had never before entered such a dwelling.

The gloom sparkled with light. The last rays of sunshine in the watersplash re-rayed on the marble ceiling, and back from there to the mosaic'd floor, flung wandering beams down the corridors on the painted bodies of the statues that stood pedestal'd in the peristyle. One, a Hermaphroditus of Silanion, showed the body of the son of Hermes united with that of the river nymph in an obscene ecstacy. A Symplegma of the school of Cephissodorus stared up in a blank, cloacal anguish at the stare of the giant barbarian.

And a sudden, wild anger seized on Spartacus. His shout brought in the Thracians. Loosening his arms from about Elpinice, he pointed to the shining figures in stone.

Then, to the crash of the breaking statues, he carried the bed-woman of Batiates to a sleeping-room.

(iv)

Up and down the atrium paced the Greek eunuch, and presently heard the screams die to a faint moaning. They moved him only to an impatient frown. How long would this delay their march? How long the Thracian waste the hours at the unclean bed of a woman in childbirth?

Knowing Elpinice an enemy of his plans, Kleon had hoped to see her die in the raid on the great Stone Way. Even when she had survived that raid, and they rode back into Lucania again, the conviction had been firm upon him that the Strategos, finding her pregnant, would abandon her by the way. What need had the slave commander to burden himself with an ailing woman when he might have women as he chose from the captives, from the hundreds of women slaves who now filled the camp under Mount Papa? But instead he had halted the march like a midwife — he who had shaped so sure in the seeming, cold and passionless, of Plato's Prince!

Going outside, the eunuch found the darkness now close at hand. He set to garrisoning the house in the pit, the hills around sloped up to the oncoming dark, the cry of the rivulet was here unceasing. Kleon stood in the dimness and looked at a star that came out and twinkled over far Papa. It was the star of the Sea-born herself.

And, for the first time since that day when the Libyans of Pacianus had robbed him of his manhood, a sick desolation came on him. Always to be alone, never to know kind hands or the lips of love! Never to see the seed of his body borne to fruit, or to hear the voice of a child. And for a moment, dreadfully, the eunuch wept. What availed him his plans or the game he played with an ancient dream from the antique times? What to him though the slaves should gain or lose, what to him life or death, already half dead, with a body mutilated to shame?

But that night Elpinice gave birth to a son, and drank warmed wine and water, and slept awhile; and woke with the coming of the morning and urged the Strategos to leave her. And this at last, though reluctantly, he did, a dreaming slave with power forgotten, and the dream that he captained a legion of men. Titul and half his company he left to guard the house, and embraced Elpinice, and saw her eyes strange, so that he remembered that night long before in the kennels of the ludus in far Capua.

Then he rode through the dawnlight to Crixus' camp.

(v)

Thoranius the quaestor had marched from Rome with the Seventeenth Legion to reinforce Varinus. He was a wily man whose father had been a freedman. Gross and uncultured, half a barbarian, he seemed to Varinus at first a worse lieutenant than either Furius or

77

Cossinus. He bellowed like a bull about the camp, and would slap his thigh with a freckled hand, stirred to mirth by his own crude wit. In appearance like a merchant and wearing his armour with plebeian clumsiness, he at first gave little evidence of the fact that he was a consummate tactician, a man whose lowly birth alone had retarded a speedy promotion.

Then, twelve hours after his arrival in Varinus' camp, he led the praetor out by the cane-brake that fringed the camp, and propounded a campaign plan plotted to the minutest detail.

At first Varinus listened to it coldly, then disagreed, then argued, then finally accepted it, though its boldness and unconventionality left him in uneasy doubt. Following his agreement, the camp hummed with activity through three long days. On the fourth morning Varinus marched out his veterans and went south into the land of ravines that led towards the sea-coast. Thereafter there departed from the camp, in bands of three hundred, eight hundred, nine hundred, and a thousand, with the space of an hour betwixt each departure, a full half of the Seventeenth Legion new-brought from Rome by Thoranius. The surrounding country had been scoured for spies or fugitives, and no eyes other than those of hawks watched Thoranius' men depart by four different routes that yet all led south.

From the slave-camp under Papa that same dawn Spartacus, newly arrived from the east, remounted his tireless stallion, and rode out at the head of two thousand slaves, Germans and Thracian, light-armed troops, Gannicus their quaestor, and marched swiftly west. Following this, ere the dust of the Strategos's departure had settled, Oenomaus took six hundred men, Greeks and Gauls, out of the camp, and marched north. After him a company of Gauls and Iberians, men capable of a pace unknown to either the Romans or the rest of the Free Legion, ran swiftly forth from the Papa entrenchments, and vanished north-westwards into the mountains. They were led by Castus. Crixus, Gershom and Kleon the eunuch were left in the camp, in command of the Gauls and the Eastern slaves, guarding not only the camp, but the companies of Roman prisoners taken in the battle near Paestum.

All night a fierce frost had held the ground, but now, under the sunlight, and with the departure of the last of the raiding companies, a mist arose and rolled over the plain. Papa stood crowned in cloud.

The Roman prisoners, digging in relays all through the previous day and night, toiled anew under the direction of Kleon.

The time was short.

Gershom ben Sanballat was uneasy, and left his Bithynians, also engaged in hasting excavation, to walk down the lines of reed huts and shelters till he stood by the side of the Greek. For a little they said nothing, watching the Romans. These prisoners, though scantily clad and ill fed on rotten corn, yet toiled under no lash, a fact which awakened more resentment in the Free Legion than any other order of the Thracian Strategos.

'They dig ill,' said Kleon. 'I think they suspect that these are Roman graves.'

The Jew combed his curled beard with his fingers, and cast quick, bright eyes over the mist-wreathed countryside. 'I would that the corpses were safe in them.'

'They'll come.'

'Doubtlessly.' The Jew's eyes lit on him in sardonic appraisal. 'It seems to me I once heard you say you cared nothing where we went or how we might fare, life being the smallest of matters to you. Yet I find you under a tribune's helmet, and in the secret counsel of the Strategos. Surely, whatever the game he plays, it's an ill thing for a Greek to serve a barbarian who eats horses and worships his dead?'

Kleon smiled, coldly indifferent. 'If he eats horses I have seen him perform greater feats. I've seen him make captains of companies eat their oaths and their pride at one meal.'

'As Jehovah is God, that's true.' Gershom ben Sanballat was pensive. 'Yet why in the Free Legion I march under the orders of an unclean Gentile, who seeks to build a tyranny on the dreams of a Corinthian eunuch, puzzles me much.'

Kleon's face flushed in a vivid anger. Then he said, in a strangled voice: 'That is an ill taunt, Jew.'

So Gershom himself knew, yet he knew no way of confessing it. The blood had stained his own face ere the words had left his lips; his fingers faltered in the glossiness of his beard. Bending forward, he cursed the Romans, and at his words they toiled with a renewed activity. Then the Hasidim guerilla turned to the white-faced Greek.

'It was ill. You're twice the man, I sometimes think, in that you are less the bull. But I grow impatient with this plotting and planning,

79

as though we were statesmen, not skulking slaves, this building of sky-republics, these secret raids and hopes. You and your Thracian build a house in sand.'

'Sand or rock, their end is the same, a dream of order on a planless earth, of endurance where all things meet and melt.'

The Jew was again the cold Pharisee. 'So speak the Hellenes, blaspheming God, as the bedmen of the Whore in Jerusalem.' His thoughts went far with his gaze. 'But she'll find that both God and I still live — if I ever win back to Kadesh.'

'Your queen?' Kleon was again indifferent. Then: 'Your Bithynians will have set half the camp with traps if you do not heed to their digging soon. They work with more heart than my Romans.'

The Jew went back to his company. Meantime the Gauls, all but a party that kept the entrenchments and several who loitered outside the dyke, lay stretched at ease, or mended their armour and tunics. From near the camp entrance the long dyke being dug by the captives and Bithynians drove straight through the lines of hutments to the far wall of the original enclosure. Towards noon the excavators abandoned the digging, and, under the vigorous direction of Kleon, set to carrying away the excavated mould. By mid-afternoon the great gape of the dyke had vanished. Roofed over with branches and turf, it seemed now a lane of solid ground splitting the camp in twain. A smell of fresh mould hung over the lines. Quietness settled on the camp.

An hour passed, and Crixus, who all day had sat on the northwards wall, descended and ran swiftly to the great camp-gate. His Gauls seemed hardly to mark his passage, unless it was that their singing and laughter grew louder as they loosened the long swords slung from their shoulders. At the gate a few Free Legionaries were already crowding, indifferently, staring upon the band that approached.

It was a straggling band of eight hundred men, escaped slaves (they shouted) who had fought their way from Apulia to join the Free Legion. They were casually welcomed by Crixus and the sentries, and entered the camp, three abreast, a disorderly throng, laughing and rejoicing.

Inside the gateway they found an abutting wall. Betwixt it and the main camp palisade was a narrow corridor that curved unexpectedly. For a moment the foremost of the new arrivals hesitated, but the pressure behind was too great to resist. The company passed in. The sentries closed in a compact body and marched in with it. Crixus, at the gate, blinked his eyes and looked northwards again.

Then, behind him, across the inner wall, arose a screaming tumult and the crackling of boughs, the hiss of arrows and the scrape of weapons. For a time the noise was deafening. Then it slowly died away. Crixus paid no heed, standing with his hand on his hip, his helmet pushed back from his forehead, his eyes blinking in the winter sun-dazzle.

Just before sunset another band of sturdy, well-fed slaves arrived at the camp under Papa. They also passed through the hospitable gate; and again, in a little, arose the terrible tumult.

The Strategos himself returned at nightfall, bloody but un-wounded, with the remnant of his companies reeling behind him in weariness. Crixus went out and saluted him in the glare of the torches, the giant slave on the giant stallion who told him the unslavelike news.

'We ambushed Varinus at Carrae, among the rocks. His Legion is destroyed. What happened here?'

Crixus laughed. 'As we planned. Though I haven't been to see.'

Together they stood inside the camp and looked at the trap into which the companies of Thoranius had walked. Shepherded by guides, they had marched in the pits dug that morning and covered with turves. As the turves gave way beneath the feet of the ostensible slaves, the Gauls had assailed them with arrows and then with the sword. Twice this had happened, and now the dyke was heaped with Roman dead.

Some had died of suffocation, some from the arrows and stones rained upon them. Some were perhaps as yet undead. But they would not outlive the night. Already from that dreadful pit, arose a fetid stench.

The Gladiator turned away, the strange barbarian moulded from a wayward slave to an archon-tyrant under the hands of a dreaming eunuch. But that ancient self that amazed his world lived in him still, if with voice less wild.

'This was your plan, Kleon. It has saved the camp. But I swear that never again we'll trap even Romans like this.'

Kleon laughed thinly, his face pallid with the stench from the pits. 'Had the Romans held this camp and slaves marched in disguised — would their deaths have come as easily as death to these? They'd have been torn again from the pits to the cross and the torturing-iron.'

'The Roman is a wild beast,' said Gershom ben Sanballat. 'They have died fitly.'

Crixus laughed. Then shivered. 'May I not die so.'

Before midnight Castus and Oenomaus had returned with their depleted companies. Yet everywhere that day the slave armies had triumphed, the two Gauls separately destroying two of the bands of legionaries despatched by the wily Thoranius in his plan to fill the slave-camp with disguised Romans. Then the two Gaul leaders had combined their forces and fallen on the Roman camp. Thoranius himself had been killed, fighting desperately, and the rest of his legion dispersed.

Meantime, through the night, northwards, Varinus fled with a small band of horse and halted not until he gained the gates of Capua.

(vi)

Spartacus halted his stallion and stared. Behind him the troop of Gladiators also came to a stop, staring at that thing that lay athwart the track. In the air was the shrill of a waterfall. The hills shelved down in a pit to the hidden Roman house.

They had ridden since daybreak to come to the house where Elpinice lay. Now, near it at last, they looked at the thing that had halted their progress. Mid-way the track lay a slave, the flies thick upon him, his tunic half-ripped from his back. No need to ask why he lay there. In his back was a hole big enough to have let out a dozen lives.

The hole had been made by a Roman pilum.

The horses shied away. Spartacus dismounted and turned over the slave. He did not know him, but the Thracian, Ialo, did.

'This is one of the men who rode with you to the raid of the great Stone Way.'

They mounted and went on. The shrill of the waterfall drew nearer. The track shelved downwards steeply. The hills drew back. Then they halted a second time, sitting very still in their saddles.

Ialo was long to remember that moment, the strange winter

82

heat and clarity, the singing of the larks overhead, and the smoke slowly upwinding from all that remained of the Roman house.

It had been burned with a thoroughness that argued practice. Its streaked walls — for there had been a fall of rain in the night — were as bare of their painted woodwork as a skeleton of flesh.

Ialo was startled by the Strategos suddenly laughing. 'Yesterday we trapped the Masters in a pit,' he said, and laughed again, terribly, looking about him in the great hill-pit that shielded the smoke-hung house. Then he dismounted, the Gladiators behind him.

They clambered up through what had been the atrium. No dead lay near. Spartacus took a great charred stake and began to lever aside the debris. Silently, the Gladiators also seized stakes and toiled beside him, seeking to uncover the passage that led to the room where Elpinice had lain.

That passage at length they uncovered. The room itself, after long toil in the cool winter sunlight, they uncovered. Then Ialo and the Gladiators stood off, and Spartacus remained there alone.

All that afternoon they waited, watching from afar. It was evening before he called to them and they came and broke down the room about the two calcined bodies. In the peristyle lay the body of a faceless slave, who had died defending these two. Ialo secretly dragged the body in beside that of Elpinice and her child, that he might guard them for ever in the Land of Mist.

They heard a strange singing in the hills, and found Titul the Iberian hiding behind a bush. He had crawled there, hacked and bleeding, the only survivor of Elpinice's guard. His tale was short.

'They came on us at noon, half a century of cavalry that had followed the raid we made on the great Stone Way. We fought, hurling great stones and javelins. But they slew us, for we had no arrows. Before they fired the house they took the woman in her bed. Many of them. She cried on the Strategos.' He paused to lick his wounds, being mad. 'As was proper. Great was the lust of men in the vanished Western Isle.'

III. REX SERVORUM

The Conqueror

(i)

NOW the whole of Southern Italy lay undefended at the feet of the Thracian Gladiator.

(ii)

A self-deputed scout, Kleon the literatus pushed northwards with a hundred Gauls through the winter-touched land. If he engaged himself more in mapping than sacking, that was a small matter to the Gauls, who sacked and looted as the mood came on them.

Once, in forced marches from Papa camp, out on some mysterious mission to the north-east, Gershom ben Sanballat, the tribune of the Bithynians, overtook the Greek and his scouts. With the Jew was a full three thousand men, his original company of Bithynians now swollen with recruitments of Syrians, Egyptians, Negroes and Greeks. But they called it still the Bithynian legion. The Pharisee guerilla grinned sardonically as he pointed to a burning villa.

'Is this the beginning of your New Republic?'

Kleon was coldly unmoved. 'We must destroy before we build.'

'As the divine Plato doubtlessly said,' growled Gershom. And then: 'Where are we to winter, Greek?'

'In Kadesh, perhaps.'

The Jew cursed him and marched away his legion. By evening that day they were beyond the furthest trailings of Kleon's scouts. Then the latter turned westward, combing the roads that ran parallel with the sea. It was the design of the slaves to intercept all travellers from the North.

These were few enough. Merchants had fled the roads, seeking Greece and Africa by sea. But that evening Kleon, sleeping in his camp, was awakened by the noise of much drunken mirth. Rousing, he rose and went into the flare of torches and found a half-score of his Gauls, much laden with wine-skins and incongruous finery, surrounding a band of travellers scooped from the northern road.

They huddled together, these travellers, or rather huddled

about one figure. Coming forward, Kleon surveyed that figure with cold, amused eyes.

She was a woman of that beauty that was singularly Roman, however she had departed from the antique codes of the Masters. Tall and full-breasted, with level brow and widely spaced eyes, she stood calm in the tumult, with a calmness that angered her captors. Kleon thrust through them and took the woman by the jaw, turning her face into the full light. She did not struggle, only looked at him with eyes into which flashed a sudden disgust and fear. Kleon knew that look — the look of a woman for the Mutilated.

'What is your name?' he asked.

'Lavinia.'

She had been the mistress of Cossinus, brought down from Rome under the protection of that Kharmides who now lay out on the great North way with his throat cut from ear to ear by a Gaulish miner. Kleon stood and regarded her with cold, clear eyes. Should he hand the woman over to the Gauls? Or was there any other purpose she could serve?

As the mistress of Cossinus she must be aware of secret matters in Rome — how the Senate had taken the defeat of Varinus and planned the new campaign against the slaves. But he himself had no leisure to question her; and, even as women sickened in his presence, so he felt for them an unquenchable loathing. With all — as all with him. Excepting . . .

He turned from that thought in a strange pain. 'I will send you to the Strategos,' he said.

Her eyes widened with fear. 'Spartacus, the Thracian?'

The Greek grinned coldly. 'Even so. But he seldom eats women.' His eyes were cruel. 'As for anything else he may do — that will be nothing unusual in your experience, will it?'

Next morning he watched her go south under the guard of ten of the most trustworthy Gauls. And for some reason he remembered Elpinice again, whom he had hated; and stood and stared after that train that carried the Roman woman to Spartacus.

(iii)

Meanwhile, marching mostly by night on their mysterious venture, Gershom ben Sanballat and his legion faded into the east. The

88

Pharisee, forced for long periods to eat of unclean meat, contented himself with little but fruit and looted corn. At night he slept on his shield. No watch-fires were lighted when the slave-legion made camp, for it might be that strong bodies of Romans were still abroad, remnants from the rout of Varinus. These the Jew had no desire to engage.

The city of Nuceria prepared for winter. It was defended by an ancient wall and ten centuries of soldiers under the command of a Greek named Glaucon. A good general and a stern disciplinarian, he had had the ancient walls strengthened as the country around began to seethe with the slave revolt. From those walls he would watch undisturbed the smoke of burning homesteads rise in the air. Nuceria they might not attempt.

Glaucon had half a dozen warnings nailed on its walls. These were the crucified bodies of slaves captured in their attempt to slip away and join the army of the Gladiators.

He had campaigned in many countries, Glaucon, and amongst his slaves had a Jewish woman, Judith. A child of the Egyptian Diaspora, she was a tall, dark woman of whom Glaucon had soon wearied as bed-woman; for even in his bed she shuddered as at an unclean touch. Amused, Glaucon had made her his cook, for she was deft in the preparation of the spiced dishes he had grown to love in the East. Also, placed on oath in the name of her God, he knew she was incapable of poisoning him.

With the passing of the years he allowed her considerable freedom and bore with her occasional Jewish insolence. Daily she went to a farm beyond the walls, bringing back fresh eggs and milk and herbs to savour her dishes.

On a day in early winter she found the farm very quiet. Coming to the rear door she entered. As she did so an arm encircled her throat and she found herself held by an armed man. He gagged her with care, and hesitated a moment in the darkness of the passage, hungering, half-minded to rape her. Then he chattered something in unintelligible Latin, and dragged her into the kitchen of the farm.

Several score of armed men — or so it seemed to her — lay on the floor, the tables, the shelves, lay everywhere, fast asleep. Only one man other than her captor did not sleep, and he looked a frowning question; a tall, black-haired man who combed at his curled beard.

'Release her,' he commanded.

Released, Judith stood and looked at him. And suddenly they both smiled; and the Bithynians woke to hear greetings exchanged in a strange tongue, and saw the woman kiss the hand of the leader of the Hasidim. She had heard of him often in Alexandria, in the days when he stayed the Hellenizing Jannaeus; who of the Diaspora had not heard of Gershom of Kadesh?

So it was that, their commander and his advance-guard secretly admitted to the city through the wall-gate of Glaucon himself, Nuceria next morning awoke to find itself in the hands of the Spartacists.

Assured of their northern frontier, the slaves prepared to evacuate the camp under Mount Papa.

(iv)

Preparing, the slaves were conscious of a change in the quality of their leadership.

No longer was each band left to its own devices, to squat by the fires and drowse on memories of the kennels and mines. Instead, centuries and exact legions were instituted, each legion composed of four thousand men, armed thus and so; and if possible composed of a definite tribe. Feuds were forbidden, or the robbery of the merchants who now swarmed round the camp to sell their wares in exchange for the loot of Metapontum and the treasure-train from Brindisium. Standards were given to each legion of slaves, insignia and tribunes bearing badges of rank. Daily the slaves were marched out to skirmish and drill, leaving their women in staring bands on the parapets of the Papa entrenchments. Those who were smiths or armourers erected crude smithies and set to the forging of iron weapons.

At this breath of Roman-like discipline, the slaves, in their hatred of the Masters, were delighted. Practising ecstatically, they imagined themselves both Masters and conquerors of the Masters. They obeyed their centurions without question, and, sweating, would leap and wrestle, naked, in the lines of long, open-air gymnasia. Even the Gauls and the Eastern men lost their shame in appearing unclad; and with bodies shining with oil would hurl the discus or practise as slingsmen.

Shouts of adulation would greet the Thracian Gladiator as he

90

passed through the sweating companies. Crixus the Gaul alone appeared unchanged, and confessed a complete inability either to drill or manoeuvre his legion. 'I am a Gladiator, no soldier. As once you yourself were,' he said to the Strategos.

The heavy Thracian burr of the Latin did nothing to guise the passionless ferocity of the words. 'Once I was also a child, Crixus. But I've stopped drinking milk. You'll drill your legion, or I'll appoint another to drill it for you.'

The Gaul stared. It was indeed a new Spartacus, this. Then Crixus went to drill his men.

That night a message was brought to the Strategos that a woman and three men captives, taken by Kleon on the northwards road, had arrived in the camp under a guard of Gauls. Ialo the Thracian brought him the message. He had now made himself the Gladiator's intimate attendant, and stood in the dark of the hut looking questioningly at Spartacus seated on a little stool. So every evening he sat in darkness, unless a tribune came seeking his counsel, or Kleon the eunuch were in the camp. Then torches would be brought and the two sit poring at a table over the plans that the Greek would sketch on his tablets or sometimes with drops of spilt wine. The Gladiator looked up.

'Bring in the four of them.'

So they were brought before him, and Lavinia, in the light of a single torch, looked at the conqueror of southern Italy, who had shaken the Republic as no other since the days of Hannibal. All Rome was a-rumour with his name and intentions, one rumour preponderating over all others. It was said that the Thracian savage was mad, mad not with the brutality that might have been expected, but insane, being clement, one who neither tortured his captives nor looted unnecessarily. And Rome had listened open-mouthed, and laughed, knowing that only the feeble-minded could antic in such a fashion; and stilled its fears, knowing the successes of the rebellion accidental after all, to be speedily nullified when the consuls took the field at the end of the winter.

So Lavinia remembered, standing dishevelled and dusty, but still with beauty upon her, in the presence of the slave who had shaken Rome. Behind him stood Ialo; the Gauls lounged at the door, slaves in authority. If the story of his reputed clemency were a lie, she shivered at the thought of what would next happen to her — had he no use for her himself. She herself had experimented with slaves in moments of idle curiosity as to how a mutilated man behaved and cried.

Then Spartacus raised his head and looked at her.

At first there was fear with her, then, as always when she met the gaze of his kind, a shuddering disgust of the slave who dared look at her with unshielded eyes, a feeling of a foul contamination. But she saw strange eyes, glowing yet dull, and minded that thing that he carried on his standards, the slave-army insignia of a Snake. Now she knew at last where they got that sign, and shivered while those dark eyes grew suddenly gold. Spartacus stood up.

In the tent were cloths Elpinice had used, a bronze mirror, for all she wore Gladiator's armour, a spatula and a horn cup. In the dark of the evenings under Papa Ialo had been wont to find the slave-leader staring at these, strangely and terribly. Now he gestured towards them.

'Take these away. What is your name, woman?'

'I am Lavinia,' she said, in a white whisper.

'A Roman?'

She found his thick Latin barely intelligible. But she understood. She nodded.

And that night, when at length he slept and she drew shudderingly back from his arms, far off and ringingly she heard a wolf howl; and, harlot though she was, listened with quivering nostrils.

(v)

All the next day and all the next night the smithy fires flared in the guarded camp of the slaves under Papa. Twice forced to evacuate it in the campaign waged with Varinus, it had yet grown homely to many of them, they had garlanded its huts and shelters with boughs; and the women in autumn days had strewn flowers in its shelters, and daubed its posts with images of the gods, while the mountain soared guardian through the passing days. Now, in the flare of the watch-fires, Mount Papa watched their last night.

There was a calling of orders, a crying of names, mustering of companies rising shrill above the noise of the beaten anvils. Slaves knelt by the fires and hammered their shield-rims or sharpened their

92

swords; a wail of unsleeping children rose all around. The legion of Thracians, appointed to march under Spartacus himself, wrought through sweating hours to forge the javelins with which he desired them to arm. As with Gershom's legion he planned to possess a body of soldiers neither legionaries nor hoplitai, but modelled on the peltasts of whom Kleon had told.

Greek literati sat everywhere, copying-slaves who had joined the revolt, making notes of provisions and armour, numbers and companies. Four men, three Gauls and a Greek, appointed spies by Kleon the eunuch, wandered from legion to legion, learning the secret opinions and complainings of the slaves. None knew what was towards in the northern march, but the wildest rumours were spread about — that Spartacus the unconquered would seize the land, and make himself king with them as his guard, and defy the power of the Masters for ever. And a growing murmur swelled to a shout, a shout that echoed through the listening hills:

'AVE, SPARTACUS! AVE, REX SERVORUM!'

Crixus, alone undisturbed, slept in his tent, dreaming of that unhomely Gaul he had little desire to regain. Elpinice came once and troubled his dreams; but in a little while his God arose and drove her back into the land of shades.

And in the early dawn the Free Legions were on the march, northward, up through the tracks they had descended early that year. But now the ground was white with hoar-frost, and a chill wind blew from Lucania. Great baggage-waggons rumbled up the track, the oxen labouring deep-breathing, dragging northwards the spoil of South Italy. Above, Papa was wreathed in mist, but the slaves knew little of augurs, for their Gods were but ill remembered.

The Gauls had wreathed their hair with chaplets of brown leaves and marched out with their helmets slung on their backs, the great Gaul swords slung with them, their spears upended as staves. Once slaves of the mine, the portico, the plantation, they led the legions north, and, singing, vanished into the morning dimness.

The German bands of Gannicus tramped heavily after. Lastly, the Thracians, three thousand strong, with new-welded javelins in their belts and Spartacus riding his stallion in their midst, marched northwards just as the wintry sunshine lifted the cloudy streamers from Mount Papa's crest.

93

Crixus, who commanded the rearguard, laden with baggage, knew nothing of this departure. He slept in the almost deserted camp till roused by a slave who desired to dismantle his hut. Thereat, yawning, he arose and went out to look at Papa for the last time. Then he looked from that to the track that led north.

'Our Gods have a Fortune awaiting us there.'

Winter in Nola

(i)

NOLA was stormed by the Gaulish advance-guard of the Free Legions. Castus hurled wave after wave of attackers upon it, and took it after great slaughter. But with its seizure the southern half of the peninsula, which Kleon and the Thracian designed to make a great slave state, was now defended by two strong towns. Nuceria was strongly garrisoned, but the body of the slave-horde quartered in Nola.

It was a bitter winter. None but velites and such light troops might move while it lasted, and throughout the months of inaction the slaves might have sunk in a placid torpor, but for the ceaseless urging of Spartacus and the eunuch Greek. These knew that unless the horde was welded into an army, the consuls would destroy them in the Spring. For now, and at last, the Republic was aroused. The Wolf had wakened on her hills, and was crying her packs to defence. It was even told that a great shipment of timber had been sent for to the Sardinian forests: to make crosses for the captured slaves.

So drilling and training in weapon-play went on unceasingly under the walls, despite the bitter winds from the north. The furnaces glowed unceasingly, while hastae and pila were hammered and sharpened in preparation for the Spring. Kleon even conceived the idea of the construction of rams and catapults for the taking of the southern cities still unmolested by the slaves. That idea might never have passed to fulfilment, but that the slave-horde was joined in Nola by a Greek named Hiketas, neither slave nor freedman, but an Argive noble. He brought with him his sister, Eradne, with whom he lived in incest. Traversing the roads from Rome, he offered his services to the staring eunuch.

'This is the slave-army,' Kleon said, with a cold distrust. 'You are of the Masters.'

The young Greek laughed; and yawned daintily, eating a comfit from a silver box. 'I am tired of this life of Masters and slaves. Your slave-bands offer diversion. So I and Eradne would join them.' He waved a negligent hand at the tall, slight figure clad as a man, who had ridden with him to the Nola guardhouse. Kleon said: 'She is your

95

woman?'

'She is my sister, and we live in incest.' The young Greek ate another comfit, and dusted his hands. 'But we've no ambition to live in this guardhouse, unless your Strategos rejects our help. In that case we've another plan to follow.'

'What is that?' Kleon asked.

'To charter a boat in Sicily and sail west through the Pillars to the Outer Seas. I'd put to the test this tale of old Plato's that the Western Isle was really sunk.'

Kleon thought of Titul and smiled on him bleakly. And then thought: 'You may join the Free Legions if you will. But I'll set a guard to watch you and your woman.'

Hiketas raised plucked eyebrows in his painted face. 'Set a legion, if you'll sleep better of nights.' And then, as he was led through Nola, broke from his half-captivity to gesture at the single ram in the market-place. 'And you hope to assail the cities with that?' He had lost his languor. 'Give me men, materials, and time until Spring. . . .'

Kleon had given him all three. And now to the other sounds of preparation the forum of Nola rang with the sound of the mallets wielded under the orders of the renegade Master, upbuilding two great helepolites for the siege of such cities as might resist the slaves, giant towers of wood that were scaled with brass. In addition to these, the Argive noble set to the construction of five tormenta, great catapults for hurling rocks on the roofs and walls of cities they might assail. Kleon withdrew his guard upon Hiketas, in time the slaves ceased to stare as he passed, and he and the woman Eradne found quarters near the Nola Forum, close to their labours. When the Springtime came. . . .

(ii)

Spartacus summoned Kleon to his quarters. It was late afternoon as the eunuch crossed the city, and the cold bit deep, for his blood was thin. Coming to the quarters of the Thracian, he passed the guard of Ialo. Spartacus sat, as of old, on a little stool, without his armour, his head in his hands.

'When will the consular armies move?'

Kleon had already debated this with him, and looked at the

brooding figure in surprise. 'Not for a month yet, I think.'

'Then we must move before them. If we wait till they are defeated, the south will stir against us. It is stirring already.'

Kleon said coldly, 'With you to order the battle, no army of the Masters can stand against us.' And thought: 'Until they bring Pompeius from Iberia.'

The Thracian nodded. 'Until they bring Pompeius. When that day comes, we can meet that day. Meanwhile, we do not risk what we've taken already. Southern Italy we can hold if we choose — yet only if we choose. I'll send Castus into Apulia to put down the country and hold the great Stone Way.'

'Castus?' Kleon shook his head. 'Now I would not send him.'

'Why not?'

'He's a lover of yours, they say.' The brooding figure did not move. 'And at least too unready to hold a separate command for long, with you not by him. There's only one tribune you can send.'

The Strategos knew it also; but he seemed to avoid the knowledge.

'The Jew?'

Kleon smiled acidly and shook his head. 'He would rend out his beard by the roots and suspect he was being sent out of the way while I prepared to anoint you king — that cry of REX SERVORUM has haunted him since Papa. Though he is faithful enough. Nor can you send Oenomaus, for the same reason that Castus cannot be sent. Nor Gannicus, for, with a separate command, he would loot and murder to his heart's content. There's only one fit commander.'

It was snowing, gustily, in a bitter wind. The two slave leaders sat at a window and looked out through the slats at the white, waving curtain, with beyond it the walls of Nola and the mountains into which they proposed to despatch an army. In the coming dark, despite the storm, the city shone lighted and secure, warming a little the Greek heart of Kleon, hating the wastes of the countryside. He sat in silence and watched the Thracian, marvelling a little that there should endure in him such love for a fellow-slave of the arena.

When even the memory of Elpinice was dead.

And thought of Elpinice came on Kleon again. She often disturbed his thoughts, reasonlessly, seeing she was dead, and if not nothingness only a pale shadow in a world of dreams — the Land of

Mist, as the Thracians called it. She had stood between him and Spartacus, and though he had no fear that this other love of the Strategos would so stand, it was the one defect he saw in that passionless statesman he was moulding from the fluid clay of the Gladiator of Capua.

Then Spartacus stood up and called his attendant, the same Thracian Ialo as had ridden with him to the Roman house in the pit of the hills.

'Bid Crixus come to me.'

Then he turned round and met the nod of the Greek. 'I'll send him into Apulia.'

(iii)

The quarters of Gershom ben Sanballat were above the wall-gate of Nola itself. From there the Pharisee hater of Gentiles saw to the guarding of the slave-host in Nola. Captain of the town's defences, his was the appointing of guards and sentinels, the periodical inspection of all the wall's circuit, the questioning of arrivals and departures of merchants. Accustomed to the bleak winds of the hills of Judaea, the winter weather had but little effect on him. Clad in a long mantle and a leather helmet, he would stride from guard-room to guard-room, followed by two Bithynians, shivering, and keeping a slight trot in order to maintain pace with their Jewish General.

Coming from his council with Spartacus, Kleon the Greek made his way to the house above the Northern Gate. Darkness had come, and all the house was in shadow but for the glow from the charcoal brazier in the room where Gershom sat. Gershom he found not seated alone. Beside him was a woman who, at the appearance of the Greek, rose to her feet and walked out of the room by another door. Kleon stopped and stared after her sardonically.

'A priestess of Jehovah, doubtlessly?'

The ex-leader of the Hasidim combed his beard. 'It is Judith, the woman who opened the gates of Nyceria for us. She is a very good cook.'

The Greek shrugged mockingly. 'And no doubt a passable bed-woman. Hear the word of the Strategos, tribune: You'll relieve all Germans from guard duties immediately, and send them armed to their own quarter.'

The Jew stood up and reached for his helmet. 'What foolishness is now afoot? Where are the Germans going?'

'Crixus is taking them into Apulia. The Strategos proposed you, but I told him you were over-busied.' He glanced at the door through which Judith had gone. 'As apparently you are.'

The Jew's brows drew into a scowling line, for a moment again the noble addressing the eunuch slave. 'Such business as I have is my own. Heed you to yours.' And added irrelevantly: 'Has not Spartacus his Lavinia?'

Kleon sat down. He nodded moodily. 'Yes, that was my mistake. I should have cut her throat on the Northern Road or else handed her over to the Gauls.'

It was Gershom's turn to sneer. 'Has she no faith in the New Republic, then?'

But Kleon was not listening. For long after Gershom had gone, to the walls and relieving the Germans, he sat in that room by the Northern Gate and stared in the brazier's glow. The Jew with his Judith, Spartacus with Lavinia — every slave who could find or steal or win a woman this night might sit by his fire in comfort and drowsing content. Or rouse into warmth and tenderness, the stinging bliss of lust. Except himself.

And that bitter hatred he had of the Masters pierced him like keen knives, till he laughed a little at himself, shakenly, and it passed. Then he went out, through the darkness and noise of Nola. The snow had cleared and far up, cold and clear, shone the stars.

He stood and looked at them for a little, and with a nameless comfort.

(iv)

Next morning half the German legion was detached from the command of Gannicus, and marched out by Crixus on the road to Apulia. And Crixus and the Strategos kissed; and the Snake standards shone above the marching slaves. And long from the walls of Nola, Spartacus watched that departure.

99

Crixus in Apulia

(i)

THAT year Gellius and Quintus Arrius were elected consuls at Rome, and waited for an unusually bitter winter to pass before setting out with the legions on the principal object of their election.

That object the Senate, at length aroused, had stressed as the suppression of the slave rebellion. Both consuls, having suffered in their southern properties from the ravagings of the Free Legions, were in complete agreement for once with the policy of the Senate.

All the forces available in Central Italy were to be taken against the Spartacists. They amounted to three legions, eighteen thousand foot and horse, besides auxiliaries brought from Cisalpine Gaul. The slave-horde under Spartacus was believed to number at least twenty thousand men. But it was composed of slaves, and the odds therefore negligible.

Yet both consuls were discreet and cautious, patricians, cold men, viewing the slave revolt with neither fear nor contempt. They did not underrate the Bandit or his power and generalship. This was a thing to be stamped upon, the slaves killed or recaptured, themselves to win credit and a triumph through Rome. So the winter passed but slowly for them.

Pass it did, however, and in the early days of Spring they took the army south, cautiously, towards Lucania. A host of spies in that country sent them constant word of the movements of the slaves. The Thracian still lingered at Nola with the majority of his following. But they learned it was his intention to attack Capua itself, with great machines built him by a renegade patrician, Hiketas. The consuls hastened their march, for Spring was quick in the land.

They came through a country as yet undesolated by the slave armies: for desertions to the Gladiators had almost ceased. All believed that the Free Legions would be crushed before summer; and, watching the passing, horse and foot, of the army of the consuls, this opinion found additional weight among the slave populace. Men and women, they would speak in their sheds over-night of the scenes to follow the suppression of the Bandit. Thinking of that returning passage of the army of the Masters they had seen press south, they would lick dry lips, the slaves, full of a sickened curiosity, seeing their endless days of toil and the whipping-block as upholding lives pleasant and safe in comparison with those who had joined the Criminals of Capua.

But at Nola Spring was also finding the Free Legions active. Bands of slaves scoured the surrounding country, for provisions and iron were running low in Nola. With knowledge of that fact Kleon the eunuch was determined to put into operation his plan of pacifying the Italiot cities and gaining them as willing allies. Gershom ben Sanballat, who had captured Nuceria, was accordingly sent to pacify that city, to relieve it from the rule of a brutal Syrian, who had been acting in a fashion semi-independent of the slaves in Nola. The Jew's instructions were to call together the principal men, propose or force an alliance upon them; and demand a monthly tribute of corn and wine. Then he was to hold south into Lucania to every town and city on the way to Metapontum, and consolidate the country into a slave province, yielding provisions and tribute.

But his legion could not be spared to accompany him. Beard-combing and sardonic, the Jew set out, taking with him fifty Bithynians and his cook, the woman Judith. Kleon watched them go, and had a cold twinge of regret. For it was a mission altogether desperate, this of Gershom ben Sanballat's. If the Syrian in Nuceria refused to be moved the Jew might well have to set to the re-conquest of Lucania and South Campania with no greater force than his fifty Bithynians. Doubtlessly his cook would prove of aid.

Meantime, to the east of the Matese mountains, the consuls learned from a captured and tortured slave-rebel that Spartacus at the head of a considerable force had broken out from Nola a month before and crossed into Apulia. Seeing no reason to doubt the news, Gellius and Arrius, having finished with the slave (who grinned and died, being a wild-humoured Thracian), turned east, left Capua to what fate might come on it, crossed the mountains, forded the Fortore into Apulia; and were presently apprised of irregularly armed bands of scouts falling back in front of their march.

(ii)

That hot Spring day when the consuls forded Fortore, the

101

tribune Crixus sat on a rock under the shadow of Mount Garganus and stared across that sea which was yet to become the Adriatic. Below his feet was the camp of his Germans; and looking down at that camp, he yawned.

'This business of commanding Germans is like milking aurochsen,' he said to the man by his side.

Brennus, lying flat on his belly, grinned. He was very content and filled with food, and blinked in the light, like a lizard. But the little tribune was wearied.

'I wish Kleon would commence the march on Capua and send us word to join him. This business of chasing Apulian sheep for fresh mutton is as tame as a day in the old arena in company with a fat instructor.'

Brennus reflected. 'When we capture Capua I'll ask Kleon for his share of the women we take. For he'll have no need of them.'

'Nor Spartacus of you. He has little patience with bulls — even wild ones from the forests of Gaul.'

'Gods!' said Brennus, 'to hear it again — a wild aurochs herd bellow on the evening's edge!'

But Crixus had ceased to listen. He was shading his eyes in the sun. 'A messenger.'

The man came scrambling up to their ledge, and halted, panting, and told his news. A minute thereafter and Crixus and Brennus had gained the camp, where already the Germans were arming in confusion. Pushing through them, Crixus reached his tent and commanded a bucina to blow and assemble the centurions. The wearied light had vanished from the eyes of the little tribune. He addressed the assembled Germans as a boy who planned to snare a fox.

'Unless the Masters know these lands well, they're already in our hands.'

'How?' asked a follower of Gannicus.

'They can attack us only from the north, and think they have trapped us here. But we have the narrow pass into the mountains to the west. That they don't know, and will pay little heed to their rear. Now, we'll await them here, but send a messenger back through the pass, to ride to Nola and summon reinforcements. Then the Strategos will bring his legions and fall on the Masters from behind.'

In an hour a messenger was riding for Nola. All that evening he

102

rode, making a wide detour to the south to avoid the Romans. He was a Gaul, one of Brennus' scouts, and spared neither himself nor his long-tailed mount. By midnight they heard him shouting outside the walls of Nola, and the Northern Gate was opened for him by Gershom's Bithynians.

One recognized him. 'What news from Crixus?'

'Good news,' the Gaul called, and rode into the winding alleys of the town.

At the house where the Strategos lodged a sleepy Thracian would have barred the way for the Gaul. 'Spartacus sleeps.'

The Gaul showed his teeth. 'We don't sleep in Apulia. Out of my way, horse-eater, or I'll damage the wall by beating your head against it.'

'Of that we'll make test,' said Ialo, helpfully, and now fully waked. But as they glared at each other an inner door opened.

'What is it?'

It was a woman, wrapped in a dark night-mantle, her hair a great shining cloak. Lavinia, the woman of Spartacus. Ialo glowered.

'This pestiferous Gaul wants to awaken the Strategos. He says he comes from Apulia.'

Lavinia considered the splashed messenger. Then, disregarding the Thracian's grumbles, beckoned him into the inner room and closed the door. Unabashed, Ialo leant his head against a crack and listened. Beyond that inner room the Strategos slept in a closet.

Ialo heard the messenger speak the message of Crixus, hurriedly, for he thirsted for action, being young, and was in no mind to miss the coming battle below Garganus. He heard the woman promise to awaken Spartacus and deliver that message. He heard the hurried steps of the Gaul returning towards the door, and so hearing, himself hastily retreated to his seat and spear, and appeared to doze.

The Gaul was riding out of Nola just as the dawn came into the sky, bright, tremulous, tremendous, a shining dawn into which he rode. By early afternoon he had crossed the great Stone Way, and in a little was amongst the mountains. He might have reached Garganus by nightfull but for the fact that in a narrow defile he came suddenly on a band of Roman velites. At that sight he laughed, then unslung his axe and spurred forward his horse.

(iii)

An hour later Crixus heard of the nearing of the Roman scouts and that the main army of the consuls was rounding the far shoulder of Garganus. This he had anticipated, seeing its purpose to drive him back against the mountain-wall. To delay its advance, he sent two hundred slaves through the narrow corridor in the hills. These went under the command of Brennus and had orders to vex the Roman rear, but to make no disclosure of how they had gained an exit from the slaves' apparent trap.

Gellius and Arrius, cautious commanders, camped for the night and were setting up the usual entrenchments when they heard the slave chant come out of the darkness to their rear. A moment later a shower of arrows skimmed over the half-erected palisades, and, with the blowing of horns and the waving of long swords, a band of barbarian slaves attempted to storm the southwards dyke.

The legionaries, hastily dropping their picks, repelled the attack with ease. The slaves faded off into the darkness, still chanting. But they did not go far. Every now and then an arrow would wing out of the darkness around the camp, quivering in the beams of the consuls' tents, or striking down a legionary through some unguarded joint. This endured until Gellius, irritated, despatched a century of horse which routed the slaves from their position.

Unfortunately, it was impossible to pursue and exterminate them in the moonless night. The horsemen contented themselves with a wide patrol of the camp.

'Where did this band come from?' wondered Arrius.

'No doubt from stray raiding or foraging,' said Gellius. 'We'll have many such bands to deal with after the killing of the Thracian tomorrow.'

And on that, in full armour, they lay down to rest till an hour before sunrise.

(iv)

All that night the armed Germans slept on edge under the shelter of Garganus. But Crixus did not sleep. He walked to and fro, hour after hour, awaiting news from the detachment of Brennus beyond the corridor. For he had arranged that Brennus, after an abortive attack on the Roman camp, should set out westwards, meet the slave reinforcements under Spartacus, and then return to bring the Germans news of these reinforcements.

But no Brennus came, and Crixus, despite his light heart, began to know anxiety. Once he went and watched the sea, and another time himself walked far up the corridor into the hills. But it was unwise to leave his Germans for long, and he speedily returned.

To ease his mind of the constant conflict of hope and surmise, he sat down in the deeper darkness that heralded the morning and began to whet his sword and polish the Greek helmet he wore. And in that hour, a great loneliness coming upon him, he sat with his head in his hands, thinking of the morrow.

His Gods were dim and he had no faith, nor even now realized the need of either. Only a wondering came on him that the blood should be so warm in his body and his fingers so swift and sure as they plied the whetstone. And tomorrow. . . .

And for some reason he thought of the woman Elpinice, and, though with dim Gods, shivered in the early mist that rose round the sleeping camp. For perhaps her spirit was still in this ill land of Italy, following in the wake of the Free Legions still. What though it did? It would never harm him, as he never it. And so strong upon him did this imagining grow that he turned his head with a jerk in order that he might look in her face. Then he laughed, and wiped his forehead, and stood up; and below him, in darkness, heard the far sighing of the sea.

An hour before sunrise, while the earth was yet grey, and the soaring heights of Mount Garganus grey turning to gold, and so slowly to the hue of blood, Brennus came back through the pass alone.

'There is no sign of Spartacus or the other legions.' And panted. 'The Masters have broken camp. I ran all the way through the pass. They cannot be far off now.'

Then on Crixus there came a fine gaiety. And suddenly it seemed to him that the air was sweet and good; though he had never noticed such things before. And in that early-morning light there clung to his eyelids a fine web from the night-time mist; and the wonder of that on his eyelids was strange on his spirit for a moment. Then he called to the bucinator to sound.

The hoarse howl of the horn was answered by the shouts of the

105

awakened Germans. From caverns and crannies, pits and lean-to's, they swarmed out, the slaves from the North, yellow-haired, most of them, though some were barbarians from a further land, furth of the great East rivers, sallow of skin, dark-haired, dark-skinned. They marshalled in hasty ranks, and Crixus mounted his horse and rode to and fro, from group to group, jesting, as was his manner.

And the Germans, beating their shields, sang the great bass war-songs of their tribes.

Soon arrows began to fall in their midst, and many lay down, while those with bows or slings endeavoured to return that arrow-hail. Then the Romans, advancing evenly across open ground, opened to allow their horse to charge.

Remembering the inadequacy of the German long sword to face charging cavalry, Crixus sent the order from rank to rank that they thrust not at the riders but at the legs and bellies of the horses. But at the first sight of the Roman charge the tribes had instinctively prepared for this. The front rank of the Germans knelt on one knee, swords swinging low, the second stood crouching, whirling their blades; and these gleamed in the early light like the wheels of chariots driven through a ford. Then, with wild yells, they received the Roman charge.

It broke and fell back and came on again. At first the slaves had taken it with the bitten lips and uncertain hearts of slaves who fronted the attack of the Masters. But now the slow German blood began to stir, and they fought with a wild ferocity. Unavailing, leaving a heap of writhing horses, the cavalry drew off and Gellius advanced his legions.

As he did so he turned to Arrius and commented with amazement on the small number of slaves opposing them. There could not be more than three thousand — a full half-legion — at the utmost. And he gave orders that Spartacus, when discovered, was to be taken alive.

Then he shaded his eyes under his helmet-rim. 'Though I see none who looks like the Thracian himself. Who is the little slave on the long-tailed horse?'

Then news was brought to him that the little man who rode the horse and shouted taunts and jests to the labouring advance of the Roman foot was Crixus, another Gladiator, and one of Spartacus's tribunes. Spartacus himself was said to be still in Nola.

106

At that both consuls knew they had been tricked by the Thracian slave they had put to torment; and the sweat pringled on the skin of Arrius at the thought of the machinations that might well take place in the Senate, to bring him to ruin because of this business: accusing him of leaving the road to Capua unguarded. And he gave orders for the immediate dispersal of the slaves in front of him.

But now they fought like wild beasts in a pit. So they were, and so they realized. Yet presently on them also, the slaves of stews and plantation and warehouse, there came something of nobility under the alien crags of Mount Garganus. Their ranks long since broken, they formed into the great fighting schiltrouns of the forests, the heroes' rings the defeated formed in the German tribal wars: and inside and without these fell in scores, butchered by the arrows of the sagittarii or the thrusts of the reeking short swords. Crixus and Brennus rode from group to group, hewing paths through a living wall, steadying the reeling circles of slaves, Brennus with his left hand and shield shorn away, and the stump bound up in a hasty twist of cloth and a wooden splint. He rode swaying and bloodless, but Crixus beside him sang and fought on unwounded.

Then the Romans drew off and reformed. And Crixus caused those that survived of the slaves, six hundred in all, to retreat up a slope, with rocky ground that would hamper the legions. So might they stand with but a frontal enemy to fight. Bleeding, fatigued, they fell back and climbed this slope, with the roars of the Roman bucinae and the methodical shoutings of the Roman centurions in their ears.

Crixus himself rode last up the slope. Then he dismounted in front of the slaves, and drew his sword and pulled his horse's mane, and laughed at the beast; and then stabbed it swiftly through the heart so that it gave a groan like a slain man, and fell at his feet. And the tribune turned to the wondering Germans.

'Comrades, there's no retreat. We die here or fight until Spartacus comes.'

And to Brennus, remonstrating and swaying in his saddle, he spoke strange words, albeit he laughed when he spoke them.

'Retreat through the pass? A General the Free Legions need? I am no General. Only a slave. Yet soon I'll be more than either slave or General — if the dark Gods leave me sleep sound. And I don't think, dying here, we'll do ill to that cause of Kleon's.'

Then he mused for a little, and beckoned ten Germans and pointed to Brennus.

'Take the centurion Brennus back through the pass, steal horses, and ride till you come up with Spartacus — or beyond that, till you come to Nola. For we cannot say if our messenger reached it. But tell them how we stood here and fought, and bid Spartacus ave from me!'

And when they had heard this message, the Germans seized the weeping and cursing Brennus, and bore him away from the tribune who cried his last ave. Then Crixus laid aside his armour till he stood in his tunic only, bareheaded, for so, he said, he would fight the lighter. And the Germans kissed in their ranks as the hail of the arrows began again.

Then the Romans stormed up the slopes; and Crixus saw that the light was dying, far away to the east, from the face of the sea.

Torment

(i)

IN the evening of the next day they saw from the walls of Nola the nearing of fatigued and mud-splashed horses. At that sight on the little-traversed tracks the walls became thronged with slaves peering into the east. Then the nearing band was descried as half a score of men, ill-mounted and beating their beasts; and presently a shout of wonder arose.

'They are Germans!'

The slaves looked at one another in speechless surmise, then crowded down to the Eastern Gate. Midmost of the riders was a man who was bound in his saddle — a man who lacked a hand. Opening the great gate Gershom ben Sanballat ran and caught at the bridle of this man's horse.

'Brennus, what news from Apulia?'

The Gaul half started awake, and stared about him with bloodshot eyes.

'The Masters caught us like beasts in a trap because the Strategos did not come. All the Germans are dead. Spartacus. I have a message for Spartacus.'

'And Crixus?'

'I saw him kill his horse.'

At that news a groan of horror and anger went up from the assembled slaves. Such townspeople as had pressed near in curiosity retreated hastily within their houses. But Brennus fell forward again in his saddle; and one of the Germans who rode with him cursed.

'Spartacus — Crixus sent us with a message for Spartacus.'

So the way was cleared and they rode through the narrow streets till they came to the great Forum of Nola. There, in the bright evening weather, the air was alive with the beating of mallets and the smell of fresh-sawn wood, pungent and resinous; and the blue smoke of the smithies rose in long lines into the windless sky. For Kleon's dream was being fulfilled with the aid of the renegade Master, Hiketas. With iron and timber commandeered at will, they were building the great helepolites and catapults with which to assault the walls of Capua. High into the air towered the great machines, ready for testing and then dismemberment, for loading in the great ox-wagons of the Gauls when the Free Legions took the field again. Amidst the din of the smiths and the hammering of the joiners Kleon, Hiketas and Spartacus stood in a little group, the Thracian silent, the two Greeks in dispute over the weight of the tormenta. Then they heard a voice call.

'Strategos!'

They turned and saw the company of Germans, with the rider who swayed and stared in their midst. Kleon's lips grew white.

'It is Brennus, one of Crixus' men.'

(ii)

And when Spartacus heard that message he wept, to the wonder and terror of those who stood round. For a little there was none who might speak, and then the Thracian broke from their midst, leaving the questioning, whispering groups of slaves to debate the news from Apulia. The consuls were in the field, the Germans dead or scattered: in a little while the Masters themselves would be before Nola. And at that thought a shudder of dread ran through the slave-horde. For they had come to believe themselves invincible and that Crixus no more than Spartacus could ever be defeated.

But Spartacus gave little time for debate. In an hour's time the citizens heard the horns blow up, and saw the slaves pouring to muster in the market-place. While yet they pondered the meaning of that muster, the first century of the Free Legions was marching furth of the gates; and after it, company on company, they saw the slaves depart. Over that road where Spartacus had watched the Germans disappear two months before wound the long lines of the slave army at a speed that presently left Nola far behind.

The women and baggage followed more slowly, with half a thousand cavalry to guard them. In the town itself there remained but Kleon and Hiketas and Gershom ben Sanballat freshly returned from the subjugation of Nuceria. With bitter faces Kleon and Hiketas, who had begged and expostulated a terrible hour with the Thracian Strategos, superintended the destruction of the great machines by Gershom's Bithynians.

They were piled in a great heap in the Forum of Nola, saturated

110

with oil, and fired, the great towers and catapults that Hiketas had dreamt would batter down the walls of Capua. Looking back, the slaves could see the pillar of their burning lighting all the western sky.

Then Gershom took his men and the two Greeks out of the city and followed the trail of Spartacus, marching hot-foot to meet the consuls.

(iii)

He met them in an unknown plain somewhere on the hither side of Garganus — the two armies sighting each other from afar, and pressing to join battle with an eagerness seldom known in history. Then Arrius and Gellius, cautious commanders, halted their troops in a place of vantage, and saw with misgivings the size of the Spartacist force.

Nor were these misgivings unwarranted, nor the fate of the battle for a moment in doubt. Attacking in his customary cuneus formation, an iron wedge at the Roman centre, Spartacus himself led the first charge, enormous, on horseback, at the head of his Thracians. They broke the lines of the legions, and once within those lines slaughtered almost at pleasure, while the Gauls fell on the Roman flank, and (with the impetus of a short slope) piled one wing in confusion upon the broken centre eddying round the carnage of the Thracians' drive. Then Gannicus and Gershom ben Sanballat brought up the main slave army, and soon the Romans were streaming from the field in the wake of the consuls — the first of their rank to meet and suffer defeat in the field for over a hundred years.

The battle was bloody and swift, but the carnage stayed when the Romans, at length terrified in the belief that the Republic was now overthrown, flung down their arms and surrendered in scores. They were disarmed and stripped, bound in long gangs, and whipped through the passes of Apulia till they came to the camp which Spartacus had built for the funeral games of Crixus.

(iv)

His body, flayed and crucified, had been recovered from an Apulian village near the foot of Mount Garganus. Castus had made

111

that recovery and, though he bore the dead Crixus no great love, had burned the village in a madness of wrath.

When Spartacus heard of this he smiled.

'Did you burn the villagers also?'

'They escaped into the mountains.'

'Then you did ill to let them go.' And the Thracian turned away, colder than ever towards the man who had hoped to take the place of the dead Crixus.

In that camp, with the Spring very green on the Apulian hills, they prepared the funeral games. Crixus, as a Gaul, was to be burned; and now swathed in purple, his mutilated head crowned with bay, he lay in a tent, drenched with aromatic perfumes and guarded by Gauls and Germans. Outside, on a level stretch of sward, the funeral pyre was prepared.

The Roman prisoners, chained in a corner of the camp, ragged and filthy, talked among themselves and jeered at the leadership and discipline of the slaves. A centurion who lay by the side of a young third tribune laughed at the fears of the latter.

'This Spartacus always spares his prisoners. He will march us around the pyre of Crixus, I suppose, and then dismiss us, disarmed. He's only a slave, with the heart of a slave; and though he can lead his Free Legions in battle well enough, he knows nothing of campaigns or the planning of a war. Had he followed up our rout by a march on Rome he might have been feasting in the Capitol to-night.'

'He is a Greek?'

'A Thracian. It's said that this Crixus was his best lieutenant, as a eunuch, Kleon, is the brain of the business. Certainly Crixus fought well.'

'You were at Mount Garganus?'

'Not I, but with Varinus in Lucania. We ran like hares. Crixus defeated us there: a little man on a little horse who sat eating a handful of plums and jesting while we charged.'

The young third tribune groaned in his bonds. Moreover, his back ached from the stripes the slaves had inflicted in the march. 'When is the burning of this Gaulish slave to take place?'

'At noon tomorrow, they say. Then we'll be dismissed.' The centurion looked round with a savage contempt. 'Wait till Rome really moves in the field. Then she'll burn them alive, these scum.'

112

Meantime the tribunes of the slaves had gathered in the tent of Spartacus. Spartacus himself awaited them. As they gave him greeting and squatted in a circle, it seemed to more than one of them that the Gladiator in his grief was near to insanity. His armour was still stained and bloody from the battle, and that cold control that had marked his bearing since the Pits of the South had vanished away. His head turning from side to side, he walked to and fro, his strange eyes bloodshot. This the Strategos!

And, appalled, they lowered their eyes.

Kleon was the last to enter the tent, though he was no tribune and his rank undefined. Then a Gladiator mounted guard at the door, and Spartacus turned and called:

'Bring in the woman.'

A portion of the rear of the tent was pulled aside. Ialo and another, a Thracian, entered, dragging between them a woman who groaned at every step. She had been put to the torment for several hours, and through the rents of her himation, worn Greek fashion, shone the bloody scars and rowellings of the instruments. The slave tribunes regarded her in amazement, for it was the Roman Lavinia.

She stared around wildly, then fell, mouthing, at the feet of Spartacus. He drew away quickly, and turned to the others.

'This is the woman who betrayed the Germans and Crixus. Speak, Ialo.'

Then the slave told of the coming of the messenger to Nola, and how he had listened to that message being delivered: how the woman Lavinia had promised to give it to the sleeping Strategos: how he himself had thought no more of the matter, believing a slave legion secretly despatched to the aid of Crixus. Only with the coming of the news of Crixus' death had he thought it necessary to speak to the Strategos.

Now, tortured, the woman had confessed she had held back the message deliberately in order that the slaves under Crixus might be defeated and the consuls succeed in capturing Nola and putting down the Free Legions.

The slave-tribunes listened in silence. Then Castus said: 'Seeing the woman has confessed, it is necessary only that she be put to

113

death.'

Spartacus nodded. 'And the manner of that death?'

Castus stared, his mild face troubled. 'She might be dragged to pieces between oxen. So malefactors are executed in Gaul.'

Kleon the eunuch literatus spoke, coldly as ever. 'Why waste time and oxen? She can die more quickly.'

'How?' asked the Thracian.

Kleon shrugged. 'A sword-thrust. Garotte. What does it matter?'

Gershom ben Sanballat combed irritably at his beard. 'Let her be stoned to death.'

Gannicus laughed his great bull-like laugh. 'Crucify the bitch by the little Gaul's pyre.'

Oenomaus moved from his customary silence. 'Why not hand her over to the legion — to the Gauls or the Germans, and let them dispose of her.'

And to all this seemed a good plan, moved with a twisted lust as they looked on the woman. For her beauty still lingered. Even with her tortured body in evidence, some of them still desired her: for those wounds added a strange and loathsome fascination. Spartacus had sat on his little stool, listening. Now he raised his head.

'Each a fine end, but I have a better.' He looked across to Ialo. 'Listen. Find a litter for this woman. Take her across the hills to the Appian Way. Take fifty of the Thracians as a guard, and leave her only when she is safe with some convoy for Rome.'

Then he looked at the grovelling woman for the last time. 'You'll carry my sign-manual to Rome, my message to it and to you: Ave atque vale.'

Kleon looked on him with a cold amazement. 'You've tormented the woman, and now you spare her. Both courses are bad and un-statesmanlike.'

Then he saw that Spartacus was smiling, terribly.

'I have ceased to be a statesman.'

(vi)

All that night the Roman prisoners heard a constant hammer-ing and shouting outside the camp, by the stream that led past the pyre of Crixus. Lights shone there from great fires, but the Romans

114

could make nothing of the commotion. Nor, but that it interfered with their sleep, did it greatly interest them.

Other things occupied their hours, for it was cold weather, and they were half naked, and mostly unfed since their capture. The centurion and the young third tribune, bound so that they might not lie at their ease, leaned against each other and dozed, glad to be freed from the daytime crowds of jeering and mocking slaves. Towards dawn the young third tribune became wide awake and watched morning coming over the Apulian mountains as Crixus had watched it come out of the sea. In the air was the smell of the morning's green coming, and somehow, despite his bonds, he felt a strange gladness upon him.

The slave army began to awake around the enclosure. The yawning Romans set to chafing cold limbs and beating the blood back into chilled bodies. Presently there arose a clamour of horns and a band of Gaulish slaves entered the enclosure. They bore food — steaming corn in great pots, and dishes of stewed lentils. Amazed at this bounty, the Romans ate ravenously; and, staring at them while they fed, the slaves laughed.

Hardly had they gone, bearing the empty pots, when another band entered the enclosure. They filed in to the number of four hundred or so, and the heart of the centurion, despite his strong spirit, momentarily failed him. For this new band was the Gladiator body-guard of Spartacus, well known to the Romans by their gilded armour and war-hardened bodies. They bore great whips in their hands, and the centurion groaned.

'What will they do?' whispered the young third tribune.

'More flogging.' The centurion had taken part in Rome in an Eastern triumph. He knew what portended. 'They will march us round the pyre of Crixus, half-flayed.'

But it seemed that he was mistaken. The Gladiators proceeded to release the prisoners, till three hundred of them had been so set free. Then, motioning towards the gates of the enclosure, the slaves cracked their whips. The Romans surged forward through the gates.

The knee of the young third tribune pained him, and he limped in the rear, till it seemed as if a red hot iron had been applied to his back. Withdrawing his whip for another blow, the great Gladiator behind him laughed.

Beyond the camp, they stood and swayed to and fro for a little like a herd of doubtful cattle.

Beside the pyre, flanked on one side by a river, on the other by scaffoldings of timber, an arena had sprung up in the night. Around it was thronged the slave army. Leading towards it was a living corridor of slaves, and down this corridor the Romans were driven.

At the entrance to it, each of them was handed a Gaulish sword.

Inside the arena they were separated into two parties. It was clear, pale weather, and the centurion saw the white apple-blossom on the orchards beyond the encampment. Then the terms of the combat were made known to them. They were not to fight as individuals, but as two parties. The conquering party would be granted the mercy of joining the Free Legions.

At first the Romans hung back in horror, and the crack of the Gladiators' whips rose in the air. Then they began to surge forward, wielding the clumsy and unaccustomed swords amidst the shouted laughter of the slaves. Presently the centurion engaged with a man he knew, and, as they hewed at each other, each warmed a little to the ring of the weapons.

In a moment, from the stamp and bloody struggle of the fight that wavered to and fro in the arena, bodies were falling with gaping wounds, sacrifices to the manes of dead Crixus. A warm, dreadful stench arose; and, drawn by the shoutings of the slaves, great flocks of carrion-birds came from the hills.

(vii)

Two hundred and eighty of the Romans perished at the funeral games of Crixus. Of the remaining score, half were so wounded that they were despatched by the whips of the Gladiators. Then, with the pyre a little hill of ash, the slaves broke camp, marching northwards with determination to break out of Italy and escape to their own lands.

IV. ROME!

The Defiles of Mutina

THEY had passed up through Italy, crossed the mountains, and entered Gallia Cisalpina through autumn-flooded lands. At one place where swamps extended for miles it seemed that they must turn aside and make a wide detour. But Hiketas had great drag-sledges made, and on these the Free Legions crossed safely. All the hills were in bloom with flowers, and it was near the reaping-time of the corn.

As they marched the slaves filled their helmets and the breasts of their tunics with corn-heads. The hungry rearguards strayed far to right and left of the march, beating off the straggling attacks of Roman velites and seeking unlooted villages. Spartacus rode in the centre, Castus with the Gauls in the van. Kleon the Greek had taken to himself a roaming commission that ranged from the van to the rearguard.

Rain in drenching torrents met them beyond the borders of Gallia Cisalpina. In the late afternoon Kleon, abandoning the draggled and plodding rear to the care of Hiketas, rode up the toiling lines of the slave army till he came to the Bithynian legion. It was still so-called, though the Bithynians had dwindled to a scarce century, and most of the slaves in that legion either Greeks or Negroes or Iberians. They marched as a disciplined cohort still, but wearily. All the slave-army was weary and dispirited.

They had met but little opposition to their northwards trek. All the country lay fear-stricken. Women had been hidden away in the hills. One town they entered was empty but for a single man, dying of plague. Rome lay silent in their rear. It was like marching in soft-raining, thundery weather, waiting for a sky-tumult that refused to burst.

Kleon shivered under his drenched abolla, and, raising his eyes, looked north. Fading into the evening light went the long slave lines, an army of forty thousand men. He saw the stallion of Spartacus white amidst the general dunness, considered that for a moment, passed beyond the moving blurs of no-colour that made up the Gauls and Germans: and met the horizon. What lay awaiting them there?

An Iberian, with a great package strapped on his back, stumbled

119

out of the way of the Greek's weary horse. He raised his eyes. It was Titul.

'Where is your horse?' asked Kleon.

'I ate it at the last halt,' the Iberian explained. 'Now I carry my treasure till we fight the Masters again. Then I will steal another.'

'You won't have long to wait, I think.' Kleon smiled at him grimly. 'And beyond that come the mountains and the cannibals. We are certainly a crafty army.'

'Cunning in warfare were the men of the vanished Western Isle,' said Titul, being mad.

Kleon smiled wryly and rode on. The Iberian was beyond irony. Had there ever been a Western Isle? He dismissed the matter, seeing in front of him a swaying litter borne between two shaggy ponies. Beside them, amidst a clump of his devoted spearmen, marched Gershom ben Sanballat, rain streaming from his beard and helmet, his tunic ragged and faded. The Greek grinned at him.

'This is a sad plight for a victorious tribune. You have lost a boot, Jew.'

'And you a Republic.'

Kleon mocked him. 'It is still — there.'

He pointed to the rain-darkened sky. Gershom grunted. He was irritable and discontented, even though it seemed that the Strategos harkened now to his counsel. But they should have dispersed and sought the sea. Into what wild mountains were they being led?

'You'll need the aid of Hiketas before you reach it.'

'We'll need his aid yet,' said Kleon, cryptically, and rode on, not turning his glance on the inside of the litter. The Jew had married his cook, seeking an heir to make sacrifice to his manes when he was dead. And that might well be soon enough.

Judith looked after the Greek, leaning from her litter. She was heavy with child. Then she sought the eyes of Gershom. He plodded through the mud to her side, avoiding the slipping hooves of the ponies.

'What did the Greek Mutilated propose?'

'Jehovah knows. He would stop this march if he could, and turn us back on the Masters again.' He spoke testily. 'What ails you now?'

She was looking in horror at his bare right foot. 'Your boot?'

'I left it in the marsh. Let be, let be. If the eunuch has his way,

120

I'll find it on the return march.' His leg was already twinging with rheumatism. He regarded the cloudy sky with louring gaze. 'And he'd find no great enemy to me in his planning, I sometimes think.'

For it was one thing to escape from Italy and the power of the Masters, and another to seek the land of the Hyperboreans and live there in unending twilight, hearing the howling of Behemoth as he hungered under the Northern night.

And Gershom cursed his ragged guard and plodded forward, the rain swift in his face.

(ii)

Day died, and the main army of the slaves made camp half-way up the La Fata pass. Here the mountains filled all the northward skyline in tenebrous outline, white and cloud-piercing; and far in their slopes water gleamed as the day waned fast. The Gauls looked on these mountains and remembered their passes as they were beaten southwards, slaves into Italy. And the sight moved them to tears, as was the easy wont of their race. But the Germans regarded them without love or fear, with impatience, seeking beyond them their forested homes.

The Negroes shivered that night, as did the men of Asia. The Greeks with patient, cold faces looked at the ragged horizon, and knew it madness to attempt this passage into a land of barbarians. How might a man live without a city? For the City was life. And the cold of Gallia Cisalpina soaked into all bones but those well-shielded in the looted fabrics of the villages fired in the northwards march.

But near midnight the rain ceased and Kleon, prowling wakeful the limits of the camp, found the sentry posted highest up the Pass fast asleep in the lee of a rock. Kleon stirred him to wakefulness with his foot, and found him the brother of Brennus. The Gaul grinned, unabashed.

'There'll be less of haughty footwork, Greek, when we pass these mountains.'

Kleon was unperturbed. The tribunes of the slave horde were accustomed to the insolence of their legionaries.

'You may soon be lacking a throat, far less feet, if you keep as poor watch as this.'

121

They listened. But there was only the sound of the rain and its thin seep on the sleeping land. And it came on the eunuch, as so often, how strange it was that men should toil and moil on this little earth that knew them not — that knew only its winds and rains and the suns that ripened the crops, and the light and glow of the imaged sun, never the seedsmen or reapers. It was the Fear of the Fates and the Gods that drove men, shadows they made in their own dark hearts.

He turned about and made his way back through the litter of the slave-encampment, coming at last to the tent of the Strategos, where Spartacus slept guarded by his Gladiators. As he came to it he heard a stirring there, and a torch showed damply through the mirk. Kleon saw it was the Strategos himself, and Spartacus recognized him.

'I'm uneasy to-night, Kleon. This mist on the Pass, I think. I'm going to ride up and see what lies beyond it.'

'But there is no seeing at all in this darkness.'

'We'll see as much or as little as the Masters.'

Kleon shrugged irritably. 'Then I'll come.'

So he did. They rode past the post of the now roused Gaul, and went up the tortuous track of the Pass. Above them its walls towered blackly. Underfoot the road was warm with a slime, and the horses slipped and plunged continually. It might have been near the third division of the night, but the darkness had not lightened at all. Spartacus said: 'I had a dream.'

'What dream?'

'One without much gladness. That I was no longer either the Strategos of the Free Legions or a hunter in Thrace, but dead and quiet, down there in the South.'

'So you'll still hold North?'

But the Thracian was not listening. He had halted the great white stallion. He motioned Kleon to silence. They listened. Nothing but the soft sound of the rain. Yet presently another sound, remote and distant.

The distant sound of marching men.

Now they were upon the Peak of the Pass. But all around was the shroud of the mist, thick as carded wool, and soft. The sound of the tramping grew in their ears.

Spartacus whispered from his saddle. 'Back. Walk your horse and then rouse the camp. Softly. Bring up the Thracians first.'

'But you ——'

The Strategos was loosening the great axe from his saddle. 'I'll wait.'

For a moment the Greek looked at him in a cool deliberation. He saw in a flash the possibilities and chances. The Strategos killed in a squabble with scouts: the Free Legions leaderless: himself the Voice: the Free Legions wheeled round to the South and the Cities ——

Spartacus heard the clop of the hooves of his horse fade southwards down the Pass.

Still he waited; but that muffled sound of marching men seemed to have ceased. He got from the stallion's saddle and knelt on the track, his ear to the ground. For a little while he heard nothing, except for the seep of the rain, the weeping countryside all about. The marchers had halted. Or had he and Kleon imagined them?

He mounted and waited. The stallion pawed restlessly at the ground and then swung its slavered head against his knee. He leaned forward and patted it, staring into the mist.

Mist. This, he thought grimly, was his future, a winding fog into which one peered, and it changed without form, taking to itself the shadowy likeness of faces and desires created in one's own heart. And queerly, like a ghost remembering life and the pain of death, he suddenly remembered Elpinice, and the slopes of Vesuvius, and the mists from the crater.

And then that went by. Her memory troubled him but little now, taking his women as he needed them, the touch of their breasts and their warmth against him, the strange, wild cries that they gave in his arms, held in his hands — finding such surcease from the flare of the days as he might in these moments that preluded sleep. But he knew as he waited in this silent hour and stared with dark eyes at the mist-hung Pass he would never again partake in such passion of pain and appeasement as he had partaken with Crixus or Elpinice.

So pain in their memory had gone as well. Some cord had seemed to snap in his brain as he watched the funeral games of the Gaul. He had wakened to that as they fought and plodded up from Italy to the raining North. And still he could foresee and plan the way, and set the array of battle-lines, cold, yet with a new, strange warmth upon him, a warmth of care and pity new in his heart. And that care and pity the slave legions that followed his command.

123

For he found himself entering their hearts and thoughts, with a new and bitter impatience upon him — often; yet also a comprehension, an understanding, as though somehow he himself were these men, these women, these lost stragglers of rebellion against the Masters and their terrible Gods; as though the life in their bodies was a part of his, he the Giver of Life to this multitude that had risen about him in the storm of days and shaken the Republic to its foundations. As though he were all of the hungered dispossessed of all time: as though at moments he ceased to live, merging his spirit in that of the horde, his body in that of a thousand bodies, bone of their bone, flesh of their flesh.

And sometimes he would think himself fey as he sat the great stallion by some rutted track and watched the northward march of the slaves; or bent his head from the saddle to see himself in a wayside pool, armed and armoured in his general's gear, with the gleaming helmet with the horsehair plumes and the lorica polished by Ialo, his guard. So long he had thought of himself as the Strategos, as the Statesman that Kleon the eunuch would have, that it was with a wrench as with bodily pain that he knew himself less and more and beyond: the crawling dirt-slaves of the baggage wains, those scrofulous, envermined, eyeless things that had once been Romans and followed the slaves because they had no other thing to follow — knew himself all these and all the slave host, bound in a mystic kinship of blood.

And the little Sicel slave Mella, freed from a farm in Umbria — once such a maid he'd have taken in haste, indifferently, after Elpinice's death; with abrupt impatience, bringing his lust to her body as hunger to a dish, after the death of Crixus. But that evening she was brought to his tent she was young, a girl on the verge of budding-time, and some strange compassion, as when gazing on the marching hosts, seized the bowels of the Strategos. He had said to her, 'You need have no fear. I don't need you for my bed, for my service alone.'

At his smile her shivering had slackened a little, she had known much of rape and wild crying in the night on that farm from which the slave-army had freed her, her overseer had found a grave goodness in the girls that were not yet beyond their ninth year, she had lain in the stifling stench of the sheds and expected no better in the tent of the Thracian who ate his dead and worshipped a horse.

So Spartacus had guessed; and Ialo had set her her tasks, to sweep the tent and bring wine, to sleep in a corner and tend him. And sometimes even now, his heart emptied of all desire, as it seemed, and filled with a burning question of the Gods and men, Spartacus would yet look at her with an ancient kindling of fire in his blood. But that had been seldom enough as the north drew near, as they piloted the dripping heights of La Fata Pass with beyond it the township of Mutina, no legions brought to oppose them, all Cisalpine Gaul lying strangely silent.

Were they to be allowed to pass on unmolested?

And then the Gladiator knew that they were not. He swung the stallion forward, and hefted his axe, and waited. The marching feet were the feet of heavy-armed legionaries.

(iii)

Gaius Cassius, the Governor of Cisalpine Gaul, had received early warning of the march of the Spartacists up through Umbria. He had groaned when he heard that his own richest farmstead, that of the Luda, had been looted by the horde, the wine drunk, and the slaves set free. For this meant that his usual supply of bedwomen would be denied him this year; and the large slave-farm in Umbria had been his passion for nearly fifty years.

There slaves had been bred in great numbers for Rome and Sicily: vulgares, broad-bodied, of German or Negro descent, specially and carefully mated in the manner laid down by experts, giving that combination of strength and docility ideal in the ordinary slave. He had also bred great men of Iberian blood to be sold as ostiarii, the porters of the markets, eunuchs and cubicularii, castrated or with artificially deformed genital organs. These curiosities were greatly in demand among the patricians in the Baths. There also he had bred slaves to be sold as runners for the fugitivarii, the capturers of Runaways.

But of his best breedings were the women-children destined for sale into prostitution at the age of ten. Of these the flower were culled and sent to him; and his overseers, freedmen, intent on enriching themselves, regarded this with a constant vexation. Early infected with the venereal diseases common to North Africa, where he had

125

served, it was but rarely that the discarded of his bed were returned to the slave-farm in fit condition for sale in the open market, naked, with whitewashed feet. In his years of debauchery he had also become infected with leprosy; and, inflamed in the colds of the northern province, this disease had vexed him to the edge of insanity again and again, finding its only relief in heated baths and the ministrations, night upon night, of great numbers of girls from the stud-farm. A patrician, Gaius Cassius was a man of culture, and knew that without the strong hand of Law men would live in misery and fear. And, groaning in pleasure, he would fondle the horrified children.

Now, in his sixty-fifth year, he heard of the coming of the great slave horde, led by a Thracian Gladiator. Together with Gnaeus Manlius, the praetor, whom he hated, he consulted on means of defence. Manlius had long since ceased to feel interest in the province, or indeed, in most other things of the life to which he had been assigned: he hungered for Rome. Large, dark and strong, like one of the ostiarii bred on Cassius' farm, he sat in the council chamber through those raining days, receiving the messengers who had circled around the slave march, and brought the instructions of the Senate. The Spartacists must be met and destroyed ere they left Italy.

'That's easier to order than to execute,' he would affirm to Cassius, squatted in a padded sedile, scratching at his ulcerated skin and drinking draughts of warmed wine brought him at innumerable intervals throughout the day. And Cassius would groan, thinking of his ruined farm in Umbria.

In the Province at the moment were three full legions, the Second, the Fourth, and the Ninth, each of six thousand men, fully armed and equipped in the new model. Besides these were the cavalry and several thousand irregular troops. Cassius made over complete command to Manlius. The latter summoned the legions to Mutina, leaving the irregulars for policework, and received news of the nearing approach of the slave army, forty thousand strong, but at least a third non-combatant, disorganized, wearied with rain and mud, hasting to escape from Italy.

And the rain fell, fell and fell continuously, as at last Gnaeus Manlius moved.

When he moved from Mutina that night his plans were still misty in his mind. But then he heard the slaves were encamped half-way up the thither side of La Fata Pass. Sending one legion on a detour of thirteen pace miles, through the shallow estuaries haunted by the sea-birds, he took the Fourth and the Ninth Legions, and with them climbed the Pass. His intent was to reach and seize the peak ere the morning came, and so trap the slave rabble betwixt himself and the tribune of the Second when the day broke.

In that upward climb, climbing west, he felt the day coming behind him, rather than saw, though he frequently looked back. He himself rode with the horse, the sound of their hooves muffled in the blanketings of fog. Winter was near and in places they splashed through freezing pools. Once they heard the howling of wolves in a little wood, and the forward velites jested among themselves, saying that these were undoubtedly Spartacists, you could tell them by their smell.

The praetor had flung out a light line of Balearic fundatores, they trotted away, short men, into the mist, their pouches swinging on their hips, climbing the Pass. At their heels toiled the legions, heavily armed, with the shorter pilum that was used in this mountain country. With the cavalry the praetor brought up the march, as swiftly as they might in that dim-veiled track.

Now, it neared the third division of the morning and from his spies the praetor knew he was near the ridge of the Pass when he heard in front a sudden shouting break out. He cursed and halted the cavalry, sending an order forward to halt the legions as well. The shouting continued, and two centuries of the Fourth climbed swiftly up to see what had caused this outbreak from the fundatores.

Then it was that the mist suddenly cleared, it went in a great waft of air from the far mountains, suddenly the rain ceased and the world sparkled frost-keen about them, on the edge of winter, and the Roman legions looked up, the praetor, dark and tall, shaded his eyes and looked at that scene in the early light.

The fundatores had fallen back after that first attack, for now the slaves had reached the peak, and the air was filled with the hiss of the light-feathered arrows. But of these things, other than shifting specks, neither Gnaeus Manlius nor his legions saw much. What they did see remained in the mind of Manlius for long, he remembered it that year he rode up the Appian Way, lined with its dripping fruit, he remembered it under the torture of Catiline, he remembered it when

127

F

he and Brutus watched the sardonic smile on the face of a bowed patrician in the Senate on an Ides of March.

For, crowning the ridge, was a still, watchful figure on horseback, helmeted in gold, armoured, immense in the spreading glow of the mist, the sun suddenly upon him. So he gleamed like a God, gigantic, and the legions stared and murmured as they looked at the terrible figure. For there was terror in it. In those mountain changes of the air they could see his face, immense and near, bearded and calm, high-browed under the helmet-rim, his eyes cold and staring upon them, yet filled with a glow like the eyes of a snake. And to the praetor Manlius, it seemed he saw more than the Strategos Spartacus, he saw THE SLAVE himself.

Then that fancy passed, the last wisps of mist went quickly, the figure faded: and Manlius was aware of the slave army already in possession of the peaks of the Pass.

(iv)

All that morning and afternoon the Spartacists fought a rearguard defence and a van attack across La Fata Pass, Gnaeus Manlius retreating as the day rose, the Fourth and the Ninth legions fighting stubbornly, pressed by the Thracian van of the slave army. Behind, the Jew Gershom ben Sanballat and his Bithynians engaged the Second legion, which had marched around the mountain and come up through the mist expecting to find the Spartacists assailed by Manlius from the peak of the Pass.

Gershom rode to and fro as the sun wheeled to the third division of the day, directing the defence of the slave rear. The mist had passed completely and from this height the one-time leader of the Hasidim could see for long miles around the shine of the wintry Italian landscape. The shivering Bithynians fought with a fury more of cold than of valour, a bare score of the original Bithynians surviving. Some had died in Lucania, some under Papa, one withered nailed to a tree in Apulia, one at the moment lay recaptured in the slave-pits of Rome. Gershom had made a stout bodyguard of the survivors, and these gave their name to the legion that kept the peak while the main body of the slaves plodded and fought down across La Fata Pass to the plain beyond, and Mutina, shining white-walled in the afternoon.

Rain came after noon and pelted the retreating armies in flying showers, the Fourth and Ninth bore it with indifference, as did their pursuers, the Thracians. But at least a third of the slaves had not been vulgares, men of the fields and open, but slaves from the kitchens and bakehouses, the vats and baths and cubicles: and in these heights and rains they shivered in a uselessness which drove Kleon to a bitter scorn. He rode beside Spartacus and watched the shivering drift that passed, into the evening lour of the battle by Mutina; and suddenly proposed that the Germans drive these weaklings down on the Roman pila.

Spartacus was riding wrapt in his thoughts, Ialo behind him, the maid Mella somewhere in the centre with the women. He shook his head.

'These folk are unaccustomed to such weathers. They'll fight better on the plain.'

'They'll fight not at all beyond the Alps, in the wild lands of the North.'

Spartacus nodded; that was true. And again, as the night before, he knew, looking at the winding drift of the slaves, that angry possession upon him — all the slaves himself, feeling the stinging pain in the torn feet of a Gaul who limped past, in the worn womb and the heavy breasts of a woman near to childbirth, straggling from the baggage centre, in the humped determination of his Thracians, marching with sloping spears in the glister of the rain. All that, but more. For he saw the glister of the unending weapons with a keen, wild pride, not in that he owned or commanded them, but that he was of the horde, among them, going armed to meet the Masters. He rose in his stirrups and looked back, and backwards, as frontwards, loomed an unceasing human drift. He turned to Kleon.

'Another might lose himself. Ride back and bring me news of the Jew.'

It took Kleon almost an hour to come to the Bithynian legion, still at the peak of the Pass, under a hail of darts and arrows from the fundatores of the Second. As he dismounted a slinger's pellet rattled on the helmet of Gershom ben Sanballat. The Jew smiled sourly, combing his curled beard.

'Easier work than I wish, fighting these light-armed scum. In a

129

little while it'll be less easy — when the legionaries themselves have gained the peak and we are retreating below.'

'They'll have you at their mercy, then,' said Kleon.

The guerilla Pharisee was sardonic. 'This comes of reading Plato.'

But Kleon saw the situation with a sudden sharp clarity. 'Bithynian, you must detach a fourth of your legion to hold the peak — hold it and die in the task. And you march down the Pass to aid the Strategos.'

'And who'll command this fourth to be sacrificed?'

Kleon looked through the rain at the far mountain-tops, those hills across which the Strategos planned to lead the slave army — into the wild, uncitied north, into a waste of barbaric fields, of forests bent at night under snow, wild oxen calling, not the criers of news, mist and beer, not sun and wine, men vulgares from kings to commons, not a single literatus to be met though you lived till Gershom's Behemoth came down and devoured the world. So he knew his answer.

'I will.'

The Jew stared at him angrily, haughtily. 'You? Is this a jest from your Plato, Thracian?'

'Nor one from the codes of Jehovah, Bithynian. Hasten your division — unless you fear to march down to the pila of the Masters below.'

'By my God, but I won't. You'll die here.'

'If I don't, I'll die elsewhere. And I've no fancy to die in that barbarian North. Hasten, Gershom.'

And at length, seeing that he would not be moved, and that so things might come to a better pass, ben Sanballat gave his orders and marched away three fourths of his legion; and he came to Kleon and kissed him, and that the Greek suffered, with a sudden twist of his bowels, the tears that might have come to one unmutilated. And he saw, terrible in Gershom's eyes, a picturing of that fate that Gershom knew to be his. Then the Jew turned, cursing his Bithynians, pulling angrily at his beard, and marched down the Pass.

Kleon found no orders to give, they awaited the nearing attack of the legionaries, for the Roman velites had now drawn back. Then Kleon turned and found Hiketas by his side, and stared at him in surprise.

130

'You here? Your place is with the Strategos.'

Hiketas yawned, delicately. 'Over-late to order that now. I'm here with my Amazon, and here I stay.'

They stood with arms entwined, like lovers on an Attic vase, the woman had her hair braided under her helmet, brother and sister, lover and mistress, they smiled in each other's eyes, and then in the cold, bitter eyes of Kleon. Then Hiketas said:

"Like yourself we've no mind to adventure among the barbarians. We've known them before. We fight against the Cities, if at all.'

So they waited. Below them, the Second legion mustered. Beyond, far to the north, the Germans and Thracians were debouching on the plain before Mutina and engaging the legions of Gnaeus Manlius.

(v)

Spartacus drew out on the plain, the Bithynian rearguard at his heels, and engaged the Fourth and Ninth legions before the praetor had time to well order their battle. Night was falling, there was no hope in retreat on Mutina, though its lights shone whitely through the rain, the great flares by its watch-gates where the shivering sentinels peered through the drizzle at the manoeuvring phalanges of the slaves. Wolves had come howling from the hills. In Mutina they could guess the reason.

Then towards the city came a stream of fugitives, the fundatores and the sagittarii pursued by the slave cavalry. One man, a Balearic slinger, was the first to reach the gates. Him Mutina saved. But thereafter so close and hot was the pursuit of the slaves, at the heels of broken bands of legionaries, not merely light troops, that Mutina refused to open and watched the slaughter under its walls. The rescued slinger told of a type of battle familiar enough to Italy of late: the Gladiator breaking the legions' formation with the impact of his iron cuneus wedge, and his cavalry slaughtering through the breach.

Gnaeus Manlius fled from the field. Gaius Cassius groaned when the news was brought to him in Mutina, scratching in his bath, winking and fluttering his eyes. The road to the North was open to the slaves. They could pass unpunished, with the flower of the enslaved of Italy in their ranks, to seize new provinces and stir the vulgares to nameless crimes. And, scratching and calling for a young maid to bring life in his rotting bones, Cassius groaned again, for this meant the end of all beauty and culture.

But Spartacus, watching the Fourth legion break, heard at last from Gershom ben Sanballat of how the rearguard came to be in action, of its fourth that was left at the peak under Kleon, to die there, as the eunuch preferred, rather than face life in the North. The Strategos clenched his hands.

'Kleon? How long can he keep the peak?'

Gershom of Kadesh looked at the sinking sun, poised on the rim of the horizon.

'Until that goes down.'

'Then we may save him yet. Call Castus.'

So Castus was called and a moment thereafter the slave horse drew off from pursuit of the flying legions of Manlius, and vanished round the bend of the hills, across the estuaries where the sea-birds nested, following the track the Second legion had taken a day before.

Spartacus camped his men under Mutina. Then he summoned the city to surrender, but it refused, strongly walled, albeit it refused with caution and offered a gift of corn.

The winter night came down with a speed unknown to the slaves from the south. At its fall Spartacus sent for Ialo and with him left the camp, they passed through long lines of little fires, where the rain fell hissing in cooking-jars and hissing on the slaves' wet hair and arms. The southern men shivered and sought to bind their wounds. A child wailed, lost, in the rain. Red eyes gleamed on the camp's outskirts.

Then, in the midst of the Bithynians, they passed a bough-shelter with a tribune's pole and heard there the wail of a new-born child. Spartacus half halted at the sound. It came again and he smiled, and walked on.

The rain cleared. Beyond the camp they came to the verge of the Pass where Gnaeus Manlius had sought to reform his legions and stay the slave-army. Here the Romans, dead and wounded, lay in serried ranks, with piercing them the cuneus dead of the slave attack. Already robbers from the slave-army were at work. Ialo plucked at the Strategos's cloak.

'There's no profit in coming here. We can spoil them to-morrow.'

'Tomorrow we march at dawn.'

And then Ialo saw a dreadful thing, that the Strategos wept. He walked with unshielded face, weeping — suddenly weeping his dead, the lost and forlorn, the rejected, those born to stripes, his people who had died here so bravely, so aimlessly, for they hardly knew what, for a hope and belief so dim, yet in which they had followed him blindly. So Spartacus wept for his dead, the first and last time, with an anger and passion that frightened the slave who companioned him. And then it was there came that resolve that altered the face of history — a resolve newborn from sight of those heapings of torn men who lay so quiet under the coming of the stars.

They came in frost. As they walked back to the camp the Thracian Gladiator raised his head and saw in the north, shining, straining in their traces, the Seven Ploughing Oxen, following the Pole-star home. For a moment he looked at these, and then went into his tent, sitting there long with his head in his hands, none disturbing him, though Ialo and the Sicel maid kept watch.

But at midnight the camp sprang to life with the coming of a fresh host down the Pass. Castus and his spent cavalry had returned, bringing with them the remnants of that quarter legion of Bithynians left to guard the peak. Castus had dispersed the Second legion, taking no prisoners. He stood blood-splashed and exhausted in Spartacus's tent, his young face weary, yet still eager-eyed for a word or a look from the Strategos.

'Kleon?'

'The eunuch has a wounded leg, but he lives.'

The Greek lay in his tent when Spartacus went to see him, following Castus, Ialo carrying a torch to light the way through the dark slave-lines. He lay and bit at his arm, for pain he could not endure. He turned a cold, bright glance on the Strategos and Castus.

'The way's open now then, Spartacus. And I — I'm saved for the cannibal pots.'

'You've been saved for the sack of Rome.'

They stared at the Thracian. Then Kleon knew.

'*Rome*? Then you're to turn back?'

'We go back to conquer Italy. It's ours — our Legions made it. And we'll march against the City itself.'

The Falling Star

THEY turned south, the winter at their heels. And turning, it seemed that new strength flowed up through their bodies from the touch of that southlands earth, even with the Gauls and Germans who at first had complained so bitterly. They crossed La Fata Pass again, down through Gallia Cisalpina and halted in Umbria, capturing a nameless city. There, in a fever of preparation, Spartacus set his tribunes to organize for that conquest of Rome that had come on him as an ultimate necessity the night he stumbled over the dead slaves on the battlefield of Mutina.

But now he saw himself neither as king nor dictator, a God drove him on, a God crowned with the knowledge that unless the Beast that squatted in the Seven Hills were killed, there would be no possible life ever again for men while the world endured. And, knowing he might fail, the Thracian knew also that he might not dare refuse that attempt with all the strength and all the force and all the cruelty the task might demand. And it seemed to him each morning of those hasting preparations that the slave-horde awoke in him, moved with his body, looked with his eyes, hungered with his hunger, tired with his tiredness, were shadowed with the hate of that same Shadow — the Wolf that looked north from the Tiber mouth.

Beating out bolts and grinding their swords, building great machines under Hiketas' direction, the slave legions toiled like men possessed through that month of the hastening Spring. The Strategos had made over to Gannicus and Gershom the administration of the legion laws and requisition of food and supplies. And Kleon the eunuch drew up a great Law, the Lex Servorum, to use in the time when the leaders of the slave-legions sat in the Senate. It dreamt, this Law, of a land of little farmsteads sleeping secure, of quiet towns with literati in the porticoes and freemen in the mills and booths, of the sea and the wind in the hair of Plato's dream. Kleon read clauses from it in the night-watches to Hiketas and his sister, Gershom ben Sanballat sitting by, sardonic, combing at his curled beard.

'In that time there'll be no need of laws, far less of this cumbrous Lex,' Hiketas affirmed. 'If it were for this only that we march on Rome, do you think I'd have joined the Free Legions or would sweat now upon my catapults?'

'Only by Law may the perfect State and citizen be created,' Kleon affirmed.

'Only by the will of Jehovah may such be done,' said the Pharisee Jew. 'And He makes no dispensation for Gentiles.'

'Only by perfect freedom may life be perfect again,' said Hiketas. 'As once it was in the Golden Age, when there were neither Laws nor swords, Masters nor slaves ——'

'Nor talkers, eunuchs, or geometricians,' growled Gershom ben Sanballat. 'When do we march?'

'In six days' time,' said Kleon. 'If the war-machines of Hiketas are ready by then.'

'They'll be ready,' affirmed Hiketas. 'And with your Lex and my ballistics — who shall resist us?'

He went smiling away with the woman who loved him, his sister and mistress; and even Kleon, cold and indifferent in such matters, believed their love evil, though there were no Gods, no Laws but those men made themselves. Gershom ben Sanballat looked on the thing with the aversion of one who had looked overmuch on Gentile abominations to be vexed from aversion to hate. To Castus it was a matter of indifference — he hungered for a love that was still denied him, that of the Strategos himself. To Gannicus it was a matter of staring amaze and jesting filth.

Spartacus slept that last night in Umbria with a soundness of sleep he had little known for months. It was a fresh Spring night, blowing from the hills the smell of the wakened earth. Ialo slept by the door of his room, and near dawn stirred at a sound. The Sicel maid Mella had entered the room and crept to where the Strategos lay. Ialo got softly to his feet and drew his gladius and came behind the girl. So he waited for her to raise her arm to stab.

But she made no effort to strike, and when the Thracian saw the look on her face he lowered the gladius, staring at her puzzled. Then he slipped back and made pretence to sleep again; and Mella went out and the dawn came in, and Spartacus awoke.

They brought him warmed wine and he sat and drank it in the chill of the morning. Then abruptly, and all around, the air was rent with the hoarse blowings of the bucinators, for the march was placed early in the dawn. The Bithynians were first to muster, the heroes of La Fata Pass, and march out southwards with Gershom of Kadesh at their head. Spartacus mounted on his great white stallion sat by the gate with Kleon and watched them march. In the baggage section of Gershom's legion went a litter with Judith and the child born on the night of the battle of Mutina. The Strategos smiled at the Jew as he saluted.

'We'll find this child a palace to sleep in at Rome.'

Gershom scowled. 'It were better if we find a cow unquartered on the march. The mother's milk has failed.'

Then the long Bithynian lines, the eastern and southern slaves, the Negro vulgares of the quarries had found great bales of red-dyed cotton and marched with their bodies swathed in the uncut web, their sword-hilts protruding from the folds, their thin-legged march raising a cloud of dust. So they went by, and then came the Gauls under Castus, with slung shields and heavy tramp, they marched because march they must. And Spartacus knew well that unless Rome was seized, as seized it must be, these would not long endure his command. Castus rode at their head and saluted, looking wistfully in the face of the Thracian. And Spartacus saluted and made no other sign.

Then came the Germans, with Gannicus also on horseback, a great roan the size of the Strategos's stallion. He scarcely saluted, Gannicus, and went by, his wild-haired tribesmen tramping behind him. Kleon said, 'I still doubt if our Sky-Republic can exist secure without the blood-offering of Gannicus.'

Spartacus said, 'This sounds like a worship alien to that of — I forget the name of your God.'

'He was no God, but a man, Plato, though men called him divine.'

'Were there slaves in that city he dreamt?'

Kleon moved uneasily. 'He lived in other times.'

'Then his time will never be ours. For this is our proclamation as we march on Rome: that we come to free all slaves whatsoever, that in the new state we'll make even the Masters will not be enslaved. We march with your Lex Servorum, but we do not march with your Plato.'

(ii)

On the borders of Sabani and Picenum they halted one night

under the fringes of a great forest, a gnarled growth of trees from ancient times. Here the Gaulish velites of the Free Legions lay down to sleep, the main slave army ten stadia to the north. All that day, a great snake with crested head, that head the shining spears of the Bithynians, the army had wound south in the dust-wake of the velites. Shepherds fled from their horrea and watched it from afar, or, with the news that all slaves would henceforth be free, flocked to join it at its halting-places.

Brennus and his brother did not sleep that night, speaking of Gaul for long together, in a strange unease one with the other. Brennus said, 'I would that we hadn't turned back. There's an aurochs follows me in dream at night, down through this ill road we take to the South. What can we do against the great city of the Masters?'

His brother grunted; but he also was sleepless. Presently they both rose and put on their abollae, and went through the lines of the sleeping velites and stood in the starlight at the edge of the forest, looking south.

As they did so, suddenly the sky rained fire. The long white arc of the heavens, a pallor, an immensity of stillness, was broken as though the stars were torn from their settings about the belt of Hercules. The two Gauls caught breath with fear.

The northern horizon flashed and winked. Then a great star fell and flamed over the forest, southwards, shedding a wan light on the countryside, rousing the velites so that they stared and covered their faces, those with Gods; and cursed, those without; and turned to sleep, those weary of both Gods and the godless. Brennus said, 'I think that's an ill thing to have seen. I'd have done better to go through the mountains alone than have looked on that, though all Rome awaits our looting.' And he brushed the sweat from his brow with his withered left arm.

The camp of Spartacus had seen the great star as well. All Northern and Central Italy had seen it. Kleon sat with his Greek scribes in his tent, he was reading for their copying the military clauses of the Lex Servorum when that light winked and flashed across the night-stilled sky. He got up and watched it, cold and secure, unmoved by the threat of the sky. For the stars were bodies of fire circling about the earth at a little distance, and had no bearing on the fates of men. The literati with him muttered and swore, till Kleon turned his cold eyes upon them, and each sought his stylus and tablet.

It roused Gershom ben Sanballat in the bed of his Judith, he muttered in her arms and she soothed him, but terrified; and they watched together that bright thing torn from the sky and flung south over the Gentile lands, some sport of the alien Gentile Gods that had meaning for Gentiles — what meaning? And Judith whispered, 'Sleep, sleep,' with her breasts warm under the head of Gershom of Kadesh.

Spartacus saw it, with Ialo, on the limits of the camp, making the round of the sentinels. Ialo muttered in fear and the Thracian stared long after that gleam winked bluely to nothingness, south. And a sudden spasm of fear went by, leaving his iron resolution unshaken. 'Our star leads us south to Rome,' he said, and Ialo was comforted at that.

The long lines of the slave army stirred. Men rose on their elbows to stare, the Bithynian women moaned, here and there the sentries forgot their posts and forgathered and whispered. But the legions were too weary to pay great heed, excepting the southern men, who knew the Gods unsleeping and fearful, and the Gauls, thinking of the sad Gods of the woods and the ancient towers, the Gods of the verdant Spring of Gaul who trailed the plague and death in their mists, death that was no resting at all, but only the beginning of lives without end — in the flow of water or a bright bird's flight, unceasing, enduring, undying in the wheel of macabre Law.

Gannicus slept.

Castus turned on his bed and thought of Spartacus, and bit upon his wrists.

And the star fell and fell unendingly, lighting up the countryside till it stood above Rome, and the people came out, and the beggars stirred in the tenements, sleeping their hundreds in one room; and on Right Bank a wail arose from the pens of the slaves, recaptured, awaiting the block on the morrow. And they cried, 'It's the Gladiator coming!'

The lions in the Luda saw the star and howled.

The Senate sat in session over the news of Mutina, as yet unknown in the Forum. But the senators knew that the Thracian had turned, had armed and re-armoured in Umbria, and was marching south with Rome his objective. Could either consul do more than snap at him as a cur at a lion? What beast was there to set against the lion?

It was then they heard the howling of the lions in the Luda, and a lictor cried the news, and they crowded, old and young, heated with debate, to watch from a terrace that waning splendour above the City.

It seemed to wheel and wait, lighting the Seven Hills on which the Gladiator marched. Then it fell and flamed and vanished in the Tyrrhenian Sea.

The augurs searched till morning in the vitals of a slain sheep for meaning of that star. And at last, in the temple of Capitoline Jupiter, they slew a slave and looked in his entrails. And the augurs' words were made known to the Senate, listening coldly, for they were the words of its own secret instructions returned to it.

'The falling star is the Gladiator's star. His march on the City will fail.'

That night Marcus Licinius Crassus Dives was chosen provincial praetor, to supersede both the consuls in the field, a small man, renowned for his greed and ability, wealthy with plunder from Sulla's time, hungering for recognition of his military prowess. But even he, appalled with thought of facing the slave hosts with the demoralized legions, advised the Senate to summon Pompeius from Iberia.

Meantime, he set to fortifying Rome.

In Sicily the pirates saw the star as the galleys wheeled out towards dawn to sail raiding down the Messine straits. It fell and hissed in the sea as the morning came, flinging the water high in a great spout.

And relentlessly, southwards, brushing defenders from their path, the slave legions marched on Rome.

(iii)

They saw it at noon, from the Campagna, from the Sabine Hills, shining below them, Mons Cispius crowned with trees and the long-roofed Doric temples, Mons Oppius shelving tenement-laiden into the sunrise's place, Mons Palatinus splendid with villas, fading into a sun-haze mist where the land fell down by Boarium to the Pons Aemilius. Aventine lay south, and north, high-crowned, the Capitoline Hill. Rome!

It was the first time most of the slave-host had seen it, the

139

legendary City of the Masters. And at sight of its shining walls, and the wind that brought its reek a fierce drift across the Campagna, a strange sound rose from the legions of slaves — a growl like a wakened beast that ebbed and rolled into the rear ranks, where the Thracian had brought up the rearguard since dawn, fighting off the detachments of light cavalry which Crassus had sent to vex their march. Kleon stared at the City with cold, clear eyes if with trembling lips, his thoughts sharp on weak points for assailing, noting the cloud of cavalry gathered on the Clovus Suburanus and the hillsides deep-trenched by the guarding Tenth legion. In the air a lark sang, shrilly, sweetly, so that the Germans raised their matted heads to look, and even Gannicus forgot to look at the City, staring instead into the sun in an effort to see the little bird.

But that only a moment. From left to right flank, where Castus and Gershom had halted by the swaying machines of Hiketas, all stared at the City below them. Rome!

Now a cloud had been over the City but that went by, the sunlight came flowing by the Circus Flaminius in long waves catching the sheen of the Tiber and from there upflinging pellets of light, dazzling, into the eyes of the slaves. So for a time they were blinded, and covered their eyes. In its sunlight, terrible, they saw it afresh, the home of the Masters; and this time it was no cry of anger that rose from the slaves, but a sound like a vast, sighing moan.

Spartacus, helmeted, cloaked, mounted on his great white stallion, sat and stared at the City of the Masters, with a coolness at first like Kleon's: but it changed with that flare of sunlight. The home of the Masters, the richest City on earth, where the Gods arose by night and closed the gates and sharpened the swords of war! Rome that had marched to uttermost Thrace, that drew in a long black stream from the shores of the furthest seas the fettered conquered to slavery, that knew no mercy, no peace, no truth, that loved pain and ruth as other men life, a squatting Beast in the glare of the sun. And the Thracian looked round at his halted host, at the men near by him, by his horse's bridle, at their poor, starved, frightened, lustful faces, their hanging mouths and their wound-scarred limbs — and back again at the City — and back again at his legions: and something like an icy hand seized on his heart. These to conquer the City that was unconquered?

140

And again over the slave army that vast sigh ebbed.

Black roof on roof, palace and tenement, the Romans crowded to look at this terror at their doors. Old men, patricians, were borne to their roofs to look on the coming of the slaves. The Senate thronged to look. Slaves peered from the sweating-dens by the Porta Fontinalis across the shoulder of the Collis Viminalis at that far halted massing of lines they had heard were the Criminals of Capua. How long, O Gods, how long?

Then they saw a strange thing, a thing that Rome might not believe, the army of the slaves in motion, at first it appeared at the legionaries' run upon the City. Then they saw it halt and split again; and then — the lines wheeled round, flashing their stolen armour in the sun.

The slaves were in retreat!

(iv)

That seemed in a day and an hour long past. Yet only another night had come, though it seemed to Kleon the space was bridged with days of fighting and pleading since that moment when the slave legions turned about, with a strange unanimity, and marched away from the sight of Rome at their feet — marched swiftly away, heart-broken and in despair, frightened with a fear that had no name, marching and marching, the cloudy gathering of horse at their heels, the tribunes riding to and fro the disordered lines, pleading, commanding, even slaying here and there. But in such places of killing the slave march broke and became no more than a streaming rout, they kissed the hands of Spartacus, of Gannicus, of Castus and even of Kleon the eunuch, they cried that these were the greatest of strategoi and that they would follow and obey them for ever — but not against the City that no men might take, where the Masters lay waiting to trap and torment.

Only the Bithynian legion wavered and shook and yet stood fast, Gershom of Kadesh riding its ranks, smoothing with a cool hand now at his beard, cursing the frightened in their Asian tongues, wary as a panther, unfrightened at the shining Wolf below. Yet presently when he sent a mounted messenger to bear the news to Spartacus that the Bithynians stood fast and so would stay while the other legions were reformed from their panic, the answer came back that Gershom was to march his legion in the wake of the slaves, acting again as its rearguard.

And at that, seeking this venture less than most, ill-omened of its success, hating and despising this life of the sword in Gentile lands, something stirred black to a tremendous anger in the heart of the Jew. For a moment indeed he sat and looked down on Rome and weighed the chances of seizing the City by himself — ill-garrisoned, fearful, rich with spoil, of seizing it or setting to it such a flame that it and its Masters would empyre the world. Then he looked over the patient troubled ranks of his legion, and tore at his beard again, that he might not weep. 'We march as rearguard,' he told his tribunes.

Only then did he remember Judith and his son, with the main body of the fleeing slave army.

Only another night. Night indeed, Kleon knew, riding to that night and their camp on the borders of Picenum, to the dream that he and the Thracian had dreamt, an end to the dream that the slaves would ever march through the Forum of Rome, seize Rome and build it anew. And he did not think that ever again, such was the thought of his bitter despair, that dream would be dreamt by men, they would cower in acquiescence to the lash and mutilation till the world ended, power and freedom put by as dreams, together with dream of the Golden Age of which Hiketas had sung.

Hiketas?

But none knew of him as the night fell; and Kleon rode hither and thither through the voiceless, marching legions, seeking in vain for sight of the Greek, or his sister and lover, or the great machines they had made in and dragged from Umbria. Then at last he heard from a centurion in the Bithynian legion that the machines had been abandoned at the Halt on Rome, and Hiketas had refused to leave them. He and the woman and a dozen more Greeks had stayed and died there, the centurion thought. And Hiketas had cried a message that the Free Legions would have no more need of machines since they had no need of the greatest of Cities.

And how and when he had died none knew, nor ever knew in the Spartacist host, nor of the eyeless doorkeeper in a Roman cellar who lived into a time when men spoke of the name of a general Caesar to one witless who strove to tell, untongued, of the Halt before Rome and the great machines amidst which his sister and lover had died in the hands of the Roman legionaries.

She had taken long to die.

They flung up a hasty camp that night, the slaves, and lay under the fall of the dew, over-disheartened to set up even the tents of the tribunes. There was no attack, though down in the south shone the watchfires of the Roman velites. A great ruined villa stood near the camp, and here quarters were found for the Strategos, he went in through a ruined atrium where the faces of the broken Penates had been smeared with cow-dung by the slaves a year before. His Gladiators clattered in at his heels and lay in the atrium, while Ialo and Mella sought to stir life in the old fireplaces abandoned to rust and damp in the narrow kitchen.

There were no stars that night. The General of the slaves sat in his sleeping-room, awaiting the meal that Ialo prepared, looking out through a slit in the walls at the land that rolled south to those watching fires of the Roman scouts. And now he felt neither the fear nor the wave of anger that had followed the fear when panic had come on the Free Legions. He felt again strong and sure, yet filled with the same dark restlessness that had turned him at Mutina. What next — where, whither, whence?

He wrapped himself in his cloak and went through the atrium and the lines of the sleeping Gladiators. Two guarded the entrance. These would have roused the others to go with him, but he motioned them to silence, and went out in the dark to wander the camp where the slaves slept in unease. In the section where the Bithynians lay he heard the weeping of a wakeful child and knew that Gershom's son was crying for milk. All about him rose the smell of sodden humankind — so familiar to his nostrils it had seldom had meaning. Now it had, a dreadful meaning — that so these would live and endure as long as the Free Legions endured. No houses or habitations, no huts they might call their own, no mornings to see the same hills, the same skies, remembered and near: but a constant marching to and fro, and uncertain campings under alien hills. Until ——

He went back to the villa and found Ialo awaiting him. Only then

143

did he know his own weariness and allow Ialo to unbuckle his lorica. He heard movements in his sleeping-room and asked who was there.

'Mella,' Ialo told him. 'Shall I send her away?'

'Let her be. Have you eaten? Or she?'

Neither had. At his order they ate with him, the Thracian and the Sicel maid, in the flare of a torch in the peristyle. On its plinth at the far end an Aphrodite smiled on them with painted eyes. And a strange fancy came on Spartacus, so that he looked from that perfect face in stone to the starved and unbeautiful face of the little Sicel maid.

So looking, he caught suddenly her own glance upon him. And he knew at once the hunger that looked from her eyes.

But desire for women had long gone from him. He needed no longer their presence to shut from his memory the faces of Crixus and Elpinice. And the strange compassion that touched his heart went by without leaving an impress thereon.

So they ate and drank in the sputter of the torchlight, Ialo and Mella glancing with still faces on the veiled snake-eyes of the Thracian Gladiator who would save them yet, and all the host. And it seemed to Spartacus that he ate and drank with the slave host itself; and again that strange feeling of identity with them, of them, came upon him. And he stared down into the future, as the three broke bread and drank wine, and saw for a moment an alien table, with alien faces about the board. Then that went by, like a shadow on the wall, and the present was at hand, and its question: Whither?

'Where were you born, Mella?' he asked.

She stammered that it was in Sicily. She had been reared on a slave-farm there, one of the greatest of the farms, her father and mother both slaves. They had been vulgares, and were long since dead.

He asked how they died and she told him they were killed together in a pit by wild dogs. They had become old and games had been declared because of the news of some General's triumph in Rome. She did not know what General that had been, but she remembered the pit and her father and mother, they had fought off the dogs for a little while.

Neither Spartacus nor Ialo asked for what crime these things had happened in the pit. Slaves over-old for toil — they had lent some

144

amusement, in the crunch of live flesh in the jaws of dogs, to the Master and his friends ere they banqueted.

But Spartacus's memory was roused.

'I've heard of this Sicily. It is an island. There are many slaves there?'

She whispered, the little Sicel, gazing at the Strategos in awe, that indeed there were many slaves there, many thousands, they had risen in revolt many times. So she herself had heard ere she was sold as a breeder to the farm of Gaius Cassius. She had been brought from Syracuse to Rhegium in windy weather, many of the slaves had been flung overboard to lighten the ship when pirates came in pursuit.

She told more of her life, in her soft, scared voice, to that listener she found less frightful now, who sometimes seemed to draw her heart from her body — the body intended for breeding slaves in the kennels of the Umbrian farm. His eyes were dark and remote as he listened, though he smiled at her in the end.

Then he stood up and went to his room, and Mella lay down and slept near at hand, Ialo across the entrance to the room.

Spartacus tramped that room in thought till the day was near at hand.

He would march the Free Legions down through the Peninsula, cross into Sicily, and seize it as a home for the slaves.

(i)

BUT next day he found that the whole of the army of Crassus the Lean, emboldened by the slave retreat, had marched out from Rome and now barred the way to the south. From refugees who straggled into camp he learned that Crassus had with him as legate one Mummius, a seasoned soldier and a skilled commander, and that the legions under their command fell little short of the fighting strength of the slaves.

To Spartacus three courses were now open: to retreat into Picenum, to march again on Rome, to force a passage southwards to Rhegium, as he had planned. But he might not attempt either of the last two courses, the Free Legions demoralized as they were. The slaves were in no condition to face the legions of the Masters: accordingly, he sent scouts forward into Picenum and prepared to withdraw into that country.

Titul the Iberian rode out at noon, commander of the slave velites. He took with him Brennus and thirty Gauls, and had orders to return before nightfall. It was a day of wind and flying cloud, and the Gauls loosened their braided hair and rode at ease.

In Picenum, hardly touched by the campaigns of the slave-revolt, the Masters were again attending their fields, long gangs of slaves at work on the land, sheep thick on the pastures under the hills; and up the hillside the light fell dark on the olive-groves of spring. But the land seemed to wilt at Titul's advance, knowing his following slaves at a great distance. Nevertheless, they attacked none, for their orders were definite. None attacked them, because of the terror of the Criminal's name: and it was as yet unknown in Picenum how the Free Legions had failed before Rome.

Yet, twenty pace miles into Picenum, riding the verge of a little wood, almost they marched into the midst of a double column of legionaries. Titul stayed his scouts with an effort, and the Gauls lay down and watched, in the sun-dapple of the leaves, the columns that marched south-east. Then they saw that two full legions were passing, legions with cavalry, the soldiers fresh and well fed. The wind had died away, and still the legions marched by, a cloud came over the sun, the legions marched without noise in the dust: and it was to the slave-

146

velites as though they watched an army of the dead. Then the columns swung eastward again, into a village in the hollow below, and seemed there to form and halt.

Titul beckoned to Brennus and another.

'I'd have the two of you go down to the village, and seek out news of these Masters' legions.'

Brennus was blunt. 'Seek it yourself. Who'd fail to recognize us as Free Legionaries? And I, at least, am unanxious to die on the cross.'

Then Titul remembered a field they had passed but a little way back, where, unobserved themselves, they had seen ten slaves and an overseer at work. 'We'll return and strangle the overseer and the two of you can divide his clothes and go into the village.'

Three Gauls rode back to the field and slew the overseer, the terrified slaves standing and watching, unhelpful. But as the Gauls stripped the body and turned to ride back to Titul and his company in the shadow of the little wood, the slaves implored the Gauls to free them. They were manacled one to the other, and when they were discovered with their overseer slain they would undoubtedly be crucified, as a warning to other slaves.

The Gauls listened and were moved a little. But they had no time to unmanacle the gang, and the slaves of it would encumber the scouts. So they left them, hearing their cries for long as they rode round the shoulder of the hill.

Then they brought the garments to Titul; and Brennus and the other Gaul halved them, and went down to the village while the rest of the company hobbled their horses under the trees and slept with one of their company for guard. In the failing of the daylight lights began to spring up in the village, and the slaves, awakening, could see that a stockade had sprung up around the halted legions. Then, as the dark came down, the Gaul who had companioned Brennus returned.

Titul was the first to hear the strange, slobbering sound down the track. He and another went forward to look, and saw what seemed to be a bear crawling upwards in the half-light. Then they saw it was the Gaul who had gone with Brennus. But each foot was a bloody pulp, and as they lifted him up his hands spattered them with blood.

He whispered, 'We were caught and crucified. Me they nailed without care, one of my hands by the skin only. I tore myself down when the darkness came.'

147

Titul asked, 'Brennus?' and the Gaul, slobbering and biting at his crusted lips said, 'He's on the cross.'

For a while, as they held him up in the shadow of the little wood, his lips broke into a meaningless babble. Then he ground his teeth into them, for he had crawled the dust and stones of the track to do more than babble. 'The legions are those of Mummius, the legate of Crassus the Lean. He is here to hold the Strategos from marching into Picenum — not to fight, but to retreat if the Strategos advances'; and he slavered in wild pain again, though they gave him wine to drink from a skin that a Gaul carried. His hands and feet had begun to swell, but still he might not die.

Then Titul took a knife from his belt and asked the Gaul if he could kill himself; and the Gaul tried, but he might not. Then two others came and held the knife and he drove it into his heart.

The slave scouts mounted and rode back in haste through the coming night to the Spartacist camp. And all that night, as the inflammation burgeoned in hands and feet, Brennus hung from the cross. As the morning came in a red flow of light, the Romans saw his tongue hanging thick and swollen from his lips; with the greater heat of the day flies came to vex him, the legionaries passed by below, indifferently, paying no heed to the humming clouds or the thickening odours of blood and excrement. But by nightfall agony had left the Gaul. And in the last of the light three legionaries passing the cross saw his body stiffen; and they stopped, idly, to watch.

As they did so, far up in the hills, there came a strange, agonized lowing.

'What was that?' one legionary asked of another.

The other was an older man. He stared, puzzled, into the gathering night.

'I'd have known that had it been in Gaul,' he said. 'It was the lowing of an aurochs.'

(ii)

A Gaulish woman, heavy with child, awoke groaning as her man shook at her shoulder. It was still night. Outside the nest of bushes and grass in which she lay she could see the stars pallid in the Italian sky, waning into dead whiteness by the east.

'It's still night,' she told him. 'We must sleep.'

'The bucina, woman! Can't you hear it? I must run to the ranks. You'll see to join the other women?'

She gave a cry of fear, but he did not hear it, in the clatter of belting himself in his sword and seeking his helmet, clumsily, with chilled fingers. He had been a serf on an Apulian farm, she the bedwoman of an overseer. Now she was with child, conceived in the cold of those winter marches while the slaves tramped into Cisalpine Gaul and dreamt that that child would see birth in Gaul itself. He patted her shoulder and she heard him run; and all around the stirring and running of many feet. The horns blew up again. She cried after the man — he would surely return.

Yet he did not return. A Negro swore over his brother wounded in a skirmish of the retreat from Rome, and shook him, and then laid him down with a groan. The blind brother cried after him, as the Negro stumbled into his rank, not looking back.

The bucinae were sounding March — all march.

Three German brothers roused in a pit they had dug to shelter them from the dews. They groped for arms and armour in the dark. One said, 'March! Gods, to Germany, let's hope!' And another panted, 'Not to Rome, anyhow, whatever the Thracian says.' And the third said, 'Gannicus'll see to that.'

Gershom ben Sanballat hurried from the villa and gained the quarters of the Bithynian legion just as the bucina sounded. In his tent Judith slept with the child, appeased with exhaustion if not with milk. He stared down at them and then shook them awake.

'We march. The Free Legions are caught between two armies of the Masters. It is cuneus order.'

She had heard of that order before. She caught his sleeve. 'But not for the wife of a tribune?'

'We take no women or baggage.'

She wrung her hands, staring at the child. Gershom's face seemed frozen as he girded on his sword. Then a quietness came on Judith. She rose and helped him, and they stared at each other. Then he took her and kissed her, and did not look at the child; and ran from his tent, cursing the Bithynians to haste as the bucina roared again.

The wolves lairing up in the hills heard it and growled and turned in sleep. The Roman velites heard it in the south, and stirred from sleep and stared at the winking watch-fires of the slaves, and turned to sleep again.

The morning came winged over Italy. The cities left in the wake of the slave-passing stirred to a furtive half-life. In the ruined fields and plantations the birds were crying from a dimness now shot and sprayed with the stippled arrow-hail of the sun. A low wind blew from Campania.

The Roman velites rode north till they came to a hill, and looked down on the camp of the slaves around the abandoned villa. It seemed as on the day before. There was nothing to report back to the main army where Crassus the Lean was now stirring from sleep.

Since the failure of the attack on Rome, it was now plain to the provincial praetor that the end of the slave-revolt was imminent. He could wait for the Spartacist army to disintegrate, and destroy it at his leisure. It would never advance on Rome again; if it marched south, he could hold it; if it retreated to the north Mummius would fall back in front of it, as instructed, giving battle under no circumstances but extreme necessity.

The slave-revolt was near its end.

The provincial praetor, the Dives, the Lean, sat waiting for news from the velites. But none came. At noon he sent a centurion of the Eighteenth legion to report on the appearance of the slave camp. The centurion was a grizzled Lucanian. Coming up with the velites who watched the camp of the Spartacists he looked across the ochre shimmer of the day at the palisaded dykes; then he rode his horse three stadia nearer.

And then he knew what trick the Spartacists had played.

He returned to the velites, cursing them.

'Send to Crassus at once. The slaves escaped during the night. They have left only their baggage and women.'

When Crassus heard this, the face of the Dives went livid with anger. He commanded that the hundred men of the velites be decimated. Then the whole army stirred at the shouted orders of the tribunes and marched north on the slave-camp.

All day the women in that camp had watched stupefied the dark hovering of the Roman scouts to the south. Now they saw that the end had come. And some were glad, wearied of this life of travail up and down the Italian roads, rain in their faces, fear in their hearts, their

150

food the leavings of hungry men. Better all ended: and for most their Gods had no terror of after-life for slaves and the simple, only death and long rest, long rest. But there were still other women of the slave-host, young, who looked at the nearing army of the Masters with hope and not fear in their hearts. Surely they would be spared, they were still young and fair, too fair for the cross; and the bed of a legionary better far than the bed of a rebel slave. And they washed their bodies and braided their hair and waited with trembling lips.

But the woman Judith watched that approach, she and a little Jewish maid; and they looked at each other and then at the child, drooling and wailing for lack of milk. And Judith knew it must be the child first.

So she took a cloth and held it over the child's face, firmly, till the limbs ceased to kick; and there came a strange heat from the small face, though her own body was set with beads of frozen sweat. And then the maid plucked at her dress.

'Look, they are coming from the north as well!'

Out of the north were coming more Romans. But it was a flying retreat of disordered horse.

(iii)

In the pace of the short trot, as near as half-trained men might come to the step of the Roman legionary, the slave army had moved north through the mists of dawn. Spartacus rode in the van, Kleon beside him, Gannicus a little in the rear. They had made their plans at the council over-night when Titul brought back the news of Mummius halted in Picenum with his two legions. Now the Thracian pondered the alternatives if these plans failed.

Once, speaking to the tribunes who rode about him, he glanced back at that hasting march of the slaves, and his heart rose high and glad. Kleon saw the Strategos fling back his great head with the clouded, wild eyes; and a queer pain held the cold heart of the eunuch for a moment. This slave who led them, whom some strange God had gifted with leadership — how he changed and altered, he whom the Italian lands knew only as the ruthless, sure Spartacus! And he thought how perhaps a time would come when historians told of this

151

revolt, and figure the Thracian as a wild barbarian, sure of himself if dim of plan. While instead —

'The Bithynian and German legions will march on the village where Mummius lies. But at sight of Mummius' camp they'll pretend to fall into confusion. Gershom and Gannicus will draw them back and appear to make hasty entrenchments, with stragglers stealing away to the hills. Meanwhile Castus and I will hold round this hill of which Titul talked and take Mummius in the rear.'

'And if he fails to come out and attack us?' asked the Jew.

'Then I'll fall on him and force him from the villate. See to your men.'

Gershom ben Sanballat fell back to his legion, his Bithynians staring at him eagerly. But he rode with a twisted heart and mind: once he half halted to order his legion to turn back and save the camp and Judith. They would obey him, so readily! He could yet save the woman and his son, march on the sea-coast, and capture those ships that troubled his dreams.

His major tribune, a little Syrian, ran to his stirrup and trotted there. 'Is it fighting?'

Gershom growled at him. 'No, no, we go for milk baths to Picenum, a land of milk. Pfu!'

The little tribune grinned, and ran by his side. In swinging strides the Gauls kept the pace. The cavalry fanned out northwards. Fanged with spears, the shining march of the slaves advanced. By noon it was not ten stadia from the village where Mummius lay.

Here Spartacus divided his forces and marched north-westwards on detour, taking with him Castus, Oenomaus, and Kleon the eunuch. Gershom and Gannicus eyed each other. Gershom curled a thick, sardonic lip.

'No doubt you'd prefer to take command?'

'That's well. Now I'll show you leadership, Bithynian.'

'That's well, Scythian. I'll watch.'

'I am no Scythian.'

'I am no Bithynian.'

It was an ill beginning. The legions straggled undecidedly, the Germans fingering their slings, the Bithynians their swords, the velites a straying pack. Gershom fell back on his legion, composedly combing his beard. Gannicus sent after him a message that the

Bithynians were to take the van.

'This is leadership,' Gershom growled to his tribune, 'the essence of leadership.'

'What?' the little slave tribune asked.

'To see that another's throat is slit in preference to your own,' the Jew answered. 'As doubtlessly the divine Plato said — but of him you never heard.'

Nevertheless, he took the van with his legion. The velites straggled intentionally now, at Gershom's order, with the appearance of scouts who had little fear of finding an enemy. They passed by the field where the ten chained slaves had watched the Gauls of Titul slay the overseer. Ten shapes lay very quiet there now: already the spot was a-caw and a-crow with ravens. Gershom glanced at it indifferently, and then turned his eyes on the ochre limning of the little wood where Titul and his company had spied on Mummius' men.

So, about the time of sunset, they came in sight of the village where the legate of Crassus the Lean sat staring moodily up at that hill. A young man and haughty, he was hated by his tribunes. Nevertheless, they feared him, as did Crassus, for it was whispered that the Vestal herself protected him, and shared his bed on occasion as well. A slave brought him wine, passing under the place where Brennus hung on the cross. The legate asked what had happened to the spy.

The slave told him the spy was dead.

Mummius drank his wine, watching the dying day. Then he looked up at the wooded knoll again, and there saw halted and staring a great concourse of armed men. For a moment he regarded them unbelievingly, then leaped to his feet and cursed and shouted for the bucinators to sound.

At the orders of a great, black-bearded leader on a heavy horse, Mummius could see the armed slave-rabble falling back in apparent confusion. His blood raced at the sight and he forgot the orders of Crassus. Calling for his horse, he determined to attack the slaves.

They camped and began to throw up hasty entrenchments. But fear was evidently upon them. From the skirts of the camp Mummius could see small bands stealing away to the hills. He resolved to assault the half-made camp forthwith, and addressed his men. They answered with stern shouts, and brandished their swords.

153

Mummius forthwith led them against the enemy. With his cavalry he attacked from the south, almost veering into the line of march on which the slaves had come. But the legions he commanded to attack the slave-camp frontally, and this they did under a hail of arrows from the slave sagittarii.

For a time the fighting was bloody and indecisive. Then the Romans heard a shouting in the village and looked back and saw there, sweeping round the northern hills at a slow, untiring trot, the Thracian Legion of the slaves, well-known now for their Greek helmets and tunics. For the Thracian arrogated to themselves the Greek name in the rebellion and took upon themselves the avenging of wrongs suffered by Greece at the hands of Rome.

Mummius, at the head of his cavalry, heard nothing of the shouts, seeking the weakest place in the slave defences. Into this, at last found, his cavalry rode, opposed by kneeling ranks of slave-pikemen. Yet scarcely had they engaged than a sweating centurion from the Roman legions was at Mummius' stirrup.

'Legate — SPARTACUS!'

Mummius looked back and down the hill in the fading light. There he saw his legions half faced about to meet the wild forfex attack of a new slave army — not the customary wedge attack of the Spartacists, but one in shape like the closing claws of a crab.

Caught in this claw as darkness fell, the Romans broke and fled, such of them as the slaves did not hew down. Spartacus took no prisoners. Mummius himself rode hard to the south, almost riding into the camp where the slave-women and baggage had been left. But he and the rest of the cavalry rout swerved aside from that, the slave horse at their heels, and so came on the halted lines of Crassus.

The provincial praetor retreated and entrenched himself strongly, showering Mummius with abuse and ordering the decimation of such of his following as straggled in during the night. Meantime, as the last of the light went, the slave legions came marching back and reoccupied their camp, miraculously saved from the Roman advance.

Quiet came down on the hasting events of the day. The Gaul woman laboured in the pangs of birth, delirious, her man dead in the forfex charge by the fringe of the little wood where Titul had waited. The Negro found his brother and embraced him. The two German brothers lay on the earth and keened the death-song for that other who had perished under the hooves of Mummius' horsemen.

Gershom ben Sanballat went to his tent.

(iv)

Reinforcements poured down from Rome to the army of Crassus the Lean, for at length the senate had recalled the legions from Africa. Daily the provincial praetor sent out his velites to reconnoitre the slave camp. The weather was now white-hot in the plains, waving its mists down over Campania. In the noon hours it grew so sultry that only Italians or Africans might bear it, peering into the shimmer of the sunhaze.

In the slave camp Spartacus had set the Free Legions to regrinding the poor iron of their swords, to raiding the surrounding regions for cattle, and to making sandals from the hides so procured. Foreseeing a long march in these preparations, the slaves sang. The Germans set the horns of the cattle on their helmets, hoping in this way to add terror to their appearance. The Gauls hung on their shields the tufted tails of the bulls, and the women fed on the meat for the moment so abundant. In the deserted villa Spartacus assembled his tribunes and outlined his plan.

'We'll march south to Rhegium, seize ships or charter them, and cross into Sicily.'

Kleon said indifferently that this plan might as well be attempted as any other. He sat and stared with cold, pale eyes into the sunhaze, and would say no more.

Gannicus growled that they should retreat again into the north. But he knew while he said the words that his plan would find no hearing.

Castus looked at the Thracian with eyes of love and said nothing.

Gershom ben Sanballat pulled at his beard. 'So we fight again for a New Republic — but this time in Sicily. It'll fail again, Strategos. Let us scatter now to the northern ports and seize ships, each to his own country. We are faced by now with the unwearied legions from Africa, led by one with the heart of a hungry sow in an orchard. Crassus the Lean is no mincing consul or swashbuckling legate.'

155

Spartacus looked from one to the other of his tribunes. And they saw he had aged, the blue gloss gone from his tended hair, the skin wrinkled about his eyes, those strange eyes shadowed. But he himself felt strangely little of this ageing, as though, a mirror for them, and no more, he reflected their lives, but in his inner self remained un-old. And he knew that without his leadership the slave-army would to-morrow fall to pieces, at the mercy of the cross and the rack and the whips of the Fugitivarii.

So long was he silent, standing there looking at them, that they moved uneasily under his gaze. For they might not forget him who had ravened like a beast at the death of Crixus — that Spartacus still shadowed their minds, though he was long dead, and the gaze of the Strategos merely one of pity, and, for a moment, a despairing compassion. Then he said:

'To-morrow we'll march south. Unless Crassus gives us passage we must meet him in the open. Here is the road ——'

He traced it with a stick upon the frescoed wall, while the tribunes sat and watched. The fresco chipped and showered in little flakes. The slave-leaders watched the line as it wavered down through the hills to the borders of Lucania.

'We should reach Rhegium ere the month is out.'

But that night a quiver of apprehension ran through the slave lines, it was Crassus the Lean himself they would face to-morrow, Crassus of whom all had heard. And even in the Bithynian Legion there was fear at that knowledge, as though the small, lean man with the bloated face and the hunger for wealth was staring at each on the slave-block in turn.

Yet with the dawn they took heart, for Spartacus was undefeated and undefeatable, as all knew. They greeted him with shouts as, mounted, he watched them march. All the camp marched out to the south, not merely the desperate cuneus which had pressed north against Mummius the legate.

Judith went no longer in her litter but with the rest of the women who panted in the pace of the Free Legions. She remembered how she had come to that camp and the child that then lived, and the face of Gershom that was now turned from her. The woman who had been in childbirth stumbled with her new-born child, panting into the sweat of the south. Mella tramped with happy, untiring limbs, loaded

156

with the gear that served the Strategos. And a great song arose from all the Free Legions, a song that was sung in the fields of harvest by the harvesting slaves.

Spartacus slowed the march to caution by noon. Then they saw that Crassus would dispute their passage, his army in battle array.

Spartacus disposed his forces, and then flung forward his Bithynians, hitherto undefeated, the terror of the legions.

But they broke and fled before the centre where Crassus himself stood. At that, on the right, the fresh African legions advanced through the arrow-hail of the slave-sagittarii, and fell on the unprepared following of Gannicus. The Germans fled.

As the night fell, Spartacus drew off from the field, his Thracians covering in ordered retreat the rout that streamed outwards, south, from the first defeat the Free Legions had met under the command of the Thracian Gladiator.

V. IN RHEGIUM

The Pirates of Sicily

(i)

LUCANIA and Brittium lay undefended. The slaves straggled southwards through these lands, the Thracians taking upon themselves the
brunt of the retreat. Behind, Crassus and the winter followed at their
heels.

The news of the slave-defeat was borne to the Senate and from
thence abroad all Italy. It reached about all the dun lands of the
Mediterranean lying on the edge of harvest, ripe with olives and the
fruits of the vine, the tale of the great slave revolt that at last was
nearing its end, brought to that end by Crassus the Lean. In Calabria
the old slaves of the farms heard the news and shook their heads,
knowing that always, till the world ended, there must be masters and
slaves. In the mines of far Cyrene came the news, and the slaves,
chalk-dusted, whispered it as they strained at back-breaking loads. It
reached to Thrace and perhaps in the hills some hunter heard of the
end of the great attack on Rome that another hunter had planned.

Meanwhile, cool, watchful, defeated but unrouted, and never
before so displaying his generalship, Spartacus moulded the slave
flight into ordered retreat; twice, on the march, he turned about and
flung the Bithynian Legion into the Roman pursuit, the Bithynians
hungering to avenge the disgrace of their cowardice in the face of the
Lean. The Roman pursuit slowed down, for Crassus saw that the
revolt still endured: in despite that littered field where Kleon the
eunuch had seen the second of his hopes of Empire crumble to dust
under the wheeling attack of the African legions.

He rode south ahead of the main slave army, two thousand men
of the Gaulish legion with him. Coming to Thurii, they found it
garrisoned. It refused the slave-demand to open its gates, and Kleon,
with a sudden cold rage in his heart, ordered assault upon its walls.
It was taken after a day's engagement, the slaves, ferocious with
defeat and retreat, clambered upon the walls like madmen, they made
of themselves living tortoises that flung a last line of desperate men
up on the walls and over them, piling on the spears of the Romans till
these had no spear-heads left and must needs take to the gladius, no
weapon to use in such desperate encounter. Kleon himself sat on

161

horseback and directed operations: at night Thurii fell and he gave it over to the sack of his Gauls.

Presently it was alight, and the Gauls sought from house to house, cutting the throats of the Masters and driving out the slaves. The women, when caught, were raped ere their throats were also cut; and Kleon, riding to the Forum, heard about him shriek on shriek from the patricians' houses and saw blood trickle from the steps of darkening atria. Then rain fell and put out the gathering fires.

In the darkness such of the inhabitants of Thurii as might fled out into the countryside. The Gauls camped in the city and slept, drunken on wine and lust and blood. Kleon lay down in a house in the Forum, assured that no other city of Lucania or Brittium would now resist without heed the passage of the slave-army.

In the morning the Gauls awoke and turned in beds where women shivered and wept, or lay still with knives in their breasts. And a great weariness with lust and slaughter came on the Gauls, and with it a sickened disgust for the Masters, their houses, and their women. They flocked out into the streets and yawned, idle and fed, and curious for sport.

In the centre of the patricians' quarter the house of the Governor had resisted until nearly dawn. Now it was taken, the Governor killed, and his women apportioned among apathetic Gauls who stripped and robbed them, and then bade them go. But one of the women was the Governor's bride, newly wed, and the tale went round among the slave soldiers that her bridal was as yet unconsummated. Immediately, in a shout of laughter, she was seized in a score of rough hands, disrobing her, a tall, dark girl: when a drunken tribune cried a better plan.

'What of our leader, the little Greek? Not his fault that he lacks the means — he's the suitable groom for the Governor's wife! The woman to Kleon!'

It caught at the humour of the slaves. They had the Governor's wife dragged through the streets to the house where Kleon sat: and had her sent in with the tribune's message. She was stripped and stood before him, young and frightened and proud, dark, and he saw in her eyes things he had seen too often to have compassion for them. And he heard the cruel jest with which she was delivered, and was unmoved by that as well.

The woman saw a man, thin and tall, with a face that held

nameless memories: a cold face, alien in its inhumanity. Then she understood the purport of the jest, and reddened darkly upon her pallor. The man was a eunuch.

'What is your name?' Kleon asked, and remembered how long before he had asked that of another Roman woman, Lavinia.

She answered 'Puculla', staring at him, her hands trembling. And then a strange thing happened. The fear seemed to fade from her eyes. They looked at each other a long moment, with the Gauls crowding in the doorway to watch. Kleon turned to them, passionlessly.

'I thank you. I'll heed to the woman.'

(ii)

The slave forces retreated slowly up through Brittium. Spartacus saw the scene with both his own eyes and those of Crassus the Lean. For himself, Brittium was the road to Rhegium and Sicily. For Crassus it was a cage in which to hem the slaves till fresh legions could be brought or raised against them: or they starved into submission. To attain Sicily the slaves would need ships. If they did not attain it —

He gave orders to strip the country in their southward march. So it was done. Trees were cut down and sawn and dragged in the rear of the army in the Gaulish waggons. Anvils and all iron things were taken from the smithies. Harvests were stripped as by locust-plagues. Herds were raided and driven together, a sea of tossing horns and humps, flowing in advance of the slave-retreat. So, more like a nation in transit than a moving army, the slaves came to the Rhegine neck and passed it.

But there Spartacus left forces on guard, Gershom and Castus with their legions; and himself pressed down to the sea-coast with Kleon and Gannicus.

It was late autumn. The sea flung long hands up on the land, there were vine-lands through which the army passed where the slaves rested and slaked their thirst, crushing the grapes on their lips in a strange, tender ecstasy. Here in Rhegium the slaves now rose, and would have massacred the Masters, but that Spartacus forbade it. And he directed that no granaries or houses be destroyed, nor women unwilling be taken to the beds of the slaves. Then Ialo found him an

163

empty house in the city that looked on the Messine Straits, and he set to reorganizing the slave-hosts for the coming invasion of Sicily.

All shipping had fled, and for hope of transport they must negotiate with the pirates of Sicily. This task was deputed to Kleon. But here, in the sound of the sea, a strange restlessness seized the Greek. Like a ghost long void of hearing and taste, yet remembering a sound and a scent, he would wander the shores night after night, smelling the sea and looking up at the coming of the stars in the quiet of the Rhegine nights. Then he would return to his room where the woman Puculla awaited him, with downcast eyes and silent lips.

And a strange relationship flowered between them, dimming his hate of the Roman and Italian name, his bitter memories — her loathing of a slave as an animal with whom no patrician might consort. At first, while Kleon slept, she would shudder at the thought that he was no man, one mutilated beyond manhood, with no lust of men that might injure her. And hate had come in her heart, unaccountably, at that thought; then it passed. In the days that now were come her eyes lost hate and fear alike, looking on the eunuch her master.

And Kleon, women-hated, women-hater, stirred to a strange, queer pity as he looked at his slave. In their third week in Rhegium, while still they awaited the coming of the pirates and their ships from Sicily, he told her she was free, she would be passed beyond the slave lines and the Romans receive her, for she had come to no harm. She bent her head and thanked him, and went soft and barefooted from his room. And Kleon stared after her with cold, green eyes, and sighed at himself — what was the woman to him, he to any woman?

On the next night he had her mounted on a Rhegine pony and himself rode with her up to the Rhegine neck, through the guarding lines of the Bithynian legion. Beyond, far in the night, were the watch-fires of the Masters. And they rode together and did not speak, and a strange peace was with them, they had laid aside master and slave. And Puculla said, gently:

'I'd have had such as you to share my bed in other times, and my children as well, O Kleon!'

And Kleon said: 'And I'd have had you, for the delight of you, and your gentle heart. But this is not to be.'

And she wept, and they kissed one the other; and Kleon saluted

164

her and they said vale, and she rode away. And she came back again and they kissed again — with a ghost of passion, the mutilated slave; with a hungry horror and pity and a weeping tenderness, the Roman woman. Then she went out of his life, he never saw her again, he went back to the Messine town. But he went back strangely altered. For that dull hopelessness that had come on him with the failure of the March on Rome now passed. And with it there passed, more ancient, he had thought it life-enduring, that frozen hate that had girdled his heart since the morning he had ceased to be a man.

(iii)

He plunged into reorganizing the slave army with a skill and fire that moved the Strategos to a look of wonder.

'You sleep seldom these hours, Kleon.'

The Greek laughed at himself. 'It's because Sicily's so near, no doubt — Sicily and Syracuse. It was there that Plato went to found the New Republic.'

Of that the Thracian knew nothing, till Kleon told him the tale. The great slave laughed.

'I'd have liked to have known your Plato. Is he dead?'

'Many years ago.'

'Had he slaves? There were slaves in this Republic he planned?'

Kleon looked away. 'There were slaves.'

'Then he was only as the other Masters. I know nothing of the histories or plans of men, but there'll never be peace or the State unshaken, with women suckling their children at peace and men at work in the fields with quiet hearts, but that slave and master alike is unknown in the land. These slaves we lead — would they be better Masters than those we go to supplant in Sicily?'

'They would be no worse.'

'And it would come to the same. If ever we build our slave state, there'll be no slaves in it at all.'

The Greek was fired by that vision a moment. 'We could do it in Syracuse — if we kept but strong enough, lived long enough, you and I.'

The great slave-general laughed again, but hardly. 'It is only the slaves themselves that can do that. Not you or I alone. We are here to

165

lead. We pass. But they endure.'

And Kleon went back to his own lodging with a strange twist to his thoughts. Would ever a time come when men were so? Would ever return that Golden Age of which Hiketas had dreamed, men hunting and living untrammelled and free, ere Cronos spun the wheels of Time? Would ever again the men of the Golden Age stir in the blind, dull hearts of the great slave-hordes? Till Puculla and Kleon and Titul might yet be one?

They awaited the Pirates of Sicily.

(iv)

And at length a bireme brought the envoy of those Pirates to treat with Kleon for the transport of the Free Legions across the Messine Straits. He was an Iberian, tall and scarred and lacking one hand; and Kleon sat and stared at him when the two Gauls brought him in. And the pirate stared also, and then gave a great cry, for he was Thoritos of the One Hand, once the leader of Kleon long before, the Greek his lieutenant in the pirate city that lay in the lee of the great White Isles.

They cried each other's names, and kissed. And then the eyes of the pirate went pityingly to Kleon's middle, as though to gaze on his mutilation: for he knew he had come to treat with a eunuch. And Kleon smiled his old smile as of old, if with less bitterness in it now.

'So they did to me, Thoritos. But you still sail the seas.'

The Iberian flushed, that his gaze had been understood. 'You've paid back that mutilation to the Masters, or the tales they tell of you lie.'

Kleon asked what tales they told, and the pirate answered that of all men who companioned the Gladiator, the Greek eunuch was known for cold-blooded cruelty, even as Spartacus for his incomprehensible clemency. Kleon said:

'If I save the slave-army the name of rapine and cruelty, and take it upon myself, how better can I serve it? But this matter of the ships: how soon can you take the Free Legions to Sicily?'

So they fell to haggling on the great sum the Pirates demanded, more (as was known to Kleon) than Spartacus had in his treasury. From that great sum Thoritos would not move. Such he had been com-

166

missioned to demand: he was no more than a messenger. And, looking out on the flying scud of the Messine Strait, Kleon guessed that he spoke truly, and by some means the sum of gold must be raised.

'Then that's agreed. Half the gold when your admiral brings the fleet for embarking; and the other half when we reach Sicily.'

But neither to this would Thoritos agree, demanding half of the gold at the moment, the other half when the fleet came. For to bring the fleet would mean great preparation, the abandonment of lucrative raids, danger from the Roman ships as never before. Kleon said: 'And what surety have we that you'll indeed bring your fleet for the passage to Sicily?'

Thoritos smiled like a wolf, scratching at his face with the stump of the arm an ancient sea-fight had left him.

'No surety.'

Kleon sent to Spartacus and told him the terms of the Pirates. Spartacus had the Pirate Thoritos brought before him; and the Pirate saluted the tall, lonely figure in the gilded armour. And something mocking and indifferent went from his eyes, looking in the eyes of Spartacus.

'We've no surety to give but our word; even as we've no surety that once your slaves are in our ships they won't seize them, and take from us both our lives and treasure.'

Now, that thought had been in the mind of Kleon, for he knew the Pirates treacherous, holding faith by nothing but gain. And how, Sicily once attained, might it be defended for the New Republic except by a great fleet? But Spartacus shook his head.

'That I swear we'll not do.'

The Pirate asked by what God he swore, and then Spartacus swore by the earth and the air (for he knew no other Gods), and by blood, for so Thoritos demanded. And the Pirate was paid his gold and went back to his bireme, and sailed into the haze of the Messine Straits; and a proclamation went through the slave camps of the amount of gold that had been paid, and the amount that must yet be raised.

Then the slaves stripped their women of gold, bracelets and brooches stolen in loot: and all gave up the gold they had treasured for the time when they should be citizens, and free, in Italy, or in their own lands. And Spartacus wore on his finger a ring Elpinice had given him, long before, and that also was flung in Kleon's scales, Kleon standing with two literati at the door of the house of Spartacus, while the slaves filed past and flung their gold in the scales against the sum for Sicily. When it came to the turn of the tribunes, Gershom ben Sanballat flung in the scales a great rope of gold that Kleon had seen around the neck of the woman Judith. Titul the Iberian stripped from his ears the rings that Petronia had worn two years before. Castus and Gannicus each gave a great sum. But Spartacus had nothing but the ring, and Kleon himself, as he thought with a smile, sardonic still, but less bitter than once, nothing at all, as befitted a no-man.

Yet at length the sum was complete, the scales turning with the two talents brought by the Sicel maid Mella who served the Strategos. She had kept them in her breast against time of need: and the time had come. A laugh arose from the slaves as she threw them in the scales, and a shout as these scales turned: and she looked at the Strategos, and he at her, and the dark compassion was in his eyes. She went comforted into his house to set his meat. And the slaves dispersed.

Still the pirates delayed their coming.

(v)

Then a great rainstorm arose. Gershom ben Sanballat, at the Rhegine neck, sent news of the Roman lines closing down on the Peninsula, so that little traffic came now from Italy, and fewer merchants than of old tried to creep through when the news came how the slaves had been stripped of gold. The army of Crassus rolled inexorably down upon the Neck.

The storm passed. Days of late autumn sunshine came. Still the Pirates delayed. From roof-top and hill the slaves watched for the sails that never came, seeing in flecks of cloud the coming galleys, seeing in a fisherman's boat, far off, scudding before the breeze, the ships of Thoritos and his allies.

Yet they came not, day upon day. The birds went south from the Rhegine land; the sun went with them, sun and swallows in long wavering flights into the brightness of the Middle Seas while still the slave host peered across the Straits. Mornings came now in a cold white mist: one morning the slaves found hoar-frost on the roofs. And still the Pirates of Sicily delayed.

Then at last, no day, but in the dead of night, Thoritos sent news in a little boat across the Messine Straits. The envoys of Crassus the Lean had come to the Pirates, bringing great bribes from the Senate if they refused transport to the Spartacist army. The Pirates had agreed.

Thoritos, that he might not offend the Gods, sent back the sum that had been his share from the slaves' first payment. But this the rest of the Pirates refused to do.

The slave tribunes sought to keep secret the news, but it ran through the camp like a fire. What next? And now?

Where?

Whither?

(i)

WINTER came. It came that year with unexampled severity, so that many of the slaves, men of the south, Africa, and the Egyptians, men of warm lands and heat-grey skies, perished. Gershom of Kadesh found his legion thinning in the unceasing frosts, the keen winds that now rang down the Messine Straits; and himself began to cough blood of a night when he woke and heard near him the breathing of Judith. Winter. And next? Where? Whither?

They were hemmed in and trapped in Rhegium. For the legions of Crassus had now set to the building of a wall and fosse across the Peninsula, to hem in the Free Legions from the rest of Italy and starve them into submission. The Lean had had great hordes of slaves driven down from Calabria, a quota conscripted from every farm, bands brought from the mines of the north, even — so the irony of the chance — galley-loads brought from Sicily. Under the lash and the shouted commands of the Roman legionaries these slaves toiled in thousands raising the dyke against their fellows, trapped in Rhegium, where already provisions grew scarce.

But for a little, in this situation, the slave army knew an unwonted cohesion and unity of purpose. The slave hosts looked out on a world of winter that hated and feared them, they saw on every side the gibbet and cross did they break or divide. The mutterings of Gannicus ceased. Nightly he led slave raids on the dyke, once beating back the Roman guards and filling up the fosse for a great stretch.

The Romans retreated in disorder to the camp of Crassus. Then to Gannicus was brought a score of prisoners, one of them a tribune, captured by the dyke. The German looked at them and brooded in the glare of the torches, his crested helmet blown in the stinging wind. Then he laughed his great laugh and gave an order; and that night the Romans in Crassus' camp, preparing an assault to recapture the dyke, heard the sound of hammering and strange cries as the darkness waned to morning.

And when the light came they found the slaves had retired a mile away, to their own lines again; and high above the ruined dyke was reared a score of crosses on which hung the Romans whom

Gannicus had captured. The tribune and one other lived when taken down; but by nightfall the others had died from the swellings of inflammation. And the Roman legions, who had thought the slave rebellion ended but for a play like firing a fox from a hole, stared south and felt little delight in the game they were here to play. Only Crassus smiled as he sat in his tent and planned the next step, the isolation of Rhegium by sea as by land.

And Gershom ben Sanballat, coughing blood at night, would think of the orange groves of Kadesh as he heard the sleep-breath of Judith beside him, and wonder in his dark, closed heart when the end would come. For he knew it would come, and yet — and yet — the Strategos had saved them before. Might he not again?

Such the hope that burgeoned through all the slave army, even while it shivered and food grew scarce. The Strategos would save them yet. And about that hope presently blossomed an insane flowering of rumour — of his power, his plans, how he had formed an alliance with the African princes, who were sailing to his aid, the legions in Iberia had revolted, Crassus would be summoned away to deal with them, the Pirates had been won over again, and were sailing back to transport the Free Legions to Sicily. . . .

Gershom knew these fancies but fancies, striding back at nightfall to the house on the sea-wall where Judith awaited him. For he had taken the woman to his bed again, in that wave of knowledge of a hostile world that had come on all the slaves, in a sudden loneliness such as he had known never before. Sometimes there came between them still the shadow of the dead child whom she had strangled in the Picene camp, he would see it in the lamplight as he watched her disrobe; and the Jew would groan, and she come to him, thinking an old wound ached, as it did, and look down on his tangled beard and tormented eyes, and ask what she might do. And Gershom would growl: 'Sleep.'

But he thought of this son who might have prayed by his side in the Temple, bringing an offering there with him, where the sheen of the plumage of doves was blue in the blue-tiled courts; who might have made the last rites over him, dead; who might have known the winds of Levant, the cry of the Hasidim bands in salute; who might have endured the holy ceremony of circumcision, consecrating him to God. And to Gershom, who had never hated the Romans as Masters,

171

knowing there would be slaves till the world ended, there came the cold Jewish fury in his heart as he looked at the broken woman who had murdered the fruit of her womb and his seed to save it from a Roman spear. If ever the Strategos led them against Rome again ...!

Twice Spartacus rode out to see the great dyke with which the Romans had hemmed him in Rhegium. Castus went with him, riding wistfully beside him that second time. But Spartacus was far in his own thoughts as he halted his stallion. Wrapped in his abolla, he looked on that line of earthworks driving straight as a sword-cut across the Peninsula, the black earth piled high on the further side, the near side a deep dyke, swimming with liquid mud, defended with pointed stakes. Beyond, and on the parapets in the cold winter light, gleamed the helmets of the Roman sentries. On the wind came the smell of their camp, the smoke and stench of a camp of the time. A little Iberian, a leader of velites, one Titul, came riding to where the two slave-generals sat, and pointed to a group of Romans riding the further side of the fosse.

'It is the Lean himself,' he said.

So, beyond bowshot of each other, Spartacus and Crassus looked on each other for the first time. In the wind Crassus' cloak was drawn tight about his mean body, his face, high and pinched, peered from under his peaked helmet, the face of a merchant, his tribunes said, cold and sharp, with clear eyes and the avaricious mouth.

'It is the Gladiator himself,' a tribune murmured.

He was mounted on the great white stallion that all Italy knew well. His abolla shook out in the wind from the gilded armour that encased his body, a great body that fitly matched the great horse it bestrode. The Romans could see the blow of the uncut Thracian hair in the wind, for the slave wore no helmet. Crassus nodded.

'We'll yet have him on the cross. Bring a sagittarius.'

So they brought an archer, and he bent a great bow, the wind in his favour, but the distance was too great. They saw the slave-general sit unmoved while three arrows were loosed. Then he turned about and rode back to his camp, and the Romans to theirs, while the stratus clouds thickened in the sky. And that night the frost began to loosen its grip on the Rhegine land.

172

Next morning the snow began to fall, at first a fairy feathering of the greyed Italian sky. But as the day increased the wind rose, driving the snow ever thicker, in great gusts. Many of the slaves had never seen snow before. They ran out of doors, the women and children, and stared at it with astounded eyes and palms extended to the sailing flakes. The Negroes thought it salt and licked their hands, but it melted, leaving a cold, brittle taste. The Gaul and Teutone legions ceased their shivering. They knew this thing and were un-afraid, and played great games in the piling drifts, rolling balls of the snow in effigies of Crassus and pelting these effigies with filth, rolling smaller balls with which they pelted the Eastern and African slaves, who stared astounded from their encampments at the antics of the Northern men. But these were remembering the long winter nights by the Baltic, forested dawns that came white in snow; and they hated Spartacus that he had led them to perish in this little Neck when they might have crossed the great mountains and by now have reached to their own lands.

Kleon was strategos of the day. He rode the Rhegine boundaries, with two Bithynians in attendance. On the Neck he came to the en-campment where Titul, the leader of the velites, crouched shivering by a fire. The Greek smiled at him, contemptuously.

'Do you fear a storm worse than the Masters, Iberian? This stuff is no more than the spittle of Kokolkh.'

Titul shivered. 'Mighty were the great White Storms in the vanished Western Isle. Do you think the God calls for a sacrifice?'

'Of Roman hearts, without doubt,' Kleon said, and rode on. At the slave dyke he found the Bithynian legion marched back to the town, and Castus' Gauls replacing it. Castus himself lay idle in his tent.

'The Romans won't move,' said Castus. 'This storm's but begun.'

'So Spartacus says.'

'You've seen him to-day? He'll ride out to the dykes?'

Kleon shook his head, with a cold wonder over this love of the Gaul for the Thracian Gladiator. Many had loved him: but this was the strangest love of all. And because in the ancient Hellas there had been such loves, acknowledged and unashamed, Kleon found the essence

173

unamazing, if the constancy of Castus inexplicable.

'The Strategos has other tasks. Give up this hoping for him, Gaul. He'll never lie in your bed, or you in his.'

Castus flushed red, his hand on his dagger. But the eunuch merely smiled his dark, weary smile, and rode away with wrapped cloak and head bent against the bitter wind-drive.

In the camp of the Bithynians he found Gershom ben Sanballat squatting over lists of gear and equipment, stores, all military supplies. Spartacus had called for these lists, and Gershom pulled angrily at his beard at sight of Kleon.

'Your work, I suppose. What need have we of these lists until Spring? We can't move until Spring — if then.'

'Spartacus makes his own plans, seeking counsel from none.'

'Unless it be the shade of the divine Plato, doubtlessly summoned from hell. Greek: Gannicus again is trying to stir revolt among the legions.'

Kleon was unalarmed. He yawned. 'We'd feel the Free Legions unhomely, were Gannicus not in our midst, attempting to stir up revolt.'

The German lay on a couch in a rough wooden shelter, drinking warmed ale, a woman on either side of him, the look of a sated bull on his face. He barely stirred at Kleon's entrance.

'There's nothing — nothing but snow and waiting here while we stagnate and the Thracian dreams.'

'And what would you have him do?'

'Drive out the Rhegine Masters. Cut their throats or drive them into the Rhegine Dyke. So we might have the food they now eat. Or send again to Sicily, offering a greater sum to the Pirates.'

'Or send to Crassus, offering the head of Gannicus as the price of a free passage. It is you who dream, Scythian.'

Evening was falling as he rode back to the town: with its fall the snow increased to a blind whirl that made seeing a matter of chance. The sky cascaded upon the earth, Rhegium was wrapped in white, its hills and dales. In their houses, country and town, the Masters, starving, crouched above low-burning braziers and knew they might not survive until Spring. Already there was famine and worse. And Crassus (they knew) would not move until Spring.

Kleon found Spartacus asleep, and Ialo and Mella on tiptoe in

174

the house. The Greek went and sat by the brazier in the room where the Strategos slept, covered with a cloth. Outside the wind whoomed through the narrow streets of the Messine town. Kleon sat and stared in the brazier, wearied with his ride, his thoughts dulled by the buffet of the storm, his eyelashes fringed with snow-rime. Once Mella came and looked in, then drew away at the vacant stare of the eunuch. Spartacus slept in the half-dark, silent, as one dead.

Whither? Where? What thing could they next attempt? Spring would come, and over the dykes that hemmed them in come the freshened legions of Rome, trained and practised all the winter months for its coming. The legions, with food and fresh-ground swords — and the starved Free Legions to oppose them. And galley-loads of Romans crossing the Straits, assailing the town, undefended, for no engineer had taken the place of Hiketas. Was this the end? — or might Spartacus waken again?

Now he could feel the house shake in each icy gust; and he thought of the shivering encampments where the slaves lay who could find no lodging in the crowded town. The women and children would perish first, that would leave more food for the men, a better defence when the Spring at last came. But in this weather even the men, the southern and eastern men, were dying thickly enough out there in the dark.

He heard Spartacus awake. The Thracian peered at him in the half-dark.

'Kleon? It is still snowing?'

'Thicker than ever,' the Greek said.

The Gladiator listened for a little to the sound of it. Then he stood up.

'We'll leave Rhegium tonight.'

(iii)

It was three hundred stadia in length, fifteen feet deep and fifteen feet wide, the Rhegine Ditch that Crassus had driven across the neck of the Peninsula. None might pass, north or south: and as the gale of that night, snow-blind, set in, the centurions withdrew their men from the emplacements on the dyke, for in the open no living thing might survive. Presently the Roman camp was white-swathed,

175

and still the gale drove black, now sleet, now snow, south-westwards in the dark. From their camp the Romans presently heard the howling of wolves, and knew the scavengers of the night were abroad, hungrier than ever in the famine that held the Peninsula.

No living thing could live or endure long in that darkness and storm. Spring would come. Until then. . . .

The slave-army marched from the Messine town. Many perished ere they had gone ten stadia. Many were lost in the blinding gusts of the wind, and strayed into the hills and next day were surrounded and massacred by the Masters. Yet the main body held together, the horse moving at the pace of the women and the loaded baggage-wains that creaked softly forward, with muffled wheels, through the snow-covered tracks. For, by the order of Spartacus, they had swathed the wheels in straw that no noise might be heard; and all gear that might tinkle or clank on slave-armour was swathed in cloth, and no light was shown in all the length of the army as it moved up through the night.

Sometimes a great gust of snow smote on the marching ranks so that the whole army paused, gasping, leaning against the wind, the Bithynians coughing and choking, the Gauls and Germans grimly enduring. Yet presently upon them all, even upon the women who stumbled and gasped through the unending darkness, a fierce hate and energy descended. Weeping and cursing, the slaves still marched forward, seeing but a hand's-breadth in front of their eyes in the snow-swirl, unaware whither they were led, how it fared in front, or who were lost behind.

Titul led the van, Spartacus and Ialo behind him, surrounded by the Gladiator guard. The Thracian Ialo had his hand on the tail of Titul's horse, the other hand grasping a dagger that he might stab his fellow-slave to the heart at the least sign of treachery. This was the command of the Strategos, who rode composed and silent, peering into the snow.

The snow fell thicker and thicker. Twice Spartacus sent back a message, asking if all was well, to Kleon who brought up the rear with stragglers. It passed from mouth to mouth, the message, the Gauls gasped the words in their clipped Latin argot, the Germans screamed it in their guttural throats, the Bithynians whispered it down the tracks, through the lanes of stumbling feet in the dark, the flash and

176

glow in the snow of swaying shoulders and desperate faces. Twice the message reached Kleon and he sent back the word that all was well, though the message lied. Then no further message came, for by then, on the Neck, in the full pelt of the storm, the slaves cursed and refused any message, believing at last the Gods were to destroy them, that Spartacus had sold himself to the Masters and now led them out to die in the storm.

Titul drew bridle. 'The Dyke.'

The Strategos rode to the verge and tried to peer down and across it. Then he turned and gave the order that it should be filled up.

It was impossible. But it was done. The slaves fought and wept in the darkness, weeping with cold, dragging up great stones to the Neck and hurling them in the Roman dyke, piling earth and trees and baggage-wains in the great dark gap. The roar of the storm grew to a scream while they toiled and fought; and a great moan went south on the wind through the Rhegine night.

(iv)

The morning came. The wind had died away, save ever and again an icy gust that flapped the soft scud of the snow into drifting wreaths over the shrouded hills. All the world lay storm-raped and still, except for the howling of the wolves in the woods, their hunger still unsatisfied as another hungry day broke.

The Roman camp awoke. Crassus had slept in his tent shiveringly, for he hated the south and the cold. Yet when they brought him warmed wine they found him already in his armour. He had resolved to leave the Peninsula, leave his tribunes to hold the slaves in their trap, and himself return to Rome and heed to his own interests until the Spring came.

He gave his orders swiftly, and a murmur of relief passed over the camp when the news was known. The legions might relax a little at last.

The guards who had withdrawn from the dyke marched back there shiveringly, and took up their posts. But when the centurions came to the southern sector they stared aghast.

Even the snow might not cover it. For a third of the dyke had been filled in the night; and, winding dark under the canopy of snow, a great black track rose out of Rhegium like the trail of a snake, and passed north, into the horizon's whiteness.

The Free Legions had filled in the ditch and marched unheard past the Roman camp in the storm. Spring was awaiting their feet as they pressed north. And once again all Italy lay at the feet of the Gladiator.

VI. THE MASTERS

Breaking-Point

(i)

THEY marched into Lucania and into the Spring, Crassus toiling wearily in their wake — despairingly, his tribunes thought, out-generalled and out-manoeuvred. And the whisper ran through the legions that he planned himself to retire on Rome, leaving the war to other hands and the return of Pompeius. Meantime, the Romans passed through a land stripped bare in the famine-march of the slaves, the Spring had wilted at their touch. Starving bands of nomads and robbers who had once been free citizens now roamed the land, with tales of the cruelties of the black Jew leader and the Greek eunuch who organized searches in houses and barns, looting everything that might be carried away, and destroying that which could not. To ease his fear and fury Crassus had numbers of these bandit nomads nailed to trees, and followed on in the trail of Spartacus.

What was now his objective? The sea? — or again to march north through Gallia Cisalpina, and escape from Italy — not turn as once before, inexplicably, he had done?

The Free Legions camped in North Lucania, near the city of Pola. There Spartacus called a counsel of his tribunes, a day of soft Italian sunlight, in the space outside the door of his tent. While they heard him speak the slave leaders lay about his feet on the ground, and Spartacus looked at them with inscrutable eyes: faces with which he had grown so familiar, the bull-like brutality of Gannicus, the haughty Jew face of Gershom, Kleon's thin, sardonic profile, the blond fairness of Castus. Oenomaus had died in Rhegium.

In the slave-camp all around was a hammering on anvils and a sharpening of swords. Spring and war on the Masters had come again.

Spartacus was short and plain in his speech. 'Tomorrow we'll march on Rome.'

With many guesses as to their nature, they had assembled to hear his plans. But none had guessed this. For a little while they said nothing. Then Kleon spoke in his thin, eunuch's voice:

'There's no other course. But I thought I alone saw that.'

Gershom of Kadesh looked from one to the other, sardonically. 'So? We'll go peep again at Rome, and lick our lips, and scurry away

181

— as we did before?'

'We'll not run this time,' Spartacus said. 'The Free Legions are of a different temper now.'

And this was true. They had been welded as a blade in a fire in the months in Rhegium. But Gershom combed at his beard.

'But Rome ——'

'It is madness.'

This was Gannicus. He spoke not with his usual heat, the bull-bellowing that Kleon and Gershom, with their southern blood, found pitiful and contemptible, but with the coolness of strength and certainty. He said again, 'It's madness. And my legions'll have no part in it.'

Gershom looked at him. 'You threaten the council?'

The German laughed. 'The Teutones need no threats to say what they will or will not.'

Then Castus spoke. 'Nor the Gauls.'

At that all save Spartacus looked on him in astonishment — he who had followed the Thracian with such blind devotion, the open mock of the slave-camps, good general though he might be. Spartacus looked from one to other of his tribunes with the changing dark lights in his eyes — sombre and deep, yet shining still like the eyes of a snake.

'We'll march on Rome.'

At that Castus flushed and sprang to his feet. His voice rose in a sudden shrill scream which startled the sentries and the surrounding slaves, so that they gathered at a distance to watch and hear.

'Rex Servorum! We know the plan of yourself and your eunuch bed-man, Spartacus. But we'll be no part to it. You plan to march on Rome and betray us to the Masters, in return for their gold and a generalship in their legions. We'll be no part to it. These are the Free Legions, not your legions, Spartacus. We march north, you'll never see us again. You hear? Never again!'

A foam had gathered on the lips of the Gaul, and Kleon saw his eyes roll like those in the head of a mad dog. The council sat astounded. Then Gannicus stood up beside Castus.

'So I say also. Attack Rome if you will. You do not do it with our legions.'

But Gershom ben Sanballat was now on his feet. 'Your legions, you slave dogs? Where would either you or your legions be but for the Strategos? Lead your legions from Italy? You'll lead them to the cross!'

Ialo had watched and heard. Now he went out secretly and summoned the Gladiator guard. They came running and surrounded the tent; and fear came in the heart of Gannicus at sight of them. He licked his lips, grown suddenly dry, bull-like in courage though he was.

Spartacus said again: 'We march on Rome. There's no other course open to the Free Legions if they'd survive at all. And the Gauls and Teutones march with us — with or without the tribunes who now lead them.'

He had not risen. He did not look up. But the blood quite went from Gannicus's face, and even Kleon, cold and imperturbable, felt a sting of fear at that icy note in the voice of the Gladiator. None spoke. Then Gannicus looked round the Gladiator guard and licked his lips again.

'You're the Strategos. So be it, Spartacus.'

The Thracian looked at Castus. 'And you?'

Castus stared back at him. Had he never understood, could he never understand? And perhaps in that moment, if but for a moment, the Thracian did. Some look came in his eyes that Castus read: and at that the foam gathered afresh on his lips. But he licked them clean. He said in a whisper, 'You are the leader.'

'We march to-morrow,' Spartacus said. 'Crassus is already on a level with us — our velites have sighted him on the right. But he camps to-night and knows nothing of our plan. Before he strikes camp to-morrow we'll be on the road to Rome.'

(ii)

But a great weariness took the heart of the Gladiator that night. All the plans were made for the march on Rome, and to-morrow drew near — to-morrow, to-morrows without end. What though they marched on Rome and took it, and slew the Beast of the Tiber and ended the rule of the Masters for ever? What peace or ease or delight might he ever find in the midst of this bickering of slaves — be they slaves in fact or but slaves by memory? And he remembered suddenly, so seldom he remembered them now, they had grown thin shadows

183

J

that came at nightfall, Elpinice and Crixus, his dead loves killed by the Masters — they with whom he had once found peace and understanding in long silences, they who could sit at meat with him and need no words to tell their love or their fear. And Spartacus groaned aloud, terrible in the darkness for the Thracian Ialo to hear.

He went and brought the Strategos wine, but Spartacus told him to go, such agony in his voice as Ialo had never heard. The little maid Mella came whispering to his side.

'The Strategos is sick,' he told her. 'If Gannicus has had him poisoned —'

But the little Sicel maid saw more clearly than that, dimly though she knew the mind of her master. She said, 'I'll go to him,' and so did, and knelt beside him. And Spartacus stirred in the darkness at her touch, and put out his hand on her shoulder, and hid his face, and groaned again. And to Ialo that was still more terrible as the hours went by and the night waned, to look in ever and again and see the Strategos still gripping the shoulders of the maid. She knelt unmoving, her fair hair falling on the dark head of the Strategos, neither sleeping with the sleeping world out-by, Ialo looked at them with weary eyes as the earth wheeled to morning. In the early hours there rose the sound of a great tramping in the eastern camps, but no horns blew, and the Thracian guard thought it but the return or despatch of velites. Then Mella came from the tent.

'He's sleeping now.'

So the Thracian saw that he did, and they covered him with a cloth and left him; and Mella lay down and slept also; and the noise of men stirring in the eastern camp died away.

Kleon heard it, in his tent by the southern entrance. Neither had he slept, all night rolling and unrolling the scrolls of that ponderous Lex Servorum he had drawn up long before in Picenum, when they turned back from the borders of Cisalpine Gaul to conquer Rome. He had taken the scroll from a chest, and he saw it already faded, the edges of it crinkled in little folds from its journeyings to and fro in the baggage of the Free Legions. And he read through the night and dreamed over its clauses, and dozed a little. And when the wind of the false dawn came stirring the air he stirred from sleep, and smiled wryly at the thought that his Lex should have sent him to sleep. He looked out from his tent and watched the breaking of the night; and

184

heard, as did Ialo, that commotion in the east, and wondered that a body of velites of such number should leave at such hour. Then he lay down and slept again.

Gershom of Kadesh had heard the noise, awakened from sleep by the side of Judith. His was nearer the eastern camp than the tent of the Strategos or of Ialo. He rose and went to the entrance and looked out. But there was no shouting, an ordered tramp, and no attack on the camp. Also, a ground mist had come down and patched the place of the encampment so that he could see but little. He smelled at the air, at the smell of the dawn in it; and went back to the side of Judith, her warmth grateful, he put a hand over her heart and she turned to him in sleep; and he remembered the dead child of her womb and turned from her roughly, gruffly. Rome and tomorrow ——

And the Thracians heard it, lying in their shelters, line on line around the tent of Spartacus, dreaming of the pits, the ergastula, some of Thrace and Greece, some of Styria, where the winds played now with the rising scents of Spring and the huntsmen trapped the wild boar in greening thickets; and some, Scythians, dreamed of their plains, bright with tamarisks, and the neighing of wild horses at night; and some of women, or lust or wine, tears and fears that their lives had known. In a multitudinous stirring of dreams the Thracians heard the noise in the east, a steady trampling on the edge of dawn.

Titul the Iberian heard it. He lay with a Greek slavewoman who had been a bedwoman in Thurii, tall and white and comely. In her arms, her passionate abandon, he found a form of sacrifice to his haunting, shadowing God. And she would rise from his bed weary and bruised, so used that the day would shame her face at memory; yet still she would return to him, with a craving lust for that dark lust of life the Iberian knew. And, her white limbs in his grasp, a shuddering ecstasy would seize the lost tribesman.

Now he moved and listened, head alert, and freed himself from the woman's arms, and stole like a cat from the shelter of boughs and sods whereunder they slept together. Velites moving at this hour?

The mist was passing. So was the sound of the marching feet. But Titul ran swiftly through the camp till he came to the Eastern Gate, running by the parapet verge of the slave entrenchments. He found the gate deserted, left over-night for the Gauls to guard; and he stopped and peered about him, his gladius in his hand. The light grew.

185

The mists drew off. With their passing a strange sight was given to his eyes.

The Gauls and Teutones had lain the night in the north-east sectors of the camp. In the evening they had flung up little turf houses, in the fashion of these northern folk, in little circles about each centurion, singing, and braiding their hair as the night came down, the Gaulish women white-breasted, half-nude in the flow of gold and flame from the lights of the fires, the naked children about their feet, a scene repeated a thousand times. Now ——

Now their camp stretched deserted under the early sun and the wheeling cry of the scavenger birds. But out to the north-east wound a track that vanished unpeopled over the horizon.

Castus and Gannicus had withdrawn their legions from the slave-army.

(iii)

No cavalry went with them, yet their march was unhindered by such bands of roving scouts as lately had vexed the flanks of the slave-army. They found all the country strangely deserted both that day and the next. Halting the first night, they flung up entrenchment against — not the Masters — but Spartacus and the slave legions that yet remained with him. Neither Castus nor Gannicus doubted but that he would pursue: not to attack, but to attempt winning over their forces.

At first, the morning they marched in secret from the camp, they had given out that they marched under the orders of Spartacus, they were to seize and hold a town in Picenum for him. But now they let it be known they were marching far to the north, marching from Italy, beyond the Mountains, seeking safety from the Gladiator and his legions, who had planned to betray them to the Masters in return for their own immunity.

Hearing this news, the Gauls held a council, the Germans of Gannicus withdrawing apart while Castus told his tale. Then a Gaul stood up, and they saw it was the brother of Brennus, the scarred slave whose ferocity towards the Masters had exceeded all bounds that even his fellows knew. Now he said bluntly: 'Of this quarrel with the Gladiator we're told only now. Why not before? If we'd desired to break away we'd have done it under a different leader from you, Castus.

186

Perhaps under Crixus: he who trusted the Gladiator. And who may now believe that Spartacus would betray us?'

But another stood up to address them, the chief tribune of Castus. And he told how soon they would gain the great White Mountains and the world beyond them, honour and security in the stockaded cities and the hunters' cotes, in Gaul with its kindly sun and fragrant rains, and the sleeping seas where never again the Masters would dare to sail. And the Gauls listened, and, as ever with them, were moved to tears with the beauty of words in the mouth of a poet: and they shouted that the matter be voted upon, in the fashion which the Greek Kleon had taught them.

And each Gaul took a little stone and flung it into one of two piles — one for return to Spartacus's command, one for marching to Gaul with Castus as leader. And in a little while a murmur of laughter rose as they saw the size of the heaps of stones. For barely a hundred had flung their stones on the pile that voted return to Spartacus's army.

But the brother of Brennus flung his spear into the centre of the great pile of stones so that the shaft stood upright, quivering. And he cried a phrase that troubled their minds, though they thought it the voice of a madman.

'Vae victoribus!'

Yet he and the others who had voted for Spartacus marched with their fellows when the march was resumed, in the rear of the horse of their tribune, Castus, riding with bowed shoulders into the north.

Near evening of the second day they came through a low pass in low hills, and far below saw the glister of a wide sheet of water, bird-haunted, its shores fringed with villages. This was Lake Lucania, and the joint legions marched down on it, land hitherto untouched in the sway and flow of the slave wars across the Peninsula. They marched up the near side of the Lake, firing the villages, looting the granaries, and killing such of the Masters as had not fled at their first glimpse of the ragged slave standards, the hammered wild boar of Gannicus's legion, the nodding Mother-Goddess of the Gauls. With the coming of night the slaves camped in the ruin of a little village. Great stores of wine had been found, and from these the Gauls and Teutones feasted, their fires wakeful over a great stretch of the countryside.

Castus, whose temperance had once been a subject for jest in his

187

legion, sat and drank with Gannicus, his eyes red-rimmed with hate as he told of the shames and slights he had endured at the hands of the Thracian. And Gannicus remembered those things he himself had endured. And they cursed the Gladiator and his host till the curses slobbered foolishly on their lips. Around them rose the sound of merriment under a gibbous moon as the night went on. Then, presently, the noise and the watch-fires began to die, except where the brother of Brennus and his century of men kept the far gate of the village.

The Gaul did not sleep, staring out from the burned gateway over the stretch of water where the night-birds cried, where long grasses rustled and moved in the night-winds of Spring; and all the earth sent forth a dry, growing smell that caught at his throat, so that he remembered himself young, a boy, with no tormented men with gouting wounds in his memory, haunting him: but only the woods and the millet patches of home, and play in the sun, and the grimed, laughing face of Brennus, whom he had tended and fought and loved, and the light dying from the forests where the aurochsen lowed. And in that chill hour on the morning's edge the brother of Brennus wept, sternly; and when he raised his head from weeping listened, and called his fellows to listen.

It was the thunder of many feet at the legionaries' trotting pace. Then the brother of Brennus saw by the mere of the Lake the glint of helmets, for the morning was near.

The army of Crassus was assailing the camp.

(iv)

There were nearly eighteen thousand men in the Gaulish and Teutone legions of the slave army. At first the shouting and the thrusting blades dazed the slaves new-wakened from sleep, in a light still dim by the shadowed lake. But they had lived too long their lives in the slave revolt to sleep apart from their arms, or not by this time to have learned the rallying-cries of their tribunes. So in this place and that a commander cried and his men came about him: and they faced a ring of spears and long swords to the gladius charge of the Romans. But Gannicus lay as one dead, they had to dash water many times in his face before he awoke: and then he muttered and raved so that the

188

slave tribunes knew there was little help in him. They ran, each for their sector commands, now wilting under the full fury of the Roman charge.

Crassus himself, as the day broke, watched the reel and sway of the battle by the lake. He sat his horse on a little eminence, watching with bright, avaricious eyes. His velites had brought him on the second day news of the departure of the Gaul and Teutone legions from the slave army; and at first, thinking them detached by Spartacus, he had made no move against them. Then a straying Gaul was captured by the velites and brought to Crassus and put to the question, and the provincial praetor learned that the strategoi Gannicus and Castus had quarrelled with the Thracian, and planned to march through Italy and escape to their own lands.

Crassus saw these seceding slaves were in his hands. Yet he followed them cautiously, unsure of the quality of either Gannicus or Castus. And there was still the Gladiator to deal with, and in greater force. What if, as the Gaul slave had babbled through his breaking bones, the Slave himself should march on Rome while Crassus hunted the lesser vermin?

But it was a necessary risk, and Crassus took it, watching with cold, narrow eyes the burning of the villages by Lake Lucania. Now he sat and watched the roused slaves twice fling back his attack in a pelting wave of routed men.

Twice. But now Crassus raised his eyes and saw a low cloud of dust to the northwards that told him the Fourteenth and Seventh legions had encircled the Lake and were marching down to assail the slave camp from a fresh angle. The slaves also saw that dust-cloud and guessed its cause. Their tribunes — a barber, a farm-slave, a circus-sweeper they had once been — held a hasty council. Their decision was swift. They must strike camp and fight out in cuneus formation.

So, twice, as twice the Roman legions had assaulted their entrenchments, they attempted to do. But already a thousand or more of the slaves were dead. And some cried for Gannicus, till the rumour spread that he was dead; and men broke from the arrow-headed cuneus march, and faltered at sight of the Roman spears. Then Crassus gave the signal for his cavalry to charge the slave camp.

Barely a third of it reissued from the tangle of the slave entrenchments. But the charge had done its work. The slave base was

189

destroyed, and, like a wounded beast, the cuneus attempted to fight its way along the shore of the lake. By this time Castus had taken command of his legion, and was cool and quick, keeping the straying Gauls at the cuneus spearhead encouraged with shout and curse. He believed Gannicus dead, and, himself planless, fought with a fury in which there was little hope.

Behind, the depleted horse of Crassus returned again to the assault.

And now at length, for the bitterness of three defeats, the Fourteenth legion reaped its revenge. At the thrust of the slave cuneus the legion deployed in enclosing forfex: then, shields low, the small, dark legionaries closed in at a rapid run, on the shaken ranks of Castus.

The Gauls saw their leader a moment, young and fairheaded and desperate, hewing with his sword. Then a Roman sprang on his stirrup and seized him by the hair, and while Castus swung round and attempted to cut him down the Roman shortened his gladius and plunged it carefully into the neck of the Gaul. Then he withdrew the blade and, pushing aside Castus' hair, again stabbed him, almost severing his head from his neck. So died Castus. Then the forfex closed on the head of the cuneus, and the Gaul formation fell to pieces.

Yet still they fought, in little wedges here and there. But the Romans drew off after a little, and their slingers and sagittarii shot their arrows and stones upon the slaves, so that the latter fell in great numbers. The women fought now by the side of their men, tall and white-breasted and desperate, a great Gaulish woman armed herself with a pilum and a Roman shield and killed four legionaries before she herself was cut down. Another, the mistress of the brother of Brennus, was young and swift, with her child in her arms, she ran through the turmoil of the battle and escaped through a segment of the Roman forfex. Almost she had reached the shelter of the village wall when a slinger killed her with a singing pellet that shivered her skull.

The Gauls knew nothing of the Death Ring that the Germans could form in a desperate hour, and formed now, the great schiltrouns of the forests. Against these for a time the Roman attack broke in vain. Then the pressure of sheer numbers broke the circles, and the legionaries slaughtered at pleasure. But even while Crassus wheeled in his horse to charge the rear of the schiltrouns a shout arose and men lifted their eyes and saw on the crest of the hills the shine of fresh standards, the serpent standards of Spartacus.

(v)

Crassus faced about his legions, but the Thracian flung the
fresh Bithynians against them, driving a wedge through the Roman
ranks, himself leading the battle, axe in hand. Crassus had his
bucinators blow the retreat, calculating to retire the legions still
unbroken.

But again his calculations missed the generalship of the Gladiator. Spartacus sprayed fresh line on line of slaves on the Romans,
wheeling off each line after it had engaged but a few minutes in battle.
No troops might withstand such onset or such tactics. The Fourteenth
legion broke and fled, pitilessly pursued by the Thracians. The rest of
the Romans drew off in good order.

The battle was to Spartacus, as once to Pyrrhus. But of the
eighteen thousand Gauls and Germans a bare three thousand survived. With these fell Castus, as has been told, who loved Spartacus,
and never knew him; and Gannicus, who hated the Gladiator, and was
killed in his sleep.

The Mountains of Petelia

THE slave army was again encompassed by mountains.

But this time it was summer and retreat, the mountains the brush-hung slopes of Petelia, not the passes of Mutina. In the dry air the withering vegetation seemed sometimes to take fire and burn before the wearied eyes of the marching slaves. High overhead carrion birds followed the long, straggling march that wound through the valleys, deeper and deeper into Calabria. The slaves marched with dragging feet and panting breath, the northern men with a lurching weariness, their tongues licking parched lips. In the rear the Thracian Legion beat forward stragglers from the German and Gaulish remnant: and themselves would pause and lean on their spears, and peer up at the enfolding mountains with heat-hazed eyes, seeking fresh-water springs where they might fling themselves full length in thirst, lapping at the water slowly, like exhausted dogs.

Spartacus pressed on, deeper and deeper into the mountains that opened, deserted, before him. Crassus' messengers had been ahead, at their orders the inhabitants had fired the crops and driven off the herds, and hidden their granaries under earth and manure. Enraged, the slaves left in their trail a line of blazing homesteads which lighted on the pursuit of Scrofas, the quaestor whom Crassus had sent to follow and keep touch with the slave retreat.

Kleon rode in the rear of the Thracian rearguard, he had taken over that duty after the desertion of Castus and Gannicus, no longer the secretary and councillor of the Gladiator but (and he thought of this with a wry twist of lips) a eunuch-general of the Free Legions. Bithynians and Egyptians well able to endure the heat rode with him a motley collection of mounts — Italiot ponies, great heavy-limbed horses from Cisalpine Gaul, a half-score light Arabs: all spoil of this battle, that raid, or yon loot. Now and again they would wheel about and stare back through the westwards valleys. But Scrofas was a dull and cautious commander, he marched many stadia in the rear of the slaves, shepherding them forward into the summer heats and famine of Calabria.

And Kleon, with his irony tempered now by the adversity that

192

ground upon it, wondered what plan the Thracian had that he led them so, wondered while he knew what the end of the venture would be. Twice they had planned to march on Rome, twice failed. The second time, even after the desertion of the Gauls and Teutones, they might still have marched on the City of the Masters, as he and the Jew had urged Spartacus to do. Let Crassus devour the deserters, and, while he devoured, the Free Legions descend on Rome and devour a fenceless city. But Spartacus had refused. 'We'll save what we can of the Northern folk. They've fought beside us long.'

So, in forced marches, they had come on the scene of the second Battle of the Lake, made that salvation that Spartacus had promised: and sold Rome in the task. Then into the mountains of Calabria.

Whither? Where?

(ii)

Spartacus halted his van that night around the buildings of a great deserted plantation. Here in other days many hundred slaves had toiled at the wheat harvests of Calabria, their kennels with their rusted chains lay broken and deserted — but for one into which the slaves peered and saw there a mouldering cadaver, a slave abandoned to die of starvation, through neglect or deliberate intention. Spartacus himself walked about the plantation and looked at the kennels of the slaves, then around him at the footsore, ragged army he had led into those mountains — he had led to so many strange ventures since that night when the first of them climbed from the pits of Batiates.

Sun and wind and rain in their faces, battle and wounds and hunger to endure, the snows of Mutina and Rhegium, the blistering heats of the hills of Petelia: yet that had been better than this once lived in these mouldering kennels before the Revolt, this life of stripes and despair and sodden hatred. And again in the great slave leader there grew that feeling of a passionate identity with the slave host that he led — the feeling that he was one with them, lived in their lives, tired with their tiredness, exulted in their hopes. His tribunes questioned his plans: the great host never did — unless deserters like Gannicus or Castus misled it with lies and rhetoric. And he knew now, with a great faith, the reason for that. None of his marchings and plannings had been his alone, but an essence of the dim wills in the minds

193

of the multitude, in the Negro slave who had starved and shivered up by the Rhegine dyke, the Thracian shepherd who limped with a bloody heel, the Bithynian porter who disputed with the Thracian land-serf the name for victory and defeatlessness. He was but a voice for many, the Voice of the voiceless.

And he knew that even in this march into Calabria, when he had seen so plainly that never now might the Free Legions conquer Italy, he followed as much as led the dim mind of the host. The Gauls and Teutones were a remnant: the rest were men of the Middle Seas, if they could reach and capture Brindisium, suddenly, by strategy, they might find there ships enough to take them from Italy.

And then the curtain closed down, he might not see beyond that.

He spoke with Kleon and Gershom that night, the three of them sitting at meat, corn and the flesh of a kid, the while the maid Mella served them. There was no sign of Scrofas: the Free Legions had yet enough food: the air was blue with the smoke of its fires, and sprayed with the warm stench of humankind. Kleon looked at the other two.

'We three alone to survive! Remember the crowded councils in Nola? Though I can remember little but the crowd, what we said or did grows dim already.' He brooded for a little, and then laughed. 'As this story will grow, dim and confused, in the ages to be, the story of the slaves' insurrection. They'll mix the marches and forget our names, and make of Gannicus a loyal hero and of Gershom here a strayed Gaul from Marsala! Poets and the writers of tales will yet tell it, perhaps, each setting therein his own loves and hates, with us only their shadowy cup-bearers. All dim and tangled in the tales they'll tell, except their beginnings with that Spring when we roused the slaves. And all the rest a dream or a lie.'

'So they do not make me a Roman,' said Gershom ben Sanballat, 'they may lie as they will.'

Then the Strategos told them of his plan to capture Brindisium, and Gershom nodded, combing his beard.

'This from the first was what I advised you, Spartacus. And now you follow my advice, and once I'd have rejoiced, pointing to my own wisdom, and scorning your lack of it. Yet ——'

Kleon smiled at him his slight, dark smile.

'And yet, Bithynian?'

'Yet the Strategos had the right of it, Scythian. Once we might

194

have conquered Rome, all Italy, we might have built under Spartacus a kingdom of slaves with the Masters underfoot. Or your Republic, with neither Master nor slave. But that a devil was against us.'

'There are neither Gods nor devils. Only the Fates, who are mindless.'

'There is the One God,' Gershom said, ritually. 'But he is reserved for the Jews.'

Then Spartacus said a strange thing, his eyes remote. 'There's a God in men. But an Unknown God.'

And they fell silent for a little, till the Thracian roused. 'We march at dawn. How is it with the Bithynians?'

'Ill enough. But they've food.'

'So have the Thracians — a little. And your Gauls, Kleon?'

The Greek smiled that twisted smile once bitter.

'They march astounded with a eunuch for leader. I think I fail in some duty they're too polite to name. Perhaps the fertilization of the Mother Goddess — for otherwise their women will be barren.'

Gershom growled, rising, 'Then they'd need of a eunuch tribune. Their women spawned litters like dogs from the day the Free Legions were formed.'

And the Greek returned to the lines of the Gauls and lay down with a light cloak over him; and the Gauls took him as their leader, for he had wisdom, though mutilated to a no-man by the Masters.

Gershom of Kadesh went back to his legion, to the tent of Judith, again heavy with child. She woke as he came and rose, stoopingly, to bring him wine. But he made her sit and share the wine that he drank. And he looked at her, big with child, with angry, kindly eyes.

'Rest, woman, for we march at dawn to-morrow.'

She asked where and he did not say. Then Judith said: 'I don't think we'll ever see Judaea again, or our unborn son either, Gershom. Yet I'm glad you have brought my womb to fruit, glad to have lain with you, though no son may ever say the prayer in the Temple when we die.'

Then Gershom saw there was upon her the fancies of a woman with child; and he answered nothing, seeking sleep; and the woman lay beside him, but not to sleep, hearing long the crying of the night-birds over the camp of Spartacus.

The Gladiator himself could find no sleep. And again, a strange

195

whim upon him, he went out alone (for Ialo had died by Lake Lucania and he had chosen no other guard) and walked through the ruined lines of kennels where once the slaves had lain; and in his heart he felt all the bitterness and tears, and all the wild stolen delight of a moment's ease, that these other slaves had known. And he cursed the Masters, yet without hate; and went back to his room in the house of the plantation, and found the maid Mella waiting him there, slight and brown, weary with her day's march up through the hills of Petelia.

But now, looking on her with seeing eyes for the first time in many months, the Gladiator saw she was a child no longer, but a woman in her few years. Under the torn tunic her breasts pushed forth their buds, red and sweet, and her throat had lost gauntness, round and full; and he saw the cloud of her hair about her watching face, and the cloud of wonder that dimmed her eyes as she looked at him.

He drew her towards him, she came with a wondering sob, he forgot the Free Legions, his hands cupping those flowers of Spring that had burgeoned in the summer heats, the curving buds of desire that awaited his coming. And the little Sicel maid sobbed again, as though a God held her; and Spartacus took her to his bed, and she wept, kissing him, shuddering to a wild ecstasy in his grasp. And all night she lay there, the God with her, and knew fulfilment and agony that merged in delight and so in sleep; and they slept together, his head on her breast, till the blowing of the bucinae roused them at dawn.

(iii)

But Scrofas gave them no rest. It seemed to him, cautious commander though he was, that this retreat into mountains had developed into headlong rout. Twice the slave army had wheeled so that, describing three-quarters of the arc of a circle, it again neared the outlet of the Petelian hills. Confident in his quarry as a panic-stricken beast, Scrofas pursued at its heels.

The heat grew ever more intense, so that Gauls and Teutones fainted in the strength of it, or straggled by the way and were cut down by Scrofas's velites. But the Eastern and African slaves rejoiced in the sun's geniality despite their footsore weariness. Marching through rugged defiles, they would lift their voices in long, wailing songs, long

196

columns marching into the haze of evening. Spartacus would rein in the great white stallion and look down at his men march past, with a new twist of compassion in his heart, hearing the voice of the Slave, a thing that it seemed to Kleon also he would never forget.

They had not realized, the slave rank and file, that double-twist back through the Petelian mountains. But both Kleon and Gershom ben Sanballat knew of it; and now at length learned the reason from Spartacus.

Scrofas knew nothing of this reason. As the slave march quickened with each day, so he hastened his pursuit. Crassus lay still in Lucania, gathering reinforcement to follow slowly and meet the Gladiator when at length he was run to earth. But what if the Gladiator should emerge from the mountains, pass the camp of Licinius in the dark, and descend on Rome in a last desperate raid?

Sweat studded the plump yellow cheeks of Scrofas at the thought. He despatched his cavalry to overtake and attack the slaves.

They vanished into the bright, crystalline air of the afternoon. The mountains towered windless, the sky unclouded, dust rose and played like a spume about the feet of the smarting legionaries. Meantime, the Thracian legion of the Spartacists, having ambushed and dispersed the Roman cavalry to the rear of a narrow and nameless defile, marched back and garrisoned that defile and awaited the arrival of Scrofas.

Spartacus detached Gershom in command, while he himself waited in the rear with the Bithynians and the remnants of the Gaulish and German forces. The Jew had great rocks gathered in heaps about the ledges of the pass. Then he commanded the Thracians to lie down amid the rocks and await the signal of the horns.

Now it was a little after noon when Scrofas and his legions came to that pass that had no name, a low defile in the mountains of Petelia. As they climbed a wild shouting broke all around them, the rallying-cry of the slaves:

'Libertas! Libertas!'

Scrofas's horse was killed under him by a rock. The mountains seemed vomiting rocks on the Roman march. Through the dust of their descent the Jew flung forward half his men.

Nothing might abide that charge. When the slave horns summoned the Thracians to retire, half the Roman force was in rout and

197

disorder. Nevertheless, Scrofas, remounted, had the legionaries lashed into rank again, and sent forward his sagittarii in an effort to dislodge the slaves.

But the rocks defended them. Then Scrofas urged the wearied Fifteenth up against the slave position. Twice they attacked, but the second time more cautiously, for news had been brought to Scrofas that a path wound round the rightward mountain whereby he might assail the slaves in the rear.

He despatched his Second legion on that mission. The sun wheeled towards evening. Then, in the pass behind the Thracian ambuscade, arose a wild sound of shouting and battle. Scrofas's Second legion had been trapped by the waiting Gladiator in the valley behind the pass.

It was the signal for Gershom ben Sanballat. His Thracians rose, freshened, and charged on the hesitant ranks of the Fifteenth legion. Scrofas saw that the day was lost, and fled through the hills till he came to the camp of Crassus.

All that night his routed legions straggled into the camp of the provincial praetor, waiting beyond the mountains and expecting to hear that the Spartacists had been trapped. But instead he heard of the slaves as victors in yet another battle, victors encamped on the battlefield and devouring the flesh of the dead Roman horses. And once again a wave of cold apprehension fell on Crassus.

The Gladiator was inconquerable. He might march from the mountains against Rome itself.

Crassus prepared to retreat.

The Stallion

(i)

THAT night, for the first time in that hot Italian summer, the rain began to fall, softly, a whisper and wisp in the darkness, shining white veils, translucent, through the slave-camp at the hither side of the battlefield. The slave host stirred to its coming with hungry lips, so slight its fall it might not dampen the fires, men lay with open mouths and uncovered bodies at that descent of the warm summer rain; and the wounded, groaning, stretched out their hands to it, raining mist from the summer night.

And the hills stirred, and the dying plants raised their heads, and the earth moved and put forth new smells, stirring to a fresh and unforeseen life, wakening and moving in the raining dark. And a little wind presently came with the rain, driving it east in the track of Scrofas's rout; and on that wind came some scent that caught in the throats of the slaves, so that they stirred to slurred speech, and a wild, strange laughter, and moments of brooding that passed into quick action, singing, and shouting, and declamation. Beyond the passes the great army of the Masters lay shielding Rome. The Masters?

Who were the Masters?

Who had bestridden Italy like a God these last two years, what army abided undefeated the attack of the Serpent standards? And the slaves wept and cursed with slobbering lips, tearing at the flesh of the dead horses, peering through the raining night into the unlighted east. The Masters ——

THEY THEMSELVES WERE THE MASTERS! These the slaves, the armies of the Republic they had beaten from battle to battle. The Masters — *these*, who fled whenever the Strategos turned upon them! And a wild pride came on the slaves, and they swore they would march no more through the mountains. Italy was theirs and lay waiting their taking. And they sharpened their swords and licked hungry lips, with the little wind in their faces that was kindling all the hills.

And the women of the slave army felt on their faces that same rain, in their hearts the same thoughts as their men. They had tramped the length and breadth of the Peninsula, it under their feet, it was theirs, THEIRS, bought in the travail of the unending roads, in the travail of wounds and death and birth, the horde of children that had been born in the snow-smitten, sun-smitten camps of revolt. The Masters — they were the Masters, they who went ragged and hungry. And they looked on their children crawling out with little eager hands to grasp at the rain and laugh at its touch; and a fierce, weeping tenderness took the slave women. These should never endure what they had endured, to them sun and security and the citizen's name when the Free Legions went down on Rome.

It was said that the Strategos would retreat again, retreat through the mountains to a port, Brindisium, and there take ship from Italy. Retreat and leave this land they had conquered, where they marched unconquerable? Some had never heard of Brindisium, some thought it a great city that lay on the other side of the world, remoter than Mutina, even; and they made it one with the hate that grew on them, gathering and accumulating throughout the night, hate and a horror of the great army Crassus had brought up below the eastern mountains. Hate and no fear — as a man turns at last on a winter road on pursuing wolves and slays and slays, heedless of tearing fangs, with hate and rage for the beasts in his heart. So it was with the slaves: they prepared for battle.

And all that night the mad brother of Brennus wandered the lines of the slave camp stirring the slaves, crying that they be led against the Masters, that they hide and retreat no more. Were they not unconquerable? And he told of Brennus upon the cross, and called to their memories their dead nailed on trees, caught in the rear of retreat on retreat. And the Gauls shouted with anger, remembering the massacre by Lake Lucania; and even the Thracians, turning to sleep, swore battle with great oaths.

And all the slave-camp slept, men drunk with a nameless wine that stirred them awake in the hours of the dark to grind their teeth and catch closer their swords. They lay with their women in a hot unease and a wild tenderness that night; and the night drew on.

Kleon turned in his bed, the fever of the wet wind upon him. He peered out in the silence of the camp, his eyes on the lightless east. Crassus? They had defeated as great as him, they might do it again. And the Greek got up and lighted a torch and took from a box two rolls of writing, and looked at them with unseeing eyes — *The Republic* of Plato and his *Lex Servorum*. And desire came on him to read them

200

again, but his eyes glazed after a little while, with weariness, and he put them away, and extinguished the torch, and lay down.

They must fight. There was no return to the mountains and a safe, easy road as the Strategos had planned, planned while he lured Scrofas into his trap. Fight, as men fought the rain and the sun, and the greedy earth that tore at their strength. Hate, as men hated the darkness and cold, the bitterness of a in and dearth and death. And he thought for a moment of his own past counsels, of caution, and now they shrivelled up: and he turned to sleep with a breaking heart.

And the rain washed on through the night.

Gershom of Kadesh heard it as he lay by the side of the woman Judith, so close again to childbed. And he combed at his beard with twitching fingers, thinking with a hate and a mounting rage of that Beast that waited beyond the defiles, that Beast that would tear and devour the unborn, that Beast they must murder ere it murdered them. Sleep now, but to-morrow. . . .

And Titul slept but little that night, dozing, the commander of the velites, at the far length of the utmost gorge, his eyes on the watch-fires of Crassus's camp. And he thought of the Masters stretched in death, in torture, of himself a high-priest of·Kokolkh, with reeking altars, in the city of Rome. And he licked thick lips and waited the morrow.

And the rain held on, in a light, sweet sheet, over Petelia and its hills till it reached the lowlands of Calabria and the vineyards of Lucania; and the earth stirred and wakened to its coming.

And Spartacus slept unmoving, the sleep of utter exhaustion.

(ii)

But about the coming of the day he awoke — awoke suddenly, his body heaving in anger. In the darkness of the tent his hands found the throat of the Sicel maid, who had slept by his side, and she also awoke with the torture of death in her throat, and cried his name. His hands loosed off in the darkness, he sighed and said, 'I dreamt'; and they lay silent one by the other, till they could see the darkness thinning a little. And Mella slept again, but no sleep came to the Gladiator, watching that slow shine of the morning down the passes of Petelia.

201

The ashes of the dream were still in his mouth; but now the fire had died away. The fury had quietened from his heart. In the growing light he looked at the head on his breast, and wound his fingers in the hair of the Sicel maid; and soothed her as she wept in sleep, weeping, and knowing not that she wept. So Spartacus waited the dawn.

And when Mella again woke, that was still closer; and Spartacus told her how he had dreamt, he had thought her the Wolf of Rome.

'And instead I'm the mate of the Serpent.'

He looked in her eyes and saw them clear, if sad: sad with that fugitive sadness that backgrounded all slave delight. But he saw her youth also, that had flowered, that he had taken, that had not gone wasted, he thought, for either. And he put her aside and went to the entrance of the tent, while she rose and set him meat and drink.

He had looked but seldom on the waking world with eyes that saw it, the lost Gladiator. They had looked below or beyond it all his life — in the days in Thrace on the chance of the hunt, in the slave-pits of Batiates, waking in chains, in the marchings of the great Free Legions to and fro across Italy. But now, unwonted, he looked on the breaking day: and something caught him rigid at the sight, and held him still, the play of colour in the sky.

Cold and pale and blue the sky and the world below. But now that pallor was fading, flushing blindly in red as he watched, on the heights the gold of the sun overflowing the red, in the sky the blue still streaked with blood. Quicker and more quickly came the day, stirring little whorls of mist on the mountain-heights of Petelia while the Gladiator watched. In those heights the night still abode, but the shadows drew back, with darkling spears, at the coming of the sun. On the ground a little mist moved off, slowly, leaving the earth, the rocks, the trees, the great gorges, sparkling with the wet of the over-night rains.

And then, as he stood and listened, far off in some deserted horreum he heard the crowing of a cock — loud, shrill and piercing against the coming of the day. Twice it crowed and then there was silence, except that audibly the slave-camp stirred from sleep at that shrill crowing up through the dawn.

But again the wet wind awoke, and the Gladiator smelled it, and felt the unease of his dream return. But was it no more than a dream? To turn from the road to Brindisium for a last account with the

202

Masters. Now, clearly and coldly, in the cold blue of the morning, he saw that venture for disaster with his exhausted, depleted legions, weary and footsore, with blunted swords, no horse to shield their flanks, the slingers without pellets, the sagittarii without arrows. Disaster.

But the sun came, and the wind; and again in Spartacus there moved with a dark, wild passion that mystic kinship with the slaves he led, the thousands who stirred about him in the camp, who had held half Italy these two long years, voiceless, but their unvoiced passion moved in his heart. Exhausted, a footsore army? But the Wolf was there, they might never now leave the Masters save as the victors of these Masters.

The sky rained blood a tenebrous moment. He looked up at it with dark, dreaming eyes, terrible, in a cold, still wrath and sadness; and then turned to the Sicel maid as she knelt by the stool where she had laid his food.

But when he turned some other change came upon him. She saw him, it seemed to her, seeing and thinking dimly, in her passion of fear and love for him, young: the Strategos who was the Strategos, neither young nor old! And he smiled at her with clear, bright eyes, moving like a hunter to her side, and sat by her and they ate together. And she was troubled with the troubled passion that had swept the camp, and would have asked him what he planned.

But he was fey and strange, he spoke of his years in Thrace, the sweep of the forests at morning, how he minded now the light on their trunks and their tall plumes as they marched into evening, north, marching legions he had seen long before any other legions, Roman or Free. And he asked if she remembered such sights in Sicily, but she did not, it was all a cloud and a blur to her; and she was too troubled to heed, staring at him. And the dried corn choked in her throat, so that she could not eat, while the Gladiator sat with his head in his hands, silent. But when he looked at her again, she saw again how young he was. And then she knew without doubt that he was a God, and shivered in fear, though she had been held by him in desire, in the terror of his strength, and he smiled at her now, and kissed her and rose and sought his armour.

And he said, 'I think this comes to a last pass, Mella. If it's so, you have your knife.' And he thanked her, and said she had served him

203

well, and then looked on the crumbs of the food he had eaten, and said slowly, as if remembering, that they had forgotten, they had made no libation. Nor ever had he done so before, that she knew; and she stared wide-eyed as he flung a little of the corn on the earth, and spilled wine, to whatever Gods there might be in these mountains and in the world.

Then she buckled on his armour for him and would have brought him his light shield that was a horseman's shield; but that he would not take, instead a heavy Samnite shield, borne by such as fought on foot. And he tested its straps and greased them; and Mella brought a double strap that would bind it well on his arm. And he took his axe in his right hand, and bound a gladius under his left arm.

And Mella saw that already he had forgotten her.

Now, all about them rose a great shouting from the slave host, the trampling of many feet, and the singing of men who prepared for battle.

(iii)

As the day broke Crassus marched out his swollen army to take the road to Rome, and straddle that road in defence against the unconquered Spartacists. Scrofas, in chains, marched in the rear, with Quintius made quaestor in his place. The disgraced rout of Scrofas's legions marched in the centre, hemmed in by the legions of Crassus.

The provincial praetor himself brought up the rear, watching the dust of the legions cloud the roads as they skirted the base of the hills and turned east. Then a scout rode up to his tribune, and the tribune swore and came riding to the praetor with the incredible news. Crassus swung round in his saddle.

The slave army, a great thronging of men in disordered, shouting bands, was debouching in pursuit from the Petelian hills. The sun shone and scintillated on their stolen armour, on the Serpent standards of the Gladiators. And then Crassus saw midway the advancing host the white stallion of Spartacus himself.

By the time the legions had halted and swung about, the slave army was only a few stadia away — a great shouting streaming horde, with wind-blown rags and flashing weapons, the sour smell of them struck in Crassus's nostrils as he stared at them with keen, avaricious

204

eyes. Then he turned to his quaestor, Quintius.

'Make camp and raise palisades. Hasten.'

So it was done. The legions wheeled with the speed of much practice into camp formation, and set to throwing up an entrenchment, thousands working as one under the cries of the decurions and centurions, the brown men of the Isles, the Romans and Italiots, the legions from Spain. The sun hid for a little while in a blink of rain and then came out again and remained unobscured throughout the rest of the day. All the Calabrian countryside seemed to stand in a deathly silence awaiting the outbreak of that conflict under the shadow of her mountains.

The legions stared at the nearing enemy, and heard their shouts and wild singing, the Harvesting Song and the Song of the Serpent, for the madness of a God was upon the slaves. Kleon and Gershom of Kadesh rode cursing to and fro their ranks, seeking to form them into the array that Spartacus had ordered as never before — the cuneus with a schiltroun base. But the women had marched with the men as well, they laughed in the faces of the slave tribunes, shaking their spears towards the Roman encampment that rose in black earthworks higher and higher. A drunken host, drunken with an insane hope, the slaves now clamoured to be led against the Masters without further halt. And they began to cry the name of Spartacus in a great shouting that stayed a moment the sweating Romans building their encampment walls.

Then these saw a great white stallion ridden to the front of the disordered slave ranks, and a whisper ran through the staring legions: THE GLADIATOR. He wheeled round the stallion, armoured with a great Samnite shield upon his arm, and cried to the slaves he would lead them without delay, but they must obey their tribunes and marshal the formation he ordered.

So at last they did, while the Gladiator watched, a smile on his lips. And he felt the blood sing through his great body, and once he looked away from the changing wheel and march of the slaves before him up at the mountains he had seen come pearl-blue. Now they towered black in the sun, peering upon him. And when at last his army was in array, Spartacus dismounted from his horse, the great white stallion captured at the Battle of the Lake long before; and the beast snuffled at his shoulder and looked at him with great eyes.

205

Then Spartacus stabbed the stallion to the heart, and it fell and died, and a great groan of wonder rose from the slaves. But Spartacus said that if they won this battle, there would be many fine horses got for him to choose from; if they lost it, he would have no need of a horse again.

And he ceased, and they knew then the meaning of the foot-soldier's shield that was double-strapped upon his arm. And for a little they stared at him, sobered, till the blowing of horns in the Roman lines kindled again the rage through their ranks.

And Spartacus, seeing that they might not be stayed, arrayed them in battle-order. In the van he placed the Bithynians, hungry to avenge that first defeat they had suffered from Crassus the Lean. Gershom ben Sanballat had also dismounted, with his tribunes by his side he ran up and down the ranks, calling last orders. And he halted and waited.

Then the slave-trumpets sounded the charge.

The air filled with the hum of pellets and was darkened by a cloud of arrows from the half-built camp. But under and through that cloud the charge of the Bithynians held fast, they clove down the nearer wall and swarmed in the ditch, and there the Romans met them, and Spartacus saw the gleam of the Serpent standard vanish around where the Jew led his legion. Then Gershom vanished in a wave of men that Crassus flung on that gaining point; and, hewing and stabbing, sobbing with rage, the Bithynians fell back as their horns sounded.

But they paid them no heed. Uncommanded, they reformed their ranks and again assailed the camp. Thrice they charged, and thrice were beaten back, but at terrible cost. Crassus saw that the charge of the Bithynians, men with blunted swords, would assuredly fail: and he rode his horse up a little eminence midmost of the camp, to watch the battle.

Then Spartacus flung the remnants of the Gaul and German legions into the breach in the camp walls, and saw Kleon at their head disappear in that fury of stabbing swords and restless spears — saw that, and the Gauls presently stream from the camp in headlong rout. So he knew that the end had come, the spare legions of the Romans advancing at a run outside the limit of the camp to fall on the fleeing slaves. And the Gladiator formed up his men in cuneus, about him the

206

Gladiator guard; and he looked at the knoll whereon Crassus was halted, and tested the buckles on his shield, and led the Thracians forward into the breach.

(iv)

AND SPARTACUS MADE HIS WAY TOWARDS CRASSUS HIMSELF THROUGH MANY MEN, AND INFLICTING MANY WOUNDS; BUT HE DID NOT SUCCEED IN REACHING CRASSUS, THOUGH HE ENGAGED AND KILLED TWO CENTURIONS. AND AT LAST, AFTER THOSE ABOUT HIM HAD FLED, HE KEPT HIS GROUND, AND, BEING SURROUNDED BY A GREAT NUMBER, HE FOUGHT TILL HE WAS CUT DOWN.

The Appian Way

(i)

FIVE thousand fled, making their way north from the battle. These were met by Pompeius, returning at length from Iberia, and cut to pieces. Wearied with slaughter, the legions under Crassus at length made prisoners; and Crassus had those prisoners numbered, and they numbered over six thousand.

And Crassus marched his legions to the Appian Way, and for three days his camp rang with the busy sound of carpenters at work. Many trees were brought to the camp and cut and squared while the slaves, bound and unfed, squatted with no water to drink and the pitiless sun on their heads. And through lighted hours and dark they heard the clink and chime of the carpenters' tools, and smelt the fresh resin of the sawn wood.

But at length all was ready. And Licinius Crassus had the slaves brought forth, all through the heat of a summer day as he marched his army slowly up towards Rome, and one by one nailed on the new-made crosses. And at length even the men of the legions turned in horror from looking back along the horizon at that stretch of undulating, crying figures fading down into the sun-haze. Some, nailed on the cross, shrieked aloud with agony as the nails scraped through their bones or splintered those bones so that ragged slivers hung from the flesh. Some fainted. Some cried on strange Gods, and now at last pleaded for mercy while the legionaries drove the nails home through hands and feet. Then each cross was lifted, and the body of the slave upon it would bulge forth and the crack of the tearing flesh sound as the cross was flung in the hole new-dug. And the smell of blood and excrement increased as the day went by, wolves gathered that night and clouds of carrion-birds, waiting. And at last the last cross was flung in the earth, and the Romans departed.

The night came, heavily with dew. And throughout the miles of the crosses a groan greeted its coming as the coolness revived fainting lips, and men lifted their swimming eyes to the cool, watchful summer stars. Few had yet died, for it was many hours ere inflammation would yet set in on hands and feet, or the blood drip away till consciousness left them. And to that groan there succeeded throughout the night a babble in many tongues, men crying to a God, men crying the names of others dead or lost, men crying in a childish clamour that was wordless. Yet presently even that ceased, for the night grew almost as warm as the day. And by morning on the long lines of crosses the slaves hung with blackened tongues projecting from swollen lips, and glazed eyes, and the drooling moans of stricken beasts.

A great concourse came out from Rome to view the crucified slaves. Merchants passing at last in safety up that long road from the coast looked and shuddered and went by, at the clouding of flies and birds that now began to settle around still bodies that still lived. And sometimes a shriek would rise, and die, and the insects rise in a lazy hum. And the sightseers saw the bodies twisted in many fashions, in the last stretchings of agony; and by another day those who passed through the dripping lines saw that many had been torn by the teeth of beasts.

'None will live beyond the third night,' they said. 'There'll never be a slave revolt again.'

And they returned to Rome and light and life and their years, and the darkness that covers them from our gaze.

(ii)

It was the fourth morning, and still Kleon lived.

When they stripped him to nail him on the cross, the legionaries had shouted in mirth to find the slave a eunuch. Then they had maimed him again so that he had lost consciousness, and did not awake till hung on his cross, and the Masters had passed on.

And then pain tore at him, and like the others he babbled curses and complaints, and bit at his lips with his teeth; and something like a wheel that was spiked with fire turned and turned in his brain; and he knew that it might not endure, that death any instant must come, because no agony like this could last. And he fainted again, and awoke to the odours of his own body and the snuffling mouth of a wolf at his feet — that, and the pain, and the growl of the beast as it fled at the shriek that came from his lips.

And the day passed, the sun swung its arc of brightness across the sky so slowly that he thought of it as many days, long stretches of darkness and long stretches of light; and his tongue swelled out

209

between his teeth; and death would not come; and the spiked wheel in his brain grew and grew till it filled the sky, till it burst from his head and he saw it the earth in torment. And about him, in little spaces between his own agony, he heard the last cry of men who died, and saw their bodies bulge and shudder and pass to ease at last.

On the third night the insects left him and the beasts came. But they found him still living, and all that night he lived; and they came not near him, tearing at other flesh in the dark. And the last time he awoke he found the morning in the sky, and before his swimming gaze saw the world lighten, greater and strange.

'O Spartacus!'

It was a cry of agony in his brain and heart, but he heard it only as a stifled grunt from his lips. Then that agony of mind went as well, in a sudden flow of memory, a glister and flash of imaged memories: the first Bithynian camp, the horreum on the road to the South, Papa in mist, the battle-games of Crixus, the defiles of Mutina, Rome shining at dawn, the snows of Rhegium, the passes of Petelia — he fought and marched and debated again, heard cry in his ears the myriad slave voices, heard the ghost of that Hope and Promise wail away as the morning came upon the Appian Way. And then again pain seized and tore at his heart and passed again; and wildly, a last wild moment, he raised his eyes.

And he saw before him, gigantic, filling the sky, a great Cross with a figure that was crowned with thorns; and behind it, sky-towering as well, gladius in hand, his hand on the edge of the morning behind that Cross, the figure of a Gladiator. And he saw that these Two were One, and the world yet theirs: and he went into unending night and left them that shining earth.

It was Springtime in Italy, a hundred years before the crucifixion of Christ ——